RECKONING

BOOK 4 AFTER THE THAW

TAMAR SLOAN
HEIDI CATHERINE

SEQUEL HOUSE

For Helen and Tanya
(and your eagle eyes)

WREN

*W*ren has never known fear to be this tangible. Perhaps she's never been this scared. It's worse than when she fought a leatherskin ten times her size. Worse than standing up to Cy, or swimming through oceans made from acid, or being dragged over the edge of a cliff.

Because all those other times, no matter how afraid she'd been, she'd thought she had a chance.

Now, her options have run out.

She's in a lab with no windows.

The doors are unable to be opened.

There's no power.

No light.

And a hungry fire is devouring the walls.

She has minutes left to live. Seconds, perhaps.

The only positive she can think of is the warm body pressed up against her.

At least if she dies right now, she has Dex with her. A small consolation but it's all she has left to hold onto.

Dex is shaking. She pushes up on the tips of her toes and kisses his cheek. It's a slow kiss and somehow the intimacy of it feels even more powerful than if she'd reached for his lips. Because this isn't a kiss of lust or passion.

It's a kiss of love.

As she draws her lips away, a piece of the ceiling behind them caves in, creating a gaping hole for the dark smoke to billow through.

Wren's pulse spikes and she lets out a gasp, staring at the devastation before her.

Dex jerks her away from the rubble, but as he does, Wren hears a shout coming from outside the lab.

"Wren! I know you're in there!"

She turns to Dex. "That's Cy's voice! He's on the roof."

"You're all going to d—"

The roar of the fire swallows the rest of Cy's words as another part of the ceiling collapses. Dex pulls Wren down the hallway away from the front door, toward the computer room, as she finishes Cy's sentence in her mind. *You're all going to die.*

He's right. They are. Cy's the only one who can help them now.

And he's chosen not to.

People are scattering all over the lab like rats in a cage, desperate to find a way out. Some are cowering in corners, others are pacing the hallway. She can hear a group of people in the dining hall, loud shouts blending in with wails and screams.

"We need to get low," Dex calls, practically dragging her into the computer room. "The secret room! It's the safest place!"

Smoke rises. Which means the secret room will be like a bunker. But surely Dex knows that once this fire takes hold properly, it's going to suck all the oxygen right out of there.

Perhaps he's thinking about the few extra minutes it might buy them? Which she has to agree counts for something. Because those extra minutes are ones that she'll get to spend with Dex.

He lets go of her hand and in the dim flickering light, she sees him crouch down, tugging at the hatch.

"It won't open!" he calls back to her.

Wren squats and finds the familiar groove in the boards and tugs hard.

But he's right. It's not budging.

"They've locked it from the inside!" Wren bangs on the timber. "Let us in!"

"There's no lock." Dex is right beside her, trying to force it open.

"Then they're holding the handle." She thumps her fist again. "Let us in!"

Dex stands up and goes to the door, then back to her, then back to the door. It's as if he can't decide what to do next.

So, Wren goes to him. Since she arrived here, he's been her rock. The one to keep her steady no matter what the world has thrown at her. That's what she needs to be for him right now.

She places a hand on each of his arms and they stand in the exact spot where they shared their first kiss. The kiss that changed everything. The kiss that made Wren's world stop, leaving her wondering if it would ever start again.

And that's what it feels like now. As if the Earth has ceased spinning on its axis. It's just the two of them. Chaos is raining down upon them, but they have each other. Steady. Solid. Anchored by their love.

"I'm so sorry," he says, cupping her face.

"Stop apologizing." She closes her eyes and leans into his hand and the comfort it brings her.

"What are we going to do?" he asks. "Is this really it?"

Her eyes snap open, even though she can't answer his questions. She doesn't want to. Because then she might have to accept what she knows is true.

They're doomed.

"There has to be something we can do." He runs his thumb

across her cheek and lets his hand fall to her shoulder. "Something we've forgotten."

"We haven't."

But then Phoenix's voice pierces Wren's consciousness with such force she has to drag in a deep breath.

"Look behind the bookshelf. The one with the jars of food on it."

What had he meant when he'd said that to her as she'd left for the lab? And was that what he'd been trying to remind her about when the radio had fallen into silence?

But is there still enough time for her to find out?

She returns to the hatch and bangs on it even harder this time.

"Let us in!" she shouts. "I have an idea!"

"Do you really?" Dex drops to his knees and joins her in pummeling the floor.

"I think I can help!" Wren shouts, as much to Dex as to whoever's holding the hatch closed. "Let us in!

And finally, sweet joy, finally, the hatch opens a crack.

Together, Wren and Dex force it wide open to find the frightened face of a man staring up at them.

"You'd better be able to help us," he sneers, disappearing into the darkness below.

"You go," Dex says to Wren. "If you really think you can get us out of here, I have to make sure everyone has that same chance."

He's gone before she can stop him, heading back out the door, shouting for people to come with him to safety.

She'd said she thought she might be able to help. Not that she could. But it seems Dex's faith in her is as strong as ever.

Wren resists the strong urge to follow him, knowing the moment she leaves the hatch, the people below will hold it closed again. They were lucky to have had this small opportunity to get inside. The best thing she can do right now is stay right here in the hope Dex will return soon.

4

Very soon.

Every second counts.

She swings one leg down onto the ladder, moving as slowly as she can to buy a little of the time they don't have. Tensions are understandably high and the patience of the people at the bottom of the ladder is only going to last so long.

Now she has to cross her fingers that whatever it is that Phoenix left behind the bookshelf is going to help them get out. He'd better not have carved her a funny picture into the dirt wall. Because if there's ever a moment for that kind of joke to fall flat, it's now.

"Hurry up!" someone calls from below. "And don't bring anyone else with you. We don't have room."

"Dex!" she calls as loudly as she can, looking toward the door in the dim light as she takes a step down.

Feeling a tight grip on her ankles she yelps as her feet are pulled from the top rung and she's sent sliding down.

She scrambles, only just managing to grab hold of the ladder halfway down, stopping herself from landing in a heap at the bottom.

"What the hell?" She climbs the rest of the way down and scans the people-shaped shadows around her. It's almost completely dark down here. Impossible to know who's here and who's not.

Someone pushes past her and scurries up the ladder.

"Don't you close that hatch!" Wren climbs up, grabbing hold of a large set of ankles that undoubtedly belong to a man. Perhaps the same one that just sent her sliding down here well before she was ready.

She hauls on him, trying to do to him what he just succeeded in doing to her. But he's bigger than her. Heavier. And she feels like a mouse tackling a lion.

"There are people up there," she shouts. "You can't lock them out."

"Then we all die." The man lifts his foot from the ladder and kicks down, narrowly missing Wren's face. "There's no more room in here."

Before she has time to think about what she's doing, she pulls her knife from the back of her trousers and raises it in the air, ready to do whatever it takes to ensure Dex isn't stranded in the deathtrap above them.

"Wren!"

The sound of Dex's voice stops her knife in mid-air. The beast of a man above her doesn't know how lucky he is.

"Dex! I'm down here." She tucks the knife back in her waistband, her eyes squinting to catch a glimpse of Dex.

"There's no room," the man grumbles. "Look how many of you there are."

But Dex and whoever he's brought with him are already pushing their way onto the ladder and Wren climbs down to get out of the way, knowing there's no way they're all going to fit. Some people are going to have to wait in the computer room while she figures this out.

The small room is packed tightly with bodies and Wren squeezes her way through, trying to get to the bookshelf. She doubts it still contains the jars of food that were down here when she stayed in this room with Phoenix. Which should make it easier to shift.

"Quick! We need to slide this shelf away so I can see what's behind it," she orders, unsure to whom she's even given this command. It doesn't matter. Just as long as they can help.

She takes hold of the timber supports and tries to shift it but it's heavy and stays in place.

"Everyone grab this shelf and slide it to the right," she shouts. "Now!"

She can't see the hands, but she feels the effect they have. It's like the shelf has grown wheels and it slides across the rough ground.

"I need a light!" she calls.

"Don't you think if we had one, it would be on," someone grumbles. "We're not in the dark for the fun of it."

"Then shift back a bit," she says, trying to get enough space to bend over and inspect the wall.

A soft glow fills the room and Wren looks up to the ladder to see a laptop lighting up all the worries on Dex's face and sending soft light filtering across the room.

"We've closed the door to the computer room," Dex shouts to her. "It'll hold the fire for a little while, but we don't have long.

Wren turns back to the wall and her eyes widen to see a black circle about three feet in diameter.

She squats down and brings her hands to it, hoping it could be what it looks like in this dim light.

Waving her hands, she feels nothing but free space. She extends her arms and a rush of hope washes over her as her hands disappear into the darkness.

"There's a tunnel!" she shouts, her heart leaping out of her chest. "Phoenix dug a tunnel!"

She pushes herself into the dark space, hoping he'd had enough time to dig it all the way to safety.

The tunnel is small, and she has to lie on her stomach to wriggle through, glad her fear is of heights and not small spaces. But Phoenix is much larger than Wren, so there's room enough for her to crawl through.

"You clever bastard," she says out loud, wishing Phoenix were here to hear her. She'd hoped for some kind of miracle and it seems it's been delivered—not by any supreme being, but by her twin.

Their father had taught them to always have an escape plan. *Always*. It seems hiding in the secret room had been no exception. It also seems that Phoenix hadn't been half as lazy as she'd thought, lounging about on that mattress. Every time she left the room he must've been digging.

She pulls herself forward a couple more yards, but then the tunnel curves upwards and hits a dead end.

"Dammit!"

Maneuvering herself with a little difficulty, she reaches for her knife and brings it forward, using it to scrape the dirt away. With any luck, Phoenix has dug this tunnel right until the point it was about to break through to fresh air.

She feels pressure on her feet as someone crawls up behind her.

"Get out of here!" she shouts, knowing there won't be enough oxygen if this tight space is full of people. "It's a dead end! Go back!"

She slams the knife into the roof of the tunnel, pleased to find the soil is soft and crumbles away with ease. But now she has a new problem. Where to put the dirt that's falling back on her? Where the hell had Phoenix put it? Then she remembers the loose grit on the floor of the secret room that she'd thought had been the ceiling caving in. If only she hadn't been so distracted, she might have noticed what was really going on.

Wren scoops the dirt away from above her head, working quickly and carefully. She blinks as it rains down on her but sticks to her task. This is their only hope. There's literally no other way out of here. Her survival and that of everyone else in the lab has come down to this moment.

It's come down to her.

She coughs as a large slab of soil falls free. Crumbling it apart she tries to push it behind her, quickly realizing it's no use. The space around her is crowding in. Soon, only a small child will be able to crawl through the opening. And then, nobody.

Phoenix must have brought something in with him to collect what he'd dug out. All she's doing here is opening up a space

8

above her and closing up the one she's already in. It's like taking one step forward, then an equal one back.

She wriggles backward, her feet hitting something solid. Most likely someone's head.

"Get back!" she yells.

But whoever's behind her doesn't budge. No doubt they have someone behind them blocking them, too.

"Get back!" she tries again.

It's no use. She can't move backward, and she can't move forward.

Phoenix hadn't delivered her a miracle.

All he'd given her had been hope. And the place in her chest where it had flared is quickly being replaced with the all-consuming knowledge that this is it.

She's going to die in this tunnel dug by the hands of her twin.

Wren brings her arms forward and folds them, turning her head to rest her cheek on one of her forearms.

She stares into the darkness and counts each of her breaths, wondering how many more of them she'll be able to take before the oxygen runs out.

One.

Two.

Three.

This fire is all her fault. It had been her suggestion to let in the guard with the flamethrower. She should've realized that hemp is flammable.

Four.

Five.

Six.

Her father could put out this fire, but he's choosing not to, even though he knows she's trapped inside. It seems his hunger for revenge outstrips even his love for his daughter.

Seven.

Eight.

Nine.

She'd come in here to be with Dex, not to die in a tunnel alone.

Ten.

Eleven.

Twelve.

A dozen breaths and, still, she's alive.

A dozen more and all her hope will be gone.

"I'm sorry, Dex."

Wren closes her eyes in the darkness and waits for death to stake its claim.

NOVA

"*S*weet Terra."

Kian only mutters the words, but there's something about the way he says them that jolts Nova awake. She pushes herself upright, her palms digging into the rough timber of the raft, her pulse spiking.

"What? What is it?"

But the moment Nova looks around, she sees what has Kian's gaze transfixed.

They've reached Askala.

And it's on fire.

The raft bobs on the gentle sea, the promise of land less than a mile away. It's twilight, which means they've made good time —the plan was to arrive unseen during the night. It also means Nova must've slept for hours.

Although, she didn't expect to wake up and see this.

Angry crimson flickers on the horizon, the flames big enough to be seen at a distance. Behind her, Nova hears a moan. She turns to find Avis clutching her middle as she rocks. Luca is tucked in beside her as he clings to her arm.

Frowning, Nova shuffles over. "Motion sickness?"

Luca shakes his head, his face tight. Nova looks closer, thinking maybe it's something Avis ate. Her skin's pale, her pupils dilated in the half-light as she pants. Her lips move, saying one word over and over. "No, no, no."

Nova glances back at the fire they're steadily floating closer to. Avis isn't sick.

She's terrified.

Luca's eyes plead with Nova to fix this. "She doesn't like fire."

Because fire destroyed half of Avis's body. Stole her children. And her life.

Nova grips Avis's arms, keeping her hands firm but gentle. "Avis. Listen to me. You're not alone this time."

Avis looks like she's been hypnotized by the flames. Nova moves to the side, breaking her line of sight with the shoreline. "You're not alone," she repeats. "We won't let anything happen to you."

Avis's gaze flickers, focusing on Nova. "I...I thought I could do this. But he's...Cy's there."

"You can do this," Nova tells her adamantly. "You're going to see Wren and Phoenix."

"My babies," Avis whispers. "It's been so long..."

Avis collapses into herself, soft tears trickling down her cheeks; flowing freely on one side, tracking through the scars on the other.

"Nova." It's Kian, his voice low and insistent.

Turning to Luca, Nova grasps his hand. "We're almost there. I want you to look after Avis, okay?"

Luca nods, his face vulnerable but resolute. He tucks his hand more firmly underneath Avis's arm. "I'll stay with her."

Nova smiles in thanks before turning back to Kian. They need to decide their next step. Flick and Shiloh are standing to his left, everyone facing Askala.

They're returning, and it's obvious the destruction has already begun.

Flick's arms are crossed tightly across her front. "Where's some rain when you actually need it?"

Kian's eyes narrow. "It's the lab."

Nova realizes he's right. The location of the fire is exactly where the lab would be.

"At least it's not the Oasis," Shiloh murmurs.

Where the people of Askala are. Except...

Kian's hand reaches out and she grasps it. They don't need to say it, but one name hangs between them.

Dex.

"We'll beach where the bridge used to be," says Kian. "It's far enough away from the Oasis, but close to the lab. We need to get a sense of what's going on."

Nova nods, her heart thumping hard. She knew this would be dangerous, but she hadn't thought they'd be facing such a volatile threat so soon.

Or that her childhood friend would be in such grave danger.

They paddle silently, keeping low over the raft. Any remains of the bridge are long gone, dissolved by the ocean, but they all know where it used to be. As the raft hits sand, Nova realizes burning the one link to the Outlands had far more consequences than Magnus and the others ever considered.

They drag the raft up to the tree line, and the scent of smoke stings Nova's lungs. There's little breeze, so a cloying cloud of ash is creeping down to the beach. Behind her, she hears another moan.

Nova turns to find Avis kneeling in the sand, her hand clamped over her mouth, her eyes wide.

She looks like she's trying not to scream.

Rushing over, Nova kneels beside her. "It's okay, Avis. It's just smoke. The fire isn't too close."

Avis's hand is white as she clutches her face. She shakes her head, her eyes scanning the trees compulsively.

"Avis doesn't like fire," Luca whimpers.

The same words he used on the raft not long ago. Nova's heart aches. For the first time ever, Luca looks like the child he is. He clings to Avis like he wants to protect her but is suddenly aware of how powerless his small body is. Without the protection of Fairbanks, Avis can't be the strong adult he modeled himself on.

Nova hears Flick behind her, talking to Kian or Shiloh. "We can't afford to have her fall apart," she hisses. "If she screams..."

Kian kneels down beside Nova, keeping his gaze steady on Avis. "We're all here for you. And we won't be going anywhere near the fire if we can help it."

Avis moans behind her hand, shaking her head violently. Nova glances at Kian. Avis can't face this right now. The prospect of seeing Ronan along with the fire is too much. Nova presses her hand to Avis's scarred cheek. "I want you to go into the forest. Once we know what's going on, we'll join you.

"Run due east," Kian urges. "About half a mile in, there's a stand of boulders. That will be our meeting point."

Nova remembers it. They'd found the small clearing littered with rocks and it had felt like a playground just for them. They'd returned several times, deciding to keep the place their little secret.

She turns to Luca. "I want you to take Avis, Luca. Help her if she gets too upset, make sure she keeps running."

Luca's young face cements with determination. "I'll look after her."

Nova glances around. Someone else needs to go with them. Neither Avis nor Luca know Askala and its terrain. She doubts they've had to navigate a forest in their lifetime. Kian needs to stay, and there's no way Flick will leave Nova.

Knowing she can't suggest Shiloh over herself, Nova stands,

resolve settling around her shoulders. She'll take Avis and Luca to the clearing, then return.

But Shiloh steps forward. "I'll take them." She glances between Kian and Nova. "You two need to stay together."

Nova bites her lip. The certainty and sadness in Shiloh's eyes are unmistakable. "Thank you," she says simply.

Shiloh is everything a High Bound should be.

She doesn't reply, kneeling down to wrap an arm around Avis. "Let's find somewhere safe."

Avis nods, the wetness on her face glistening in the twilight. She allows Shiloh and Luca to lead her toward the tree line as they angle away from the fire that's not far away.

Kian's jaw is tense. "We'll join you as soon as we can."

With a small, tentative wave from Luca, they're gone.

"We need to approach cautiously." Kian grips Nova's hand as he speaks softly and urgently. "We don't know what we're walking into."

The moment they're surrounded by trees, the smoke thickens, harsh and cloying in Nova's throat.

Flick presses close to her. "Why the lab?" she whispers hoarsely.

"Probably to prove what he's capable of," Nova offers, dread sitting heavy in her gut. "He's showing he's serious."

"And to wipe the history of Askala from existence," Kian adds flatly.

Which means the Oasis could be next. Although surely, Ronan wouldn't destroy the one safe haven on this island. The only place protecting them all from the fury of Mother Nature after everything humanity has done to her...

They creep forward, the flames flickering brighter, the smoke becoming thicker. Nova can't help the gasp that escapes her when they reach the edge of the trees.

The lab is ahead, but what used to be a stoic building that represented the determination to survive is now half eaten by fire. They're on the side of the walled-off courtyard, much of it yet to be destroyed, but on the far side, the flames leap for the sky, dancing with delight at the fodder they've been given. The heat hits Nova, licking at her skin as she chokes back a cough.

They all recoil behind the trunks of trees when two men come striding around. They stop, wiping the sweat from their dirty brows, jostling each other as they take in the destruction they're wreaking.

From the other side of the building, a voice roars. "This is the price you pay, Askala. You've brought this on yourself!"

Nova waits, breath held, but no reply comes from the lab. No screams, no begging for mercy. Who is Ronan talking to?

The men pause, seeming to wait, too, then shrug and keep walking.

Kian shakes his head. "It's too late for the lab. It's going to burn to the ground."

Nova hesitates. "You don't think anyone's in there? Dex or Callix?"

"If they did get caught in there, they would've found a way out the moment they realized the fire had started. They're both smart—they'd face Ronan rather than go down with the lab."

Nova nods. Dex was always a fighter. He's probably in the Oasis somewhere reassuring everyone Ronan can burn the lab, but he won't destroy their spirit.

"I say we go find Avis and the others," whispers Flick. "There's nothing we can do here."

Nova senses the acceptance in Kian as his shoulders sag. Still, he doesn't move, facing the growing flames like he can extinguish them by force of will.

She grasps his hand. "Buildings can be rebuilt. It's the people of Askala we need to save."

Swallowing, Kian nods. "We'll come back tomorrow, after some rest. Then we find a way to make sure Ronan can't hurt the people of Askala."

They meld back among the trees, the shadows cool after the heat of the fire. The roar of the flames that was steadily growing louder mutes, and Nova's tension dials down. Watching the lab burn had been hard. It'll be a relief not to see what will be left behind.

But after a few steps, Nova glances over her shoulder one last time. Although she knows it will cause her nothing but pain, she needs to remind herself of what Ronan is capable of.

Her eyes widen as she sees Phoenix rush around the courtyard, stopping at the gate. Frantically, he shoves at it, but it doesn't move. He steps back, looking both ways before raising his boot and kicking it with all his might.

The gate splinters, the sound fracturing through the growing noise of the fire.

Nova grips Kian's arm. "Kian. What's he doing?"

"Probably trying to help it burn down quicker," Kian mutters.

But something about Phoenix has Nova pausing. She retraces her steps, stopping at the edge of the trees. Phoenix stands at the opening to the courtyard, once more glancing around like he's worried he could get caught any moment.

Nova sucks in a breath. The ash on Phoenix's face is streaked with tears.

"Something's wrong," she says, already taking a step forward. The boy who cared for Nova during her fever is scared. No, he's panicking.

Kian appears by her side, the lines of his face taut in the flickering light. "He's Ronan's son, Nova."

"But he's Wren's twin. And Avis's son."

"Wait here," he mutters, striding forward only to find Nova right by his side.

"Together, remember?"

Kian nods sharply, probably not liking that Nova's stating

the truth. Flick appears on Nova's other side, her frown determined. "We're making it a threesome."

Phoenix has already disappeared into the courtyard. They leave the protection of the trees, rushing to follow him so they don't get seen.

Inside, Nova braces herself. There could be more of Ronan's men. Fire. Phoenix holding a knife and proving her wrong.

But Phoenix is kneeling a few feet from the lab, illuminated by flames. Holding a branch, he's furiously stabbing at the soil.

"Phoenix," Nova calls out gently. "What are you doing?"

Phoenix leaps to his feet, the branch ready to swing like a bat. "Stay away! I'll kill anyone who tries to stop me!"

Kian puts out a steadying hand. "It's us, Phoenix. We're not here to fight."

Phoenix blinks, registering who he's looking at. "Thank god!" His arms drop, the end of the branch hitting the ground. "You have to help me. Wren and the others are trapped inside."

Fear punches through Nova. "What? How many?"

"About forty." Phoenix rubs his hand over his head in frantic strokes. "Including Wren and Dex."

Kian rushes to the door. "Then we need to get them out!"

Phoenix shakes his head. "My father cut the power. I don't think the doors can open. They would have come out otherwise."

Sweet Terra. Ronan has turned the lab into an oven. An oven full of humans.

"But—" Kian has to modulate his tone, conscious of the guards. "His daughter's in there!"

"She chose Dex," Phoenix states simply.

Wren chose someone else over her father. For Ronan, that would be the ultimate betrayal.

Phoenix picks up the branch again. "There's only one way we can get to them."

Kian rushes to the tree at the other side of the courtyard. "The tunnel!"

"You know about it?" Phoenix asks in surprise.

Kian jerks at a branch, wincing at the crack that snaps through the air. "Dex hid me down there before I left for the Outlands. I got curious about this room I had no idea existed, so I had a look around."

Flick rushes to stand beside Phoenix. "You mean there's a way out?"

Phoenix jabs the end of his branch into the soil. "The tunnel's not complete. We're going to have to reach them."

Kian stares at the ground, his eyes flicking to the wall of the lab. He takes a step to the left. "Here. This is where it'll come out."

Phoenix pauses, and Nova's about to point out that Kian knows Askala like he knows the layout of the Oasis—intimately —when Phoenix joins him. "Then let's dig."

They quickly establish a rhythm, each slamming their branches into the soil and breaking it up. Once they've fractured the top layer, Nova tells them to stop. Kneeling down, she scoops out the soil as quickly as she can. Flick joins her, and within seconds they've scraped out a shallow depression.

"Again," growls Phoenix.

Nova and Flick scuttle back as Kian and Phoenix establish their rhythm again, ramming the soil like pistons. The sounds of the flames grow, and Nova covers her mouth as a cough climbs up her throat. It won't be long before the fire reaches this part of the lab.

Please, let them get to the others in time.

"Hey! What are you doing?"

Everyone spins around to see two of Cy's men at the entry to the courtyard.

The same guards who were doing the rounds earlier step in,

shoulders expanding as they register what's going on. "Cy's orders were to let it burn to the ground," one of them sneers.

Kian takes a step forward. "There are people inside."

One of the men, the smaller of the two, curls his lip. "They're Unbound according to our new order. We're doing them a favor."

Phoenix steps up beside Kian. "Which makes you no better than the Askala you're trying to destroy."

The man cracks his knuckles. "If you want to die along with them, that's fine."

The two men fan out, flexing their shoulders as their bodies harden. Kian and Phoenix take another step forward, each holding a branch.

The shorter man takes a step backward, eyes flicking to the two lengths of solid wood facing them. "You stand guard, I'll warn the others."

He's realized they need back up.

"We need to rush them," mutters Phoenix quietly.

Nova's gut clenches. They can't afford for the other guards to find them. Beside her, Flick wraps herself around Nova's arm, a quiet whimper escaping her throat.

Nova knows she's thinking of the men in the Outlands, when they were trapped in the hut.

When Thom died protecting them.

Phoenix may be a seasoned fighter, but Kian isn't.

Nova slowly straightens, not wanting to bring attention to herself. This time, she won't sit by and watch. She clasps her hand to her belly. *We're going to fight, little one. Too many lives depend on us.*

The shorter one must read the intent on Kian and Phoenix's faces because his eyes widen a split second before he spins around.

Kian and Phoenix launch after him, but he's already at the gate. Nova's stomach plummets. Their chances of getting to him in time are non-existent. Especially not carrying the branches.

Which would leave Kian unarmed.

Except the second guard whips his arm out, driving his fist into the other guard's face. The first guard's momentum means the sound of his nose breaking is unmistakable, the crackle of cartilage competing with the flames. His body arcs through the air, driven by the fist in his face.

Kian and Phoenix jump back as he slams into the ground, already unconscious. They turn to the guard still standing at the entry.

Phoenix lowers his branch. "Ah, Jagger. What just happened?"

Jagger shrugs. "My dad traded me in exchange for a hut to live in. I never wanted to be part of this." He looks toward the burning lab. "And I sure as hell don't want to be part of that."

Nova freezes, the exchange from the Outlands assaulting her mind.

"They needed recruits for their army." The man had flexed his bicep. "Said he came from good stock."

"Did he want to go?"

"You ask like there was a choice."

Could this be the son of the man who tried to attack her?

There's no time to find out, because Jagger strides over to his comrade, dragging him beside the wall. "I'll get him out of sight, then tell the others he's taking a leak or something." He straightens, dusting his hands off. "You guys dig."

Phoenix and Kian glance at each other. Kian nods. Phoenix lifts his branch. Within seconds they're back at the depression, breaking up the soil. Nova joins them, Flick alongside her. They establish a rhythm.

Fracture the soil. Scoop it out. Fracture the soil. Scoop it out.

The hole steadily grows, Nova having to reach further and further down. But so does the roaring and spitting of the flames. To her left, the night sky steadily brightens as the fire devours more and more of the lab.

Nova suppresses a cough just as voices trickle over the wall of the courtyard. "Where's Garth?"

They all pause, breathing heavily and conscious they're running out of time.

"Probably slipped over in his own piss, for all we know," Jagger replies. "I'll go tell him to hurry up. You keep an eye on the door on the other side. They might try to get the security screens up."

"You always were a thinker, Jagger."

When there's nothing more, they resume digging. Sweat streaks down Kian's temples as Phoenix keeps muttering, "I'm coming Wren. I'm coming."

Nova's nails are chipped and her fingers bleeding as she scoops out the next layer of soil, but she ignores the stinging pain. The lab will be full of smoke by now. They could be too late...

She reaches down, only to freeze when she hears a faint voice. "Hurry! The fire!"

"Wren?" Nova gasps.

Digging furiously, she spears her fingers into the loose soil. "I can hear Wren!"

The others fall to their knees around the hole, scrabbling and scooping out the dirt. "We're here, Wren. We're going to get you out," calls Phoenix.

Nova's hand burrows down, gravel and rocks biting at her skin. Suddenly, she feels something different.

Something moving.

She wriggles her hand, the soil crumbling around it as she grips warm, gritty skin.

Fingers. Wren's fingers.

They've reached her.

KIAN

*R*elief washes over Kian at hearing Wren's voice, but it's short lived. The sound of crashing echoes from the other side of the lab, making everyone instinctively duck.

"The lab is collapsing," moans Flick.

Immediately following the wave of destruction, a roar of victory from Ronan's men chases the flames to the sky, sparks crackling and flashing like fireworks. Kian grits his teeth.

They need to get these people out. Now.

"Move back, Wren," Kian says, still scraping the soil as Nova grips Wren's hand. "We're going to make the hole bigger."

"No can do, my friend," she calls back. "There are people behind me. We're jammed in like the intestines of a leatherskin down here."

Phoenix replaces Nova's hand with his, indicating she should step back. "Close your eyes, little bird."

He looks to Kian, who understands what he's planning to do. Kian reaches down, too, wrapping both hands around Wren's exposed upper arm. "Ready?"

"Pull!" grunts Phoenix.

Digging his feet into the ground, Kian hauls up, tugging on Wren's arm like it's attached to a weight. At first, there's nothing but resistance as Kian's hands begin to slip and the cords on Phoenix's throat strain as he pulls. For a brief moment, Kian fears they're going to dislocate Wren's arm, but then she comes up an inch. Then another.

And another.

With a last great heave, Wren's torso breaks through the soil. Kian and Phoenix fall backward, releasing her arm.

"Wren!" Nova gasps with joy.

Wren's covered in soil, her face brown and streaked. She pulls in a giant breath and then another. "Man, that feels good."

She looks down at her waist, the rest of her below ground. She pushes and wriggles as she tries to work her way out. "Now I know how the undead feel."

Phoenix grins at her. "Half a sister is better than no sister."

"Zip it, Phee, and help me get the rest of these people out of here. I could smell the smoke in the tunnel."

They spring to work, Kian and Phoenix taking a hand each and pulling while Nova and Flick wrap their arms around Wren's waist. A few hard yanks and Wren pops out like Mother Nature just gave birth to her.

Kian turns back to the hole, watching the soil crumble away as it widens. He joins Nova as she falls to her knees, frantically scooping it out so it remains open.

A second later, two eyes blink up at him from the gloom. "Help us," the man cries feebly. "The fire…"

Kian juts his arm down. "Take my hand. We're going to get you all out."

Nova stands. "We need to get them into the forest." Without waiting for a response, she grabs Flick's hand and walks to the opening in the courtyard.

Kian and Phoenix repeat the process as they haul the next person out of the tunnel, Wren anxiously hovering behind them. The man blinks even though it's now dark, as if he can't believe he's out in the open. He turns to look at the lab, taking a startled step back. "Sweet Terra. It's almost all gone."

Kian doesn't bother to answer. They already know they're running low on time. The heat from the flames is stinging his skin as the smoke fills his lungs. He reaches down into the hole. "Next person. Let's keep this moving."

A hand latches onto his and Kian pulls, Phoenix quickly grabbing the other as the woman emerges from the black. Now that the tunnel has been excavated, they pull this person out easier. Directing the woman to Nova and Flick, Kian focuses on the next person.

And the next, and the next.

Behind him, he hears Nova telling them to run to the forest and the meeting point. Knowing all they can do is hope Jagger keeps the other guards away, Kian focuses on hauling the people trapped in the human oven Ronan has created.

With each body that clambers out, Kian sends a prayer of thanks. He recognizes them all beneath the dirt—Callix. Thea. Aarov.

Behind him, Kian hears Thea's gasp and he knows she's seen Nova. She cries out and he winces. The reunion is going to be a happy one, but it needs to be quiet. And brief.

More people exit. Each one frightened. All relieved to be alive. When they pull Bea out, she wraps her arms around Kian in a tight hug, muttering a "thank you" before rushing away.

But with each person freed, Kian's heart thumps a little heavier.

They're not Dex.

Kian senses someone behind him but he stays focused on his task. "Do you have many more?" Jagger hisses over his shoulder.

Kian's counted about thirty people. "How many were in there?"

"About fifty," Wren replies flatly.

Surprised to find her standing by his side, Kian nods. This girl chose his cousin despite what Ronan told her was true. She'd be just as worried about Dex as Kian is.

Fifty. Which means they've still got quite a bit to go.

"Keep them busy." Kian glances at Jagger. "We're almost there."

Jagger shakes his head. "We have different definitions of *almost there.*"

The next person to pull themselves out is Vern. He glances around frantically. "Where's Bea? Is she okay?"

"She's by the gate," Kian replies, panting from the strain of dragging people up. "Take her to the forest. Nova will tell you where."

Vern nods and is about to rush away when Kian grasps his arm. "Have you seen Dex?"

Wren pushes forward, just as keen to hear his response.

Vern pauses. "He insisted on being the last to come up. The smoke was really filling up in there…"

"Bloody Dex," mutters Wren. "Of course, he'd do that."

Gritting his teeth, Kian bends over the hole again. He'll go down it himself if it means getting Dex out.

The fire is a ridge of heat beside them as the next five people exit the tunnel. Embers sprinkle down like raindrops, the smoke making Kian's eyes sting as if he's just swum in the ocean.

Thirty-five people. That's still fifteen more to go.

This time when he leans over the hole Kian's surprised to find a flat, black rectangle poking up. He grips it, realizing it's a laptop.

"Will you just take it?" comes Dex's voice. "This is hard enough as it is."

The grin that explodes across Kian's face is reflexive. He takes the laptop and passes it to Phoenix, quickly grabbing the hand that was holding it. With a burst of strength powered by joy, he drags Dex up into the smoky air.

Wren launches herself at him the moment Dex is upright on solid soil. As if he was expecting it, or maybe he was needing to hold her as much as she was him, Dex's arms open wide then clamp around her.

They hold each other for long seconds, eyes closed as their breathing slows.

Dex steps away, turning to Kian. "Good timing, cousin."

Kian's grin returns. "I couldn't let you have all the glory."

Their hug is fierce and short. They still have to get their people to safety.

Stepping away, Kian glances at the tunnel. "I thought there were others."

Dex's shoulders slump. "I tried to get them to shelter in the secret room." He looks away. "Some thought it was safer to stay where they were. Others figured there was no point trying..."

Kian swallows. "So that's everyone?"

"Yeah, that's everyone." He looks around. "Speaking of everyone, where are they? Where are Ronan's guards?"

Looking around, Kian registers Nova and Flick are shepherding the last of the people through the gate. To their left, the tree is already alight, the flames licking along the branches and flaring with each leaf they find.

"We're going to the forest while the guards are being kept busy." Kian glances at Wren, knowing this isn't the time to mention Avis. "There are others there, waiting for us."

Dex nods. "Let's get moving then."

Nova's pale skin is streaked with soot, her eyes wide with worry as they join her. "Some didn't make it, did they?"

Already grieving for the souls who lost hope, Kian nods. "We were too late."

Wren shakes her head. "You got here in time to save those you did. Ask them how they feel about that."

Dex slips an arm around her shoulder. "I'm pretty glad you turned up."

Kian's about to respond when the tree explodes into a fireball. He pulls Nova to his side, shielding her head with his hand. He has to raise his voice to be heard above the roar of the flames. "We need to go."

Just as he says it, the wall they were digging beside topples, a screen of fire the only thing between them and Ronan. Keeping low, they sprint for the trees.

Kian's heart is thumping hard as they blend into the cool darkness. Were they seen? Have they gone through this all just to be discovered?

Holding onto the trunk of a tree, he peers around, but all he sees is smoke. Maybe it was enough to conceal them...

A body materializes, wide and tall like all of Ronan's guards, and Kian freezes only to relax when he recognizes Jagger. Holding his hand out so the others know to stay put, he steps out. "Everyone who survived is out."

Jagger nods, the weight in his eyes telling Kian he understands what that means. "Cy has no idea. He'll think you all died in the fire."

Kian's eyes sting with more than just the smoke. "There will be human remains for him to find."

Jagger keeps his gaze averted from the fire that's now ravaging the courtyard. "I doubt there will be much more than ash."

Nova slips her hand into Kian's as she comes up beside him. "Come with us, Jagger."

But he shakes his head. "If I go missing too, there'll be questions. I'll stay here, do what I can..."

For the people of Askala.

Kian grips his shoulder, squeezing it in gratitude. "You saved a lot of people today."

Jagger's lips twitch. "Who would've thought, huh?"

"It shows you're more than your legacy, Jagger," Nova adds.

He stills. "It seems so."

Kian glances down at Nova, wondering at her words, but another voice calls out, making them all freeze.

"To the Oasis! We have cause for celebration."

It's Ronan, and the cheers that follow his announcement make Kian's stomach clench.

Nova gasps. "He believes Wren died in that fire."

In fact, Ronan chose to leave his daughter to die rather than see her turn her back on him.

Jagger turns to leave. "Now you know what Cy is capable of. Don't forget that."

Kian nods. This will be forever branded in his memory. "Stay safe."

Sauntering away like he's looking forward to celebrating their victory, Jagger punches his arm in the air and whoops. "Long live the Commander!"

The echoing shouts make Kian wince. It makes him realize there will only be one way to end this. A solution he never would've thought he would contemplate.

Ronan has to die.

Nova tugs on his arm. "Let's get these people away from here. Several of them have smoke inhalation, they'll need medical attention."

Kian squeezes her hand and releases it. "We have a hike ahead of us. You take the lead with Dex, Wren and I will come up the rear."

Nova hesitates then nods. If anyone were to try and follow them, they need their strongest as protection.

The procession starts as Wren falls beside him. She nods at Kian but says little else, her eyes sharp and alert in the gloom. Kian takes comfort in her vigilance...and in the way she rests her hand on the knife tucked in her waistband.

A few steps into the forest, and Kian glances back at the lab.

The building is a burning pile of destruction. Soon, it will be nothing but ash and bones.

His people's bones.

Askala has been irrevocably changed.

And he's willing to do whatever it takes to heal the damage.

DEX

*A*s much as Dex hates to have been separated from Wren again, he's pleased to have Nova by his side.

She loops her hand into the crook of his arm as they make their way through the trees away from the smell of the fire.

"Stop thinking about it," she says, gripping him a little tighter.

He doesn't have to ask how she could possibly know what he's thinking. Nova's been his friend since forever. She's fully aware how difficult it was for him to leave the lab knowing there were still people trapped inside.

People he'd led there.

And now they'll never leave.

"I tried my best." He swallows, resisting the urge to turn around. Because he knows if he sees who's walking behind him, then his memory will fill in the blanks and he'll also see who's not.

"I don't know what happened, but I do know your best is always amazing." Nova shoots him a smile in the fading light. He tries to offer her one in return but fails. "And I'd like to bet that every one of these people following us is alive because of you."

"It wasn't me." He shakes his head. "It was Wren. She saved us. And you and Kian. And Phoenix."

Dex's father speaks up from behind them. "Nova's right, Dex. Nobody would have been there to save without you having brought them to safety in the first place. And you put yourself at risk to go back to get more people when most would have just saved themselves first."

Dex shakes his head at his father, not daring to believe this. It's hard to think of the people he saved when so many were lost.

"He's right, Dex," says Thea, who hasn't allowed herself to be more than a few feet away from Nova since they were reunited. Which also means she hasn't been far from Felicia, who seems just as glued to Nova's side. "I'd have been burnt to a crisp if it weren't for you hauling me back from that door when I tried to get out."

"Mom!" Nova looks horrified. "What did you do?"

"I was worried about you." Thea smiles at her daughter. "I should've known you'd be okay. Kian wouldn't let anything happen to you."

Nova gives Thea a sad smile and they walk on ahead. Clearly, not everything went well for her in the Outlands. She seems older somehow. Tougher. Like whatever it was she went through has changed her in ways she hadn't wanted to change. Dex is desperate to ask her about it, but now's not the time.

They need to reach the boulders before it gets much darker. It's dangerous out here at night. The exact reason why he'd brought the people to the lab. But still, it has to be better than the situation they'd ended up in.

He'd rather face a polar grizzly than Ronan any day of the week. He'd have a far greater chance of survival.

But hopefully they don't need to worry about Ronan for a

little while. Phoenix had stayed behind, along with that guard who'd helped them, to try to throw Ronan off the scent. With any luck he won't have realized that anyone got out of that lab alive.

Nova leans into Dex as they walk. "Kian told me you and Wren kissed."

"That guy's mouth is even bigger than his biceps," Dex grumbles as he suppresses a smile.

Nova nudges him and he winces, halting his steps for just a moment.

"Are you hurt?" Nova's face is stricken. "Dex, what's wrong?"

"It's okay." He picks up his pace again, pushing down his pain. "Nothing serious."

"Was it Ronan?" she asks. "How da—"

"It's okay, Nova." He really doesn't want to upset her. And he *is* okay. Wren completed their entire Proving with bruised ribs and barely complained once. He can do it, too. Every day he feels a little better. Although, crawling through that tunnel hadn't felt especially good.

"It's getting dark." Nova lets go of Dex so she can hold her hands in front of her.

"Let me walk ahead." Dex tucks Nova behind him. "If there's one thing I've become good at lately, it's moving about in the dark. Put your hands on my back."

Nova does as he suggests and they move forward a little slower than before.

Kian told him which boulders to head to and thankfully they're not far. What Dex hadn't had time to ask was why the others were waiting there for them instead of helping get them out of the lab. They could have used Dean and Thom's strength to pull them out. Or is it possible they hadn't come back from the Outlands with them? But surely if Felicia made it back alive then two strong men would have, too.

He shuffles forward with Nova's palms pressed to his back,

warning her when there's a branch on the path, half pleased at having a moment to sort out his thoughts. The laptop is tucked safely under his arm, although he's not sure what use it's going to be. It had just seemed like it was something he should take with him. There'll come a time when they'll want access to the Oasis. They can't stay out in the forest forever, nor can they let Ronan continue to ruin the lives of those who stayed behind.

Drawing in a deep breath of fresh air, he's never been more grateful to be outside. His clothes are hanging loosely on him now, making him aware of the weight he's lost. If only Kian had chosen the lake for their meeting point. He'd love nothing more than to sink into the warm depths of the water and wash away the stress of his ordeal.

"Did you hear that?" Nova grips the back of his shirt and pulls him to a stop.

"What?" He'd been so lost in his thoughts he'd failed to hear anything.

"There's something out there."

"I heard it," says Thea.

"Me, too," says Felicia.

The group of people pause and wait. He can feel their eyes on him in the dark and he cringes, reminding himself of his responsibilities.

Just as he's about to reassure them that whatever they heard was nothing, footsteps come rushing up from the back of the group.

He tenses, then relaxes as the soft moonlight reveals Kian's familiar shape.

Kian.

Thank Terra for his cousin. A natural born leader. The true heir of Askala.

Dex sighs as the weight of responsibility shifts from his shoulders. There's no need for him to say anything right now.

"Quiet, everyone," Kian hisses. "We need to be sure there's nothing out there. Don't move. Just listen."

Dex curses himself. Kian has just said the exact opposite of what he was going to suggest. Further proof of who makes the better leader. He feels like hugging him for returning, except he's just been told not to move...

Everyone is holding so still that Dex can barely hear anyone breathing. He blinks in the dim light and listens, hoping Wren is okay to hold up the rear of the group without Kian.

At first he hears nothing except the sound of a few crickets in the distance. But then there's a crack of a twig and the sound of something scratching in the dirt.

"The boulders are just through there," Kian whispers to Dex. Or is he whispering to Nova? It's hard to tell.

"Could it be the others?" Nova keeps her voice low in response. "You know Luca can't sit still."

Who is Luca? Dex shuffles his feet, hoping whoever Luca is, he's on their side.

"Stay here, everyone," says Kian, as loudly as he dares. "Dex and I will check it out."

Dex's heart hammers at the sound of his name. It seems his responsibilities haven't been entirely lifted after all. But that's okay. He got these people into this mess. He needs to do what he can to get them out.

Kian leads the way, Dex just behind trying to match his light but certain steps. They break through the trees into the small clearing around the boulders. The night sky lights their surroundings just enough to make out the shadows.

Dex is just about to slap Kian on the back to celebrate the empty clearing when his cousin lifts his hand, warning him to keep quiet.

"Look," he whispers. "Under the rock."

Dex strains his eyes, then pulls back when he sees what Kian's pointing at.

There's a huge polar grizzly asleep, having made a den at the bottom of one of the boulders that sits on a lean.

This was why Dex had taken the people to the lab. There are so many dangers out here.

The bear groans and moves about on the ground, scratching at the dirt as if that will make the hard ground more comfortable. Dex isn't sure if it's the same beast that tried to attack Nova, but it could be. It's certainly big enough.

Kian takes a cautious step back and nods at Dex.

Dex tips his head in return and they walk as noiselessly as they can until they reach their people. It's darker underneath the trees and Dex blinks, trying to get his eyes to focus. At least he can see some shapes out here, unlike when he'd been in the lab.

"It's a grizzly." Kian keeps his voice low, but it's enough to travel across the group. "Turn around. Stay calm."

Silently, the long line of people retrace their steps. Any normal group would probably panic. But not this one. They've been through so much already. This is a minor blip to them. Just as long as that grizzly stays asleep…

Wren will be in the lead now. Dex is glad she didn't follow Kian. He trusts her to take them to the safest place she can.

If such a thing exists.

Kian is walking backward, his eyes glued to the end of the path that opens up to the clearing, his ears tuned. Dex presses his back against Kian's as they take their cautious steps so that his cousin can step more confidently. He can feel the tension running down Kian's rigid spine. It's a comfort to know he isn't the only one out here to be afraid.

The line of people continue on, then bend to the right and take the path that leads to the cliffs.

Of course, that's where Wren would go. She loves feasting her eyes on the view up there. Well, apart from the steep drop of the cliff. And they've never seen a bear up there.

But Kian isn't seeming to like this idea so much. He's agitated, his whole body reacting to this change in direction.

"What's wrong?" Dex whispers. "What can you see?"

"We need to stop," Kian hisses.

Dex's father hears Kian's urgent call and sends the message further up the chain where it's passed on again. The long line of people draw to a halt and Nova slides past Dex to Kian's side.

"We can't leave Luca!" she says in an urgent whisper.

Luca again! Who is this mysterious guy and why is he so important?

"I know," says Kian. "We'll stay behind. Dex and Wren can take these people to safety."

"Do you think he's still with Shiloh and Avis?" she asks.

At last a name he knows. Shiloh. But who in sweet Terra is Avis?

"They won't separate." Kian's voice may be low, but it's determined. Dex wonders if he's trying to convince Nova or himself.

"We're not separating either." Dex pulls back his shoulders and stares at Kian's shadow. "I've had enough of that."

Dex's father looms closer. "It's not safe here, Kian. I'll take the people to the cliffs and we'll wait for you there. You do what you have to do here, then join us."

"But it's dangerous out there," says Dex.

"And what am I?" his father snaps back. "A rotten pteropod? I've been around a lot longer than any of you. I can take care of them. Besides, these people are some of the bravest I've ever seen."

Dex swallows. His father's right. Dex shouldn't underestimate him.

"I'm staying as well," says Felicia.

"No!" Nova is so adamant she almost shouts. "You're still not strong enough, Flick. Stay with Callix. He'll get you to safety."

Felicia huffs, then somewhat reluctantly agrees. It seems

whatever happened in the Outlands has drawn Felicia to Nova's side, making Dex even more curious about what they've been through.

"Get moving, Callix," Kian orders in a whisper. "We'll meet you up at the cliffs as soon as we've located the others. Hurry!"

It's now that Dex realizes his error. In insisting he stay with Kian and Nova, he's separated himself from Wren.

He clears his throat, needing to make things right. "I can't—"

"What's the hold up?" Wren's small frame emerges from the shadows as she hisses her question at them, practically gluing herself to Dex's side. "You trying to make sure the grizzly has time to catch up?"

Dex lets out a long breath. It seems Wren is having just as much trouble staying away from him as he is from her.

"Callix is taking the people to the cliffs," says Kian. "Nova, Dex and I are going to find...the people we came here with."

"I'm staying with you." Wren puts a hand on Dex's back. "I know how to handle a grizzly. You need me."

"What am I?" Dex rolls his eyes in the dark. "A rotten pteropod?"

"Huh?" Wren pulls back slightly and he realizes she hadn't been there when Callix had made his early comment.

"Doesn't matter." Dex shifts the laptop under his arm so he can stand just that little bit closer to Wren.

"We'll get moving," Dex's father says.

"We'll join you soon." Kian steps forward. "Go."

"Take this." Dex shoves the laptop at his father who takes it without question, his shadow disappearing as he moves into the darkness.

The people shuffle ahead and Thea embraces Nova and whispers urgent pleas to take care of herself.

"I'll see you soon," Nova promises. "I've survived far worse than this. Take care of Flick."

"Be careful, Nova," says Flick before they walk away.

Aarov appears at the back of the group as they move on, no doubt having been asked by Dex's father to take Kian's place. Forever the loyal soldier. Thank goodness he's on their side.

Their shadows blend into the night as the people walk on.

And it's the four of them once more.

Dex. Wren. Kian. Nova.

Together.

Alone.

United.

"We're going to need a group hug," says Dex wrapping one arm around Wren and the other around Kian.

"I guess we can't call it a brug this time." Kian pulls Nova closer and she puts her other arm around Wren to form a circle.

"Um, what's a brug?" Nova asks.

"Never mind." Dex tips his head forward. "Secret men's business."

They fall silent as they stand in their huddle, and Dex focuses on being grateful for this moment. His three best friends are here with him. There was a time when he'd thought he'd never see any of them ever again.

"What's the plan?" Wren asks as she breaks from Nova but continues to hold onto Dex. "I'm ready to do whatever it takes."

Dex's heart surges with love for the little ball of muscle beside him. How wrong Phoenix got it when he'd called her little bird. She's more like a little shark. So brave. So fierce. And a little intimidating if he's completely honest.

"We need to find somewhere safe to hide," says Kian. "There were three others we left behind when we came to help you. They should've been waiting at the boulders for us."

Nova lets out a whimper. "You don't think the grizzly got them, do you?"

"Luca would spot a bear from a mile away," Kian reassures.

"Okay, enough about this Luca." Dex steps forward. "Who is he and why is he so important to you?"

"He's just a kid," says Nova. "But an incredible one. He came back with us on the raft."

"You brought a kid here?" The incredulity is clear in Wren's voice. "I mean, the Outlands is bad, but this place right now—"

"We didn't really get a choice," Kian cuts her off.

"And who else is with him?" Dex asks.

"Shiloh." Nova sounds hesitant and Dex waits to hear who else was with them.

"So, just two of them." Wren has clearly missed what Dex picked up on. "We can handle that."

"There's three actually." Nova sounds even more hesitant now and Dex holds his breath. He knew there was more. "There's…a woman, too."

"Fine." Wren speaks with such certainty Dex wonders if he'd imagined the reluctant tone to Nova's voice.

Nova and Kian don't say anything to each other, but Dex can sense something passing between them. No, he hadn't imagined it. There's more to this story than they're being told. But for now, he has no choice except to trust their reason for keeping quiet.

"Come on." Kian leads them a little further down the path to a wide shrub that opens out like a tent. They crawl underneath and crouch down, peering out between the branches.

"Is this seriously the plan?" Wren asks. "We wait here to be eaten?"

"Keep your voice down." Kian's annoyance is clear.

Dex smiles. It's nice to know with everything that's changed in Askala that some things have stayed the same. Wren and Kian may have a newfound respect for each other, but they still know how to rub each other the wrong way.

There's a glimmer beside him and Dex realizes Wren has her knife out. Or is it his knife? It really doesn't matter. Whoever's knife it is, it's best placed in Wren's hands. She's the one who knows how to use it.

"Where are they?" Nova asks, her voice no less anxious than it was before.

"Shiloh will know what to do." It's like a different person is speaking when Kian talks to Nova. There's no trace of the annoyed tone he'd just used with Wren. "She probably saw the bear and took them somewhere else."

"How's your baby?" asks Wren. "Are you still..."

Dex's heart stills. He hadn't thought to ask Nova that. He'd just assumed...

"The baby's fine," says Nova and relief slides through Dex.

"Felicia lost hers, didn't she?" asks Wren.

Dex's eyebrows shoot up at Wren's question. How could she know that?

"She did." Nova's voice is full of pain.

"Figured that. What about Thom?" Wren asks. "You haven't mentioned him."

"Thom's a hero," says Kian, before Nova gets a chance to answer. "He died protecting Nova and Felicia."

Dex fights down the pain expanding across his chest. Thom's dead. Surely, this can't be happening.

"The bastards," Wren mutters. "I thought you'd be safe if you had a big guy like Thom with you."

"But Finn and Dean are okay," Nova adds, seeming to be trying to ease the gravity of Kian's words. "They decided to stay behind. Dean's putting an army together to help us. And Finn found love with a beautiful girl called Dharma. We're happy for him."

Dex doesn't say anything to this. What can he say? Finn finding love doesn't seem enough to take away the sorrow at losing Thom.

"You sure Dean's army is going to help us?" Wren asks. "Or is he going to help his beloved brother?"

"We don't know," says Kian. "But I don't think we should

factor him into any plans we make when it comes to over-throwing Ronan."

"Shh," warns Wren, scrambling to her feet and crouching beside Dex with her knife held out. "There's someone out there."

"Hold still," hisses Kian, just as something rushes at them, rolling under the shrub and landing at their feet.

Dex's heart pounds so hard he's surprised it doesn't burst from his chest as Kian throws himself at Wren to keep her from attacking.

"Luca!" Nova cries far louder than she's supposed to.

"Nova, I found you," a small child whimpers.

Dex doesn't need the daylight to know that this child is wrapped in Nova's arms. He can almost feel the love radiating from their direction.

"Kian?" the child asks, and Dex hears his cousin leave Wren to join the reunion.

Dex shuffles over to Wren and helps her back up to a seated position. "You okay?"

"I'm fine." Wren brushes herself down and nestles in beside him. "Luckily Kian lost a bit of weight in the Outlands."

"Luca, where are the others?" Kian asks. "What are you doing out here on your own?"

"They're hiding from the bear," comes the small child's reply. "They fell asleep, so I thought I'd look for you."

"Luca!" Nova scolds. "You should have stayed together."

"I could hear you, though," he says. "You whisper real loud."

Dex stifles a laugh even though he knows he should be afraid. This kid sure has some personality. It's no wonder he made such a big impression on Kian and Nova.

"We need to be more careful." Kian's voice is even softer than before. "If Luca could find us then so could that grizzly."

"No way," says Luca. "That bear snores even louder than Avis."

Dex feels every one of Wren's muscles tense beside him.

"What did you say?" she asks. "What name did you just say? Who's with you?"

"Only Avis," says Luca and Wren shifts on the ground beside Dex.

"Who's Avis?" Dex asks, desperate to know why Wren is having such a strong reaction to her name.

"Avis is the woman who saved me," says Luca.

"And she's the one who abandoned me." Wren chokes out her words. "Avis is my mother."

WREN

*A*vis.

He said Avis.

There can only be one Avis in the Outlands.

Wren's head spins and her foot taps. She needs to burn off this tsunami of emotion that's washing through her body, cell by cell. But she can't step out from under this shrub or she could become a polar grizzly's midnight snack.

Avis is supposed to be dead. Killed after she'd run off with a man from the village. Cy had been very clear about the way she'd abandoned them. Phoenix may have found this hard to accept, but Wren hadn't. She believed every word of it. Because what kind of excuse is acceptable for leaving your young children with a man like Cy?

Absolutely no excuse. And knowing now that she's alive only makes it worse. Because it means she not only didn't take them with her. She also didn't come back.

Bile spears up Wren's throat and she leans out of the shrub to vomit.

Dex rubs her back and she shakes him off, not wanting to be

touched, not even by him. The betrayal that's coursing through her body is too much.

Mothers are supposed to protect and love. Not disappear for over a decade then pop back into your life the moment you need them the least.

"Why didn't you tell me?" She directs her words at Nova and Kian, not caring who answers.

"We didn't have time," says Kian. "There was too much else happening."

"And we weren't sure how you'd react," adds Nova, getting closer to the truth.

"Is that Wren and Phee over there?" Luca asks.

Wren shakes her head at the use of the shortened version of Phoenix's name that he clearly learned from Avis. That's supposed to be just for the people who love him. Which doesn't include their mother.

"My name's Dex, but this is Wren." Dex uses the gentle voice Wren's heard him use with children before. He doesn't know that children in the Outlands don't get spoken to like that.

"I thought you'd be happy to see Avis," says Luca. "She's sure been looking forward to seeing you."

"Shh, Luca," hushes Nova. "Wren's just surprised."

Wren wipes her mouth on her sleeve and slumps back to lean on Dex, needing his comfort just as much as she'd been repelled by it moments ago. He wraps an arm around her and drops a kiss on top of her head.

"I'm here," he soothes. "I'm here."

Stubborn tears sting her eyes. She knows he's here. He's been here for her since the moment he first laid eyes on her. He'd never walk away and leave her behind, no matter how bad things got.

"Where's Shiloh?" Kian asks Luca. Wren rolls her eyes at the omission of her mother's name. It's not like she's going to forget. He may as well mention her.

"Thirty-nine big steps that way," Luca replies and they all know he's pointing somewhere in the dark. "Avis's burns were hurting real bad after the acid on the raft. Shiloh put some sap on them and they both fell asleep."

"They'll be worried about you when they wake up," says Kian. "How about we go and let them know you're okay?"

"We'll stay here," says Dex, tightening his grip on Wren and saving her the trouble of speaking up.

"I'll go with Kian and Luca," says Nova. "Give you guys the chance to talk."

Wren says nothing. What can she say to the people who brought her mother back to her without asking what she might think about it? Not everyone has a happy family like the people here in Askala.

"Thanks, Nova." Dex's voice is full of the sort of kindness Wren just can't summon right now.

There's a shuffling in the dim light and Wren buries her face in Dex's chest as she waits for them to leave.

And then it's just the two of them. The only other human she ever wants to see again.

"Did you know she was alive?" he asks. "You told me she was dead."

"I thought she was," Wren answers quickly. She doesn't want Dex thinking that she lied to him again. "Cy told us she left our village with another man and died shortly afterwards."

Dex lets out a slow breath. "Wren…"

"Don't Dex." She sits up a little straighter. "Please, don't tell me that Cy lied to me. Don't tell me that there could be another side to this story. She left us! Nothing excuses that."

"I wasn't going to tell you any of that." He pulls her back to him. "I have no idea what her reasons were. I was going to say that I'll support you however you want to respond to this. If you're mad at her then I'm mad, too. If you forgive her, then I forgive, too. We're in this together."

"Why didn't she come back for us?" Wren asks, unable to help the question from leaving her lips. "If she's been alive this whole time, why didn't she come looking for us?"

"I don't know." Dex shifts on the hard ground so she's sitting between his legs, cradling her with his whole body now and she leans into him.

"We won't always know why people do things," he says. "I don't know why someone killed my mother. Or why they hurt me. I don't know why they chose us. I've had to learn to live with that and it's hard. But maybe this is your chance to find out. You can get the answers I'll never have."

"But what if they're not the answers I want?" she asks, putting her greatest fear into words.

"At least they're answers."

"Maybe not knowing is better than knowing."

"Maybe." He kisses her forehead again. "Maybe not."

Wren falls silent, pressing her head against Dex's chest and listening to the sound of his beating heart, thankful that whoever took his mother's life chose to spare him. Her experience in Askala would have been entirely different if she hadn't met him. Who knows, perhaps she'd be sitting in the Oasis with Cy right now if she hadn't crossed paths with Dex?

She closes her eyes and wonders if that could possibly be true? She's always known Cy is cruel. But she'd thought his love for her had outweighed that. After all, he'd been the parent who'd stuck by her and that had to count for something.

But in the end it hadn't.

Wren's tears fall in the safety of Dex's arms as she allows herself to fall apart.

She's not crying for the person she is now. That person will be okay. She's crying for the girl she once was. The small child who'd clung to her twin brother's hand like her life had depended on it. Which perhaps it had. The child who'd grown rather than been raised. The child who'd learned to watch her back and be brave instead of learning to trust and love. She'd missed out on so much.

Yet...

Somehow she'd risen above it. She'd learned to trust. She'd found love. She'd become a person she didn't entirely hate.

Her tears continue to fall and Dex holds her. The night passes slowly, Dex's grasp never weakening, even when they doze off and wake to find the sun peeking through the branches hanging down around them.

"Are you awake?" she whispers, aware they can't stay in here all day. They need to get to the others at the cliff. She needs to face the mother she never wanted to meet.

Dex groans as he tries to stretch his back.

"Thank you." Wren kisses him on the cheek, enjoying the warmth of his skin. Everything always feels better in the morning, even when it isn't.

"You don't need to thank me." Dex leans into her, rubbing his fingers down her face. "I'm always here for you."

"And I'm always here for you." She kisses him again. "Except right now I really need to stand up."

Dex laughs. "Yeah, I think my body's frozen into this position. Not sure I *can* stand up."

Wren crawls out from between his legs and emerges from the shrub, blinking in the morning light. The forest is so much less frightening when you can see the dangers that surround you.

"How did I become a hundred years old?" Dex limps out from beneath the branches and rubs at his ribs.

"How are they healing?" she asks, gently touching his middle.

"Getting there. I'm okay."

It's clear he's playing his injury down, but Wren decides to let it pass. All she can think about right now is that she's sharing her breathing space in this forest with her mother. No matter how long she's had to think about this, it still doesn't feel real.

"Where do you think they are?" She looks around trying to remember how many paces Luca had said and in what direction she'd heard them disappear.

Dex shrugs and turns his neck to the side and lets it crack.

But they don't have to wonder for long as Nova steps out from behind a wide tree trunk.

"Hey there," she says. "You guys all right?"

"We're fine, thanks." Wren keeps her tone brisk, hating that she's mad with Nova but unsure about how to let that feeling go.

"I'm sorry, Wren." Nova comes closer, stopping when she's a few feet away. "We should've warned you. We thought we were doing the right thing. Avis loves you so much. She—"

"Enough!" Wren holds up a hand, unable to bear hearing any more. "People don't leave people they love."

"Ronan told her he'd kill you if she came back." Nova's eyes are wide. She clearly believes what she's saying. "She was protecting you. She was so scared. He did terrible things to her."

"He did terrible things to me and Phoenix, too." Wren crosses her arms. "Terrible things that he wouldn't have been able to do if she took us with her when she left."

"Perhaps you should go on ahead, Nova," suggests Dex. "Take Wren's mother to the cliffs and we'll meet you there."

"We're safer together." Wren shakes her head, knowing she can't put this off forever. Their safety has to come first. "I can handle it."

"We know you can." Nova dares to step a little closer. "You can handle anything. And Avis is really wonderful. I think you'll—"

"Nova." It's Dex who cuts her off this time. "She's not ready to hear that yet."

"Of course." Nova turns in the direction she came and looks back over her shoulder. "Come on. I'll take you to them. They're just over there."

"Any sign of the grizzly?" Wren asks.

"It's gone." Nova walks away. "Come on!"

Dex reaches for Wren's hand and they follow Nova.

"It'll be okay," he says.

She nods, even though she knows it won't. He's not the only one who can play down his injuries. Even if hers are ones that can't be seen.

They pass the tree to find a group of people ahead. There's Kian and Shiloh. A small boy who must be Luca. And a woman with her back turned.

She's short.

Like Wren.

Dark hair in a tangle.

Like Wren.

A strong, lithe body.

Just. Like. Wren.

They walk closer and the woman turns. Wren's surprised to see she has some kind of netting draped over the right side of her face.

More secrets.

What is she hiding?

The woman blinks at Wren, tears spilling down her face and Wren gasps. She has an older version of her own face. It's like looking into a time machine.

"Wren!" Her mother's voice is trembling and she reaches out a tentative hand.

Wren freezes, holding tightly to Dex. She can't do this.

She can't!

But she has to.

"My daughter." Her mother comes closer and Wren studies the netting on her face, wondering what can be so awful that she feels the need to have to cover herself like this.

"I thought you were dead," says Wren, surprised these are the words that chose to come out after all the possible options she'd dreamed up overnight.

"In some ways I have been," her mother says. "I'm nothing without my children."

She reaches for Wren, but Wren steps back. It's one thing to be face to face with her—well, face to half-face—but it's another to allow her mother to touch her.

"What happened to you?" Wren asks, still focusing on the side of the face she can't see. "Why are you covering yourself?"

"I didn't want you to be afraid." Her mother lifts her hand to the netting. "People don't usually like what they see when they meet me."

"Show me." Wren's come this far. She needs to see the face she thought she'd never lay her eyes on again, no matter what she's hiding under there. She has no memory of what she looked like. Wren had been too young when she'd left them.

Her mother pulls on the netting and it falls away, revealing layers of deep scars covering the entire right side of her face. It would be fascinating to study if it didn't look so painful.

Wren blinks, her heart healing and breaking all at once. Her mother has suffered in just the way Wren has spent her life wishing upon her. But now that she sees her, she can't be glad. All she feels is an overwhelming sadness.

"I'm sorry for what happened to you," Wren whispers.

"Wren, I'm the one who's sorry," her mother pleads. "Cy told me he'd hurt you if I came for you."

"Nova said that." Wren doesn't want to hear this again. The words hurt too much.

"And you don't believe it?" The hurt in her mother's eyes is clear, but Wren doesn't know what to do about it. She can't heal her mother's wounds when her own are still running so deep.

"It seems my whole life has been a lie," says Wren.

"Please, Wren. May I hold you? Just for a moment. I've waited so long." Her mother reaches out her hands, stopping short of touching her. Waiting for permission Wren doesn't want to give, but also doesn't know how to deny.

Wren lets go of Dex's hand and nods.

Her mother steps up to her and reaches out her quivering arms. She pulls Wren to her, pressing the undamaged side of her face to Wren's cheek as she embraces her.

Wren forces her arms to lift and she places them on her mother's back, enduring this hug that's both too much and far too little. She's nowhere near ready for this, but she can see that her mother has waited long enough.

"You're beautiful, Wren." Her mother pulls back and looks at her, drinking her in with an expression of such love that Wren has to look away. "I knew you'd be beautiful. How's Phoenix?"

"He looks like Cy." Wren bites her lip wondering how she always manages to say the wrong thing.

"I've heard," her mother says. "But I'm sure his heart is different."

Wren nods. "Phoenix is a good person. He saved all our lives at great risk to himself."

"I heard that, too. I'm proud of both of you."

Wren is just about to ask what right she has to be proud of anything they've done when Dex steps up beside her. Forever the peacekeeper, he must've sensed her change in mood.

"We need to get to the cliffs," Dex says. "If that's okay?"

Her mother steps back, tucking the netting that had been used as a scarf into the waistband of the elaborate skirt she's wearing.

She sees Wren watching her. "It's to—"

"Keep the bugs off," Wren finishes. "You've been living in Fairbanks?"

Her mother nods.

"But it's dangerous there." Wren's brows shoot up, surprised anyone could survive in the old city for so long.

"It is." Her mother pulls back her shoulders, and Wren gets a glimpse of the hard woman she's become. "But there are places far more dangerous than Fairbanks."

Such as the one you left me in.

But she doesn't say this out loud. There will be time to talk later. Time when she's had a chance to process that massive curveball her life has just been thrown.

"Let's go, already," complains Luca tugging at Nova's hand. "I want to see the cliffs. Are they like my tree?"

"They're different to your tree," says Nova.

"How different?" he asks. "I can't imagine what they look like."

"Sometimes life has surprises that are hard to imagine." Nova shifts her gaze from Luca to Wren and her mother. "Sometimes they turn out to be the best surprises in the world. We just need to give them the time they need so we can see them through a new lens."

"I hope so," Wren's mother says as she turns and follows Luca who's already skipping down the path.

"I hope so, too," says Wren, safe in the knowledge that her mother's too far away to hear.

It seems Dex was right. She has some answers.

The only problem is that they're to questions she never wanted to ask.

NOVA

They find the people of Askala not far from where they spent the night. It seems they didn't want to hike in the dark. Thea cries out as she rushes toward Nova and engulfs her in a hug.

They hold each other tightly, tears brimming and lips smiling that they finally have time to reunite properly. "I was so worried," her mother says. She pulls back. "You look tired. Are you okay? And the baby?"

"Sucking up every drop of energy I have," Nova grins.

"You were the same," her mother smiles proudly. "I wanted to sleep for three months straight."

They pull back, knowing they need to get to safety. Too many lives depend on it.

The walk to the cliffs is punctured with the sporadic sounds of coughing. Nova walks slowly, giving these people's lungs time to cope with the slow ascent. Her mother bumps her arm repeatedly, she's walking so close and Nova smiles inside. She's slowly accumulating people who won't leave her side. Her mother. Flick. Kian.

Luca grips her hand. "You wanna rest?"

Nova almost rolls her eyes as she squeezes his hand. He's about the tenth person to ask her that question. "I'm fine. Thank you, you're doing a very good job of looking after me."

Luca puffs out his chest. "That's what Kian said."

"Besides, we're almost there."

Only a few more yards and the rutted path opens out, expanding to reveal rocky ground and blue sky. Luca releases Nova's hand, streaking to the edge. For a moment, Nova's heart leaps to her throat and she almost calls him back. But Luca stops, his little body frozen as he sees the beauty of Askala from this new vantage point.

The others fan out along the tree line, finding some shade to sit under. They've grown up with this view, and their tired bodies and shell-shocked minds don't have the energy to appreciate it right now.

Nova walks over to Luca, resting her hands on his shoulders as she stands behind him. "It's beautiful, isn't it?"

Luca can't take his gaze off the vista bathed in sunlight. Birds flit and dip over the canopy that extends before them, the contrast stark to the world he grew up in. "Askala is so...different," Luca breathes. "I didn't know there were that many greens in the world."

Just like Nova discovered how many shades of gray existed when she came to the Outlands.

"Nova and I grew up in that forest."

Nova startles only to settle as everything becomes right in her world. Kian wraps his arms around her, pulling her against his front.

"That's a lot of trees to climb," Luca says, obviously impressed.

Nova smiles. "It was."

It's a childhood Wren should've had, and Luca now has a chance to have.

Luca turns, looking over his shoulder at Kian. "Your job is to protect that forest, isn't it?"

Nova feels Kian's sigh rather than hears it. "It is. And the people who live in it."

Which is where the challenge lies. Save the people of Askala. Defend the world they depend on.

Nova winds her fingers through Kian's, telling him he won't be facing this alone.

Luca turns back to the view, scanning the world coming to life before them. "I'm going to help you," he states resolutely. Nova can't see his face, but she can imagine the determined set of his jaw.

She squeezes him, pulling him closer against her. "We're all going to."

"We just have to figure how," murmurs Kian.

Nova looks over her shoulder, her gaze connecting with Kian's. "Together."

She knows it won't be that simple. That a war is about to be waged. But they've proven what they can achieve when they're united. She has to believe that's enough.

Kian's dark gaze swims like troubled waters. He nods, even though they don't calm. "Together."

"Together," adds Luca in a whisper.

Kian's arms tighten and Nova's eyes sting. Her heart has never been fuller. And yet her future has never been more uncertain.

The sound of movement reaches them and Nova knows they need to speak to their people. They'll be wanting to know what happens next.

How will they survive out here?

What do they do next?

How do they defeat Ronan...

Wishing their moment could've lasted longer, Nova turns as Kian pulls away. Their responsibilities await.

They've just turned around when Wren strides toward them, Dex right behind her. "Nova, we have a situation."

Nova keeps the frown from her face as she rushes to her. "What? What is it?"

"Our..." Wren's jaw works. "Our mothers want to go find food."

Nova blinks. "Oh. That seems like a good idea."

"They're saying we need to go with them."

Nova realizes the issue. The reunion between Wren and Avis had been painful to watch. Poignant, bittersweet, so fragile Nova hadn't wanted to breathe. Avis probably thinks going in a group is a gentle way to spend time with her daughter.

Except Wren isn't ready.

Kian comes to stand beside Nova. "I think we need to talk as a team. We have some decisions to make."

Wren visibly relaxes. "Damn straight we do."

"But first we need to organize food and shelter."

"Of course, we do," she mutters.

Nova places a hand on her arm. "No one does anything they're not comfortable doing."

Dex elbows Wren. "Like going near the cliffs."

Wren's lips twitch. "I'd prefer to do that than go on a family picnic."

They make their way back to the people. Over thirty of them, they huddle in small groups. Bedraggled and covered in soot, they look like the refugees they are. They turn their faces to the four of them and Nova feels the weight of their gazes.

They're waiting to learn what happens next. More than that, they're waiting for reassurance.

"Good morning." Kian scans them one by one. "Despite the difficult circumstances, it warms my heart to see you all. I know things have been uncertain and frightening. It hurts to know not everyone who stood up against Ronan is here."

The people shuffle, glancing at one another. Bea nods from

where she stands beside Vern. "It's good to see you back, Kian." Her face softens as she looks at Nova. "You too, Nova."

Nova's mother presses her hand to her mouth, obviously trying to contain tears again. Nova smiles at them both. Bea had embraced her before rushing into the forest. Her mother had held her like she didn't plan on letting go.

"Right now," Kian continues, "we need food, shelter and fresh water. I propose we form teams to secure each of those." His gaze flickers to Wren. "We'll need some raven eggs, both for protein and to purify the water."

Callix raises his hand. "I'll lead that."

Nova guesses that Callix realizes that if he set such a task for their Proving, then it should be something he's able to do himself.

Two more, including Aarov, volunteer to help.

Kian nods. "Be careful. The ravens are territorial." He scans the others. "We'll need people to find food and firewood."

Avis steps forward. "I can collect the pods of the mangrove pine and prepare them to make flour." Her gaze flickers to Wren. "I'll need some others to help me."

Thea raises her hand. "I'd like to learn more about this. I'll go."

Luca leaps to Avis's side, seeing an opportunity to finally head out on an expedition. "Me too."

Several others move beside them, including Shiloh. Nova feels Wren tense. She knows her mother wants her to join the group. Nova's not sure which is the better outcome—Wren forcing herself to do this or watching Avis's face fall as Wren rejects her.

"Our last task," Kian calls out in a strong, firm voice. "Is to build shelter. We'll need the strongest and most able for this." He looks to Wren. "And any of those with experience."

Wren arches a brow. "Well, I'm no Phee, but surely it can't be that hard."

Kian nods, his dark eyes glinting with understanding. "Excellent. We'll build as many as we can before nightfall." He turns to the Askalans. "Each of you is the shining light Askala needs in this time of darkness. You've already proven that together, we're strong. Together, we'll make this right."

Some people nod, the odd person smiles. They all move with renewed purpose now they have a task.

Dex slaps him on the shoulder. "You always did that better than me."

But Kian doesn't smile. "It wasn't enough. We need to figure out how we get their home back."

Nova places a hand on his arm, noticing the tightness in his muscles. "Like you said, we'll figure it out. Right now, let's focus on this."

His shoulders unwinding, Kian nods. "That, I can do."

"We're going to need branches," says Wren. "And a lot of them."

Dex waves his arm in the direction of the forest. "What my girl wants, my girl gets."

They begin snapping off branches, Kian instructing them to not take more than two or three from any particular tree.

Slowly the pile of building material grows. With each jerk and snap, Nova feels her arms tiring. Occasionally, she stops, not wanting to admit how exhausting this is, but not wanting to draw attention to her need for a rest. Every time it seems someone glances at her. Kian. Dex. Wren. Flick.

At one stage, her mother and Avis return with bags of mangrove pine pods wrapped in material. Her mother rushes over as if she needs to touch Nova just to make sure she hasn't disappeared.

Avis glances at Wren, but her daughter is already turning away. "Come on, Thea," she says quietly. "I have another idea for what we can eat."

Nova and Kian glance at each other. "Let's hope we can get a fire going," Kian mutters, his eyes glinting.

The thought of raw cockroaches has Nova shuddering as she smiles back.

As the afternoon wears on, Nova starts to look forward to crawling under one of the shelters they're about to build and sleep for a week. She brushes her hand over her belly. "Growing you is exhausting," she whispers.

An arm slips around her waist, drawing her against hard, familiar muscles. "What did you just tell our daughter?"

Nova glances up, her heart smiling at Kian's words. "Our daughter?"

Kian's hand splays across her stomach, his face gentle. "Just hoping. A little girl would be pretty cool."

"With your strength and determination," Nova breathes.

"And your compassion." Kian's warm eyes narrow. "And your work ethic." He glances around, seeming to spot something. "I want you to sit over there and rest while we build these."

Nova opens her mouth to states she's pregnant, not sick, when Flicks loops her arm through hers. "You heard the boss. We have to work together, remember? That means not making trouble."

Flick pulls her over to sit beneath the mangrove pine Kian indicated and Nova lets her. They've barely eaten today, drunk even less while they wait for Callix and the others to purify some water with the raven eggs. She'll be no help to anyone if she collapses.

Nova sits back and watches as the others get to work. Wren instructs while the others drag branches over and work to lean them up against each other. There are grunts and mutters as pine needles poke eyes. There are frowns and disagreements as branches don't sit where they're supposed to.

But what really catches Nova's attention is the way Wren and Dex frequently touch—when passing a branch, when brushing pine needles from the other's back. When Dex presses a quick kiss to Wren's temple. When Wren leans in for the briefest second, her face focused on the task at hand although her whole body smiles.

Nova caresses her stomach, looking forward to the day it grows to accommodate her child. "These people are the ones who will help raise you. They'll show you that *together* is just another word for *love*."

"If you're going to keep up that sappy stuff, your kid is gonna grow up to be as wussy as his dad."

Nova spins around, her eyes wide as she recognizes the voice. "Phoenix!"

He holds his fingers to his lips, eyes twinkling. "Hey, Blondie. It seems I arrived just in time."

He points at the others and Nova follows his gaze. Kian, Wren, Dex, and Flick are all standing back admiring their first shelter.

Dex angles his head. "Is it leaning a little to the left?"

"It's fine," Wren assures. "I've seen Phee build heaps of these. I know what I'm doing. Whoever gets to sleep in this one will be thanking us."

Just as she finishes her sentence, the structure collapses, causing them all to jump back. The branches crumple, tumbling and falling over each other as they flop to the ground, pine needles quivering in the aftermath.

Flick lifts her hands to her hips. "Well, I'm glad this one isn't mine."

Phoenix pushes to his feet, sauntering over. "Me, too," he drawls. "You're far too beautiful to be turned into flatbread."

"Phee!" Wren squeals, rushing at him like a bullet.

She leaps and Phoenix catches her, his big body engulfing hers. He spins her around before setting her on the ground. "Good to see you, little bird."

She grins. "It sure is."

He glances at the pile of mangrove pine branches. "Good thing I'm here from the looks of things."

Kian steps forward. "What news do you have of Ronan?"

"He thinks I'm off hunting deer. Seems he's got a taste for venison." Wren winces but Phoenix glances at her as if to tell her there's more coming. "He wants a celebration dinner after the lab burned down with everyone in it."

Dex's arm tightens around Wren and she grips his hand. "So, the bastard thinks we're all dead."

"Yeah. The bastard does..."

Nova stays where she is, frozen with the pain that's filled the air around them. Wren's father left her to die in that fire. He's celebrating not only her death, but the people he murdered.

And now he believes the people here don't exist.

There's a rustling from the trees and Nova's mother and Avis appear, more material bunched in their hands.

Thea glances at Nova. "I can't believe you ate these things," she states, eyes alight with humor before she realizes everybody around her has lost the ability to move.

Avis drops her bundle, small bugs scurrying everywhere, her eyes wide and round as she takes in her son. She walks forward, the tears already tracking down her face.

Nova leaps to her feet and rushes over. "Phoenix, this is Avis. She came with us from the Outlands."

He blinks rapidly as he tries to assimilate that. He looks from Avis to Wren and back again. "My mother."

Avis lifts her hand only to drop it. "Phee, I'm so sorry. So, so sorry. I never wanted to leave you."

Now, his eyes are so wide it looks like he may never blink again. "I didn't believe you did."

Hope dawns across Avis's face. "Cy said he would..." She shakes her head. "It doesn't matter. Just know that I didn't have a choice."

"What did he do to you?" Phoenix chokes as he scans her scars.

Avis holds herself there, her body quivering with the need to hold her son as she shakes her head. No doubt Wren's struggle to accept her is holding her back.

But Phoenix decides for her. With one stride, he envelops her in a hug. Avis collapses in his embrace, her tears wetting the shoulder her head is resting on.

Nova holds still although she wants to press a hand to the heart aching in her chest. The moment is poignant and touching, but this would be difficult for Wren to watch.

In fact, Wren jolts into action, kicking a branch by her feet and stalking away. Avis and Phoenix separate, their faces differing shades of anguish as they watch her leave.

Dex takes a step to follow but Nova holds up her hand. "I'll go. You stay and learn how to build these so we have somewhere safe to sleep." It's only a matter of time before a storm arrives.

Dex hesitates but then nods. "She knows I'll be there the moment she blinks my way."

Nova brushes a hand down his arm as she passes him. Dex will be by Wren's side before she's even turned her head.

She finds Wren only a few feet into the trees. She's picking up stones from the forest floor and hurling them at the exposed area where a branch has been snapped off. Nova wonders if Wren's aware of the symbolism of what she's doing—taking out her anger on an existing wound.

Nova stays a few feet away. "Did I ever thank you for saving me from the polar grizzly? I don't think I've ever been more scared in my life."

Wren doesn't turn around, instead flinging another pebble at her bullseye. "About a thousand times."

"Well, that aim of yours saved my life."

Crack! A stone hits its mark. "Cy taught me how to use a

slingshot." *Crack!* "I learned pretty quick because every time I missed he whipped me over the back of the legs with a cane."

Nova winces. "It wasn't okay that he did that."

Wren finally looks at Nova, her dark eyes swimming with anger...and grief. "After coming here, I realized that. I also realized it's even more wrong for a mother to leave her children with a man like that."

"You would've felt helpless, Wren." Nova's chest aches with the pain vibrating through Wren's small body.

"I made myself strong because I had no choice." Her face turns fierce. "I knew there was no one to save me. And I wasn't wrong."

Nova nods. "You're the strongest person I know, and not because of what your father did to you. It's because you overcame that. You're kind and fair and fight for whimpering girls cornered by a polar grizzly. That's the heart Dex fell in love with."

Wren overcame adversity to be someone she should be proud of, just like Avis did. Nova hopes Wren will be able to see how similar they are, but right now, her pain—the abuse, the abandonment—needs to be acknowledged.

Wren pulls in a shuddering breath then pauses. She hikes her hands to her hips. "You know this isn't going to work."

"What isn't?"

"This agreeing with"—she waves her hand like the words she's hurled are still hanging in the air around them—"everything I've said."

"The fact that your father was a violent, abusive man? That you needed a mother to protect you?" Nova shrugs. "It's all true, Wren."

Her hands clench. "My mother left me, knowing I could die. My father left me, intending me to die."

Nova nods, acknowledging the pain those words must inflict. "But your mother came back."

Wren jerks back, turning her face away as if she can deflect the truth. But it's been said, and that's enough for now.

Nova glances over her shoulder. "We should probably check that Phoenix hasn't built a two-story mansion that Ronan will be able to see from the Oasis."

Wren straightens her shoulders like she's shaking off everything that's happened, probably hoping to leave it behind in the forest. "You're right. When we were stuck down in the secret room he said something about molding branches into arches."

They walk back and Nova stays close to Wren's side, conscious that Avis is probably there. After Phoenix's welcome, she wouldn't be leaving his side. Avis has looked forward to reuniting with her children from the moment she was forced to leave them.

The shelter is almost finished, looking far sturdier than the first effort. Wren stops even though they're barely out of the forest. "You've got to be kidding me."

Except she's not looking at her mother. She's looking at Phoenix...and Flick as she works beside him. He passes her a branch, instructing her on how to weave it into the one beside it as his hand guides hers. There's a slight flush on Flick's cheeks as she spends more time glancing over her shoulder than focusing on her hands.

Nova raises a brow. "Well, that's...cute."

"Not the word I was thinking," mutters Wren as she stalks over.

Instead of heading to Phoenix though, she moves toward Dex. He holds out his arm and she slips underneath, slotting in and holding tight. Wordlessly, he presses a kiss to her forehead and Nova almost smiles.

Dex has a lot of love to give, and Wren's had a life deprived of love. The fact she has the capacity to give it is a testament to her resilience.

Kian comes to join Nova, drawing her in the same way.

"Phoenix is going to stay and build a couple more but then he has to go back. We can't have Ronan becoming suspicious."

Nova nods. "We should be able to take it from there. His help has been invaluable."

"Once he's gone, I think the four of us need to talk."

Heaviness settles in Nova's gut at the resolve in Kian's voice. She knows it's inevitable, she knows it's necessary, but the thought of what has to come next scares her.

They have to decide what to do about Ronan.

KIAN

*P*hoenix doesn't make a move to leave until early evening, stating he'll tell his father he was tracking a stag. The prospect of putting up a set of antlers up on the wall as a symbol of his domination would be enough to explain Phoenix's absence, and for Ronan to demand his son go out hunting for as long as it takes.

By then, seven shelters have been erected, allowing almost half of them to sleep under some protection. Luca had quickly appointed himself as Phoenix's assistant, studying his every move and insisting he's going to build a shelter for Kian and Nova. This high and far away, Ronan's unlikely to find them, even if he were to take a stroll to the cliffs.

Callix, hands bloodied and hair disheveled, has created wrapped bundles of raven eggshells to filter water through. Avis and Thea have ground mangrove pine pods into flour and collected bugs for those hungry enough to eat them.

Kian watches as Phoenix says goodbye. Avis hugs him hard and it's obvious she doesn't want to let go. Kian can't blame her —the son she just reunited with is going back to his father...the man who was willing to watch his daughter burn because he believes she betrayed him.

Wren stands back, arms crossed, her frown only deepening when Felicia walks over, passing Phoenix a piece of uncooked flatbread. "For the trip home."

Phoenix grins. "Thanks, gorgeous." He leans in closer, winking as he stage whispers loud enough for Kian to hear several feet away. "Think of me as you sleep in the shelter I built for you."

Felicia flushes but quickly recovers, flipping her curls. "Think of me as you eat that bread."

Phoenix laughs, and it's nice to hear such a light sound as everything weighs so heavily around them.

With a last embrace, Avis bids Phoenix goodbye. Wren's already stalked away.

Luca stares at Phoenix as he disappears like he's made from shiny gold.

Kian sighs. Families are the most complex system of all.

As Thea checks in on Nova before heading off to collect some more firewood, Kian wonders how he can make sure these reunions aren't short-lived . Somehow, they have to fix this.

Avis joins Thea, the two seeming to have become fast friends. Kian raises his hand to gain their attention. "Fires after dark only, when Ronan and his men won't see the smoke. A few small fires are better than one large one. And they need to be out before morning."

They nod in understanding even though they're going to have to wait to bake the flatbread and cockroaches. Everyone's been told that Ronan believes they're dead. It's the only advantage they have right now.

Wren plants herself in front of him. "Now we talk?"

Kian nods. "Now, we talk."

He catches Dex and Nova's gaze and they walk over,

knowing this was coming. The four of them head for the trees and the little privacy they can afford. The others need decisions right now, not to overhear what obstacles they have to overcome to reach them.

Only a few feet into the forest, Kian stops. It'll be dark soon, and it's already a deep shade of gloom here. He wants to see the others' faces as they discuss this.

Lives are at stake.

And they're the only ones who can save them.

Wren leans against a tree as Dex rests a shoulder against the trunk beside her. Nova slips in beside Kian, winding her fingers through his. It's a wordless show of solidarity that warms his heart and he squeezes a thanks.

"So, we know what we're all here for," Kian starts.

"To bring that bastard Ronan down," growls Dex.

Kian nods. "The question is, how?"

"We have the element of surprise," says Nova. "When we attack, Ronan will never see us coming."

When we attack…

Kian sighs at the crux of the matter. "We have nothing to attack with. Just an army of people who've never fought a day in their life. Against two dozen men who have weapons and training."

Wren pushes away from the tree. "Well, fourteen men, now. We've lost a few along the way. Thirteen if you count Jagger as being on our side."

Dex dips his head toward Wren. "Plus, we have one person trained here."

"Two, if you include my brother," adds Wren. "If you give us a little time, we could give everyone some pointers."

Kian doesn't speak, letting the information digest. Fewer of them than he'd thought. And *us*—a physically and emotionally tattered bunch of peace-loving Askalans—talking of overthrowing them.

"And there's Dean..." murmurs Nova.

Kian tenses at the words. He's already thought of that. "I don't like any plan that depends on that guy."

Nova shrugs. "But if he does turn up with reinforcements, we'd be tipping the scales in our favor even more."

Dex rubs his chin. "When did you give him till?"

Kian reflexively glances at the sky, even though he can't see it through the canopy. Even though he already knows there will be the slightest sliver of moon up there tonight. "The night of the new moon. Tomorrow night."

"I don't like the dude any more than you do," says Dex. "But more people, particularly those from the Outlands, could really make a difference."

It could be a deal breaker in their ability to win this.

Kian nods. "So, we wait."

"We have the essentials—shelter, food, water," Nova says quietly. "It'll give people a chance to heal and get strong."

As long as there are no big storms and they don't get discovered. They have a reprieve, but it won't be forever.

Wren cracks her knuckles. "And Phee and I can train everyone in the basics while we wait. Nobody will go into this unprepared."

Kian has to work not to wince. Talking of taking his people into a battle against violent men with flamethrowers makes his stomach churn. "Thank you."

He's about to suggest they go back and let the others know when Dex steps forward. "And what about our people back at the Oasis?" His gaze catches Kian's. "Like your father."

Kian has to work to hold his stare. Of course, Dex would've thought of this, too. Magnus is his uncle. Callix's brother.

And the leader of Askala for most of their lives.

"It's my understanding that as long as the people on the Oasis do as they're told, they'll be okay."

Wren nods. "The more loyal they appear, the more they'll be rewarded."

"But Magnus is in the brig," says Nova quietly, not adding what everyone else is thinking.

He was the one who banished Ronan and seeded this hatred.

Kian looks to Wren, wishing he didn't have to ask this question. "What are his chances?"

Wren bites her lip, considering her answer. She looks away and Kian knows he's not going to like the words that come next. "His only chance of survival is not to be there."

Ronan's shown what he's capable of in the name of revenge.

Nova moves closer to Kian. "We need to get him out."

Kian's eyes shut as he tries to contain the pain. He already suspected this. As he's watched the family reunions around him —Nova and Thea, Avis and Phoenix, even the fragile connection trying to stretch between Avis and Wren—he's thought of his own family. His father a prisoner. His mother desperately doing what she can to save their children. The siblings Kian was supposed to build a future for.

"Having Magnus back would give our people hope," Nova muses, almost.as if she's turning this over in her mind.

It would give Kian a shoulder to lean on. Someone who could reassure him he's getting this right.

That they're going to win.

Kian considers waiting for her to reach the inevitable destination that track of thought will take her, but he can't. It's less painful for everyone if they acknowledge it's a dead end. "We have no way of getting him out without risking too much. Ronan could discover we're still alive."

And then he'd send out his men to finish what he started.

Nova sags against him and Kian wraps an arm around her shoulder. It's not an easy truth to accept.

But then she slips her arm around his waist. "I'm so sorry, Kian."

Kian blinks. She wasn't seeking comfort. She's comforting him. Kian presses his face to her hair, drawing her scent deep into his lungs. One word fills his mind.

Together.

Straightening, he turns to Dex and Wren. "We have a plan. Wait to see if Dean arrives. Train in basic fighting techniques. Continue to do what needs to be done to survive."

The others nod, their faces grave. The final step is to attack Ronan and free the Oasis.

Dex nods, pushing away from the tree. "I'll talk to Dad about having someone monitor the beach." He startles as something strikes him. "The laptop! I could ask him if it opens the doors remotely."

Wren's eyes widen. "If it does, we could totally look at getting Magnus out. We'd just have to time it right."

Kian doesn't let hope spark in his chest. There are too many 'maybes' in their plan as it is.

If Dean arrives with reinforcements.

If they can continue to survive up here.

If they're successful in defeating Ronan.

He moves back so he can grip Nova's hand. It's almost dark meaning they need to get back. "Let me know what he says."

Silently, each absorbed by their own thoughts, they walk back to the encampment. Hopefully something in their stomach and sleep will mean things look a little brighter tomorrow.

They've just exited the forest when Luca leaps down from a tree as if he was waiting for them to return. "About time," he grumbles.

Nova steps a little closer to him. "Is there something wrong?"

"Yes, there is. I want to get more firewood but Avis said I'm not allowed to go on my own." Luca rolls his eyes as if Avis is being unreasonable.

Nova sighs, but Kian jumps in before she can talk. The girl

who holds his heart has been wilting before his eyes. Although he can't do more than help her to rest right now, at least he can make sure of that.

He indicates to Luca. "Let's go then. There's no way I'm eating raw cockroaches."

Luca wrinkles his nose. "That's just gross."

Kian turns to Nova. "We won't be long." She hesitates but Kian is already shaking his head. "We're going to disagree about the sleeping arrangements, yet. Let's save it for then."

Nova's lips twitch before she presses them to his. "That will be easily solved. Where you are, I am."

Kian shakes his head and he turns back to the forest. Without enough shelters for everyone, there's no way he's sleeping under one. At the same time, Nova needs rest and protection. She should be sleeping under one of the shelters.

But that argument can wait. Firewood while it's still dry is the priority.

The others leave as Luca starts collecting small branches and twigs from beneath the tree they're standing beside. Kian bends over beside him. "Break off all the needles, they'll give off too much smoke."

Luca nods, focused on his task. "We need to make sure the others stay warm and we can cook the food."

Kian smiles. Luca is a wise old man and brave little boy all rolled into one. They spend several minutes filling their arms up with twigs and branches before Luca speaks again.

"Kian?"

Kian pauses, registering the note in Luca's tone. This isn't going to be a simple question about building fires or cooking food.

"Why is Nova missing a finger? I thought it was just something she and Flick had, but lots of people back there have lost one."

Now frozen, Kian blinks in the dark. "Well, it was something we did in Askala. To show who…" Was good enough. Was worthy. "Passed some tests."

Now it's Luca's turn to pause. "Are you going to keep doing it?"

The horror in his tone is like a spear in Kian's chest. "No, we're not. We thought it was necessary." The right thing to do. "But we were wrong."

Luca relaxes. "Good. Because you said our job was to look after them. Look what you did with the forest."

Healthy. Vibrant. Thriving.

Luca shrugs. "The people here should be just like that."

Kian nods even though Luca is no longer looking at him, his logical solution having calmed his worries.

He reaches out to ruffle Luca's hair. "You're a good kid, Luca."

With his quick mind and big heart, Luca probably would've been a Bound. No, not Bound. Those divisions will no longer exist. Luca would be someone who could lead Askala in the direction it needs to go.

Luca looks up, grinning. "I'm glad you think so." His smile grows. "Because I think I should be your baby's big brother."

Kian's eyes snap open in surprise. Nova and he haven't spoken about it, but he can't deny the bond they've already forged with this little boy.

Before he can answer, there's the rustle of footsteps approaching.

It's Dex, with Wren right behind him.

"I spoke to Dad." Before Dex says the next words, his tone already tells Kian it's not good news. "The laptop can't work remotely."

Kian doesn't even blink. "Thanks. I had a feeling that would be the case."

He tries to stem the disappointment. He told himself he wouldn't get his hopes up.

But it still stings his tongue, bitter and sharp.

Wren steps around Dex. "It doesn't matter. I have another plan."

Dex looks at her in surprise. "You do?"

Kian waits, wondering why Wren hasn't discussed this with Dex first.

Wren raises her chin, her dark eyes glinting with determination. "I go back and beg Cy's forgiveness."

DEX

"*You* are doing no such thing!" Dex crosses his arms, aware he just gave Wren an order.

She looks at him with a pained expression. "Think about it. It's a good plan."

"He. Tried. To. Kill. You." Dex shoots her the sternest look he can muster. "Which part of that don't you get?"

"He didn't try to kill me." Wren purses her lips and taps a foot. "He just didn't try to get me out."

Dragging his fingers through his hair, Dex takes a few steps away before stopping abruptly and turning back. The frustration sweeping through his body takes on a life of its own as it threatens to consume him. "That's semantics, Wren and you know it. Going back to Ronan is suicide."

She shakes her head. "You don't know him. Not like I do. He gets caught up in the moment and does things without thinking them through. Phee's already told me he's struggling with the way he left me in the lab."

"I'm not sure it's a good idea, either." Kian steps forward and Dex could just about kiss his cousin for agreeing with him. "If you go back, then Ronan will know more people got out of there alive."

"I'll tell him the others were too stupid to save themselves." Wren juts out her chin in the way she does when she's serious. "He'll believe that. I'll say it was his training that saved me. His ego is easy to feed."

"Luca, can you go back to Nova now?" Kian ruffles the small boy's hair. "Make sure she's okay for me."

"You just don't want me to hear what you're talking about." Luca looks disappointed.

"That's true as well," says Kian. "But I need you to do this for me. Please? Then later we'll talk about what you just asked me. When we're all together."

Something lights in Luca's eye and Dex wonders what he could have asked that needed to be discussed together. But now's not the time to pry.

Luca dashes away and Kian turns back to Wren. "It's more important that we keep you safe than getting my father out of the brig."

"You heard what Nova said." Wren bites down on her bottom lip. "Getting Magnus out will give the people hope. And if I can tell you one thing about battle, it's that people fight far better when they still have hope. They're so deflated right now. This is exactly what they need."

Dex watches Kian as he wraps his mind around this, his heart breaking the moment he sees Kian relent.

"No, Kian!" Dex grabs him by the arm. "Don't do it. Don't agree with her! It's too risky."

"This whole thing has been too risky from the start." Kian shakes his head. "And she could be our person on the inside."

"Get Phoenix to talk to Ronan." Dex lets go of Kian to focus on Wren. "He's his son. He can do just as much as you can."

"You don't get it, Dex." Wren kicks at the ground. "I'm his

favorite. I always have been. He's hard on Phoenix. Far harder than he is on me. I can do things he can't."

"And he left his favorite to burn in the fire." Dex also kicks at the ground but stubs his toe and winces from the pain. "Some way to treat the person he's supposed to love most."

"He regrets what he did." Wren's tone is hard. Clearly, it hasn't been easy for her to accept her father's actions.

"You're not softening toward him, are you?" Dex holds his breath as he waits for her answer.

"How could you think that?" Wren paces and Dex lets out a long sigh, only to suck it straight back in. "Do you even know me at all?"

"Kian, maybe it's time for you to have that talk with Luca," says Dex. "I need to speak to Wren alone, if you don't mind?"

"Of course." Kian nods. "Come and find me when you're done."

Dex waits for his cousin's footsteps to retreat and he's alone with Wren. Deep enough in the forest that they have some privacy to talk, but not too far away to be in danger.

He looks at Wren.

Still pacing.

Still seething.

Still the most beautiful girl he's ever seen.

"Why do you have to be so difficult to be in love with?" His words bring her pacing to a halt. "Why couldn't I have just fallen in love with some sweet girl who was willing to go through life without wanting to turn it upside down and inside out every five minutes?"

"Then stop being in love with me." She stands in front of him to amplify the power of her glare.

"Believe me, I would if I could." He reaches out and cups her face with his hand. "But doing that would be like choosing not to breathe. It's impossible."

She leans into his hand, his words seeming to have

simmered her anger. "Then stop trying to pin me down, Dex. Stop trying to change me."

"I'm not trying to change you." He lets his fingertips trail from her cheek to the back of her head, urging her face up to his. "I'm just trying to keep you safe."

"I managed to keep myself alive all those years before I met you." She pushes up on the tips of her toes. "I don't need you to look after me."

"I know you don't." He feathers a light kiss across her lips. "But that doesn't stop me wanting to try. Can you try to understand that?"

Her response is her kiss. Her words are the way she melds her mouth to his. Her refusal of his need to protect her is the grip of her hands around his waist, pulling him tight against her body until they stumble and end up with her back against a tree.

He leans into her, his mouth still pressed against hers as a whole new set of needs ignite inside him.

He loves this girl.

Inexplicably.

Inexpressibly.

And somewhat inexpertly, he decides, as their kiss escalates beyond anything he's experienced before.

Before he can even think about stopping himself, his hand runs down the length of her body, coming to rest on the curve of her waistline. He groans, desperate to explore more of her, to feel her bare skin under the palm of his hand, but he doesn't dare move for fear of being disrespectful.

Wren takes hold of his hand. Firmly. And without hesitation. And guides it to the buttons of her shirt, urging him to undo them.

Powerless to argue, he does as he's told, gasping as her shirt falls open and he takes in the sight of her.

Her skin is soft under his touch and his ragged breathing

fights to gain some kind of control inside his lungs as he kisses her with the sort of passion he'd never imagined.

This girl has him body and soul. He'll do anything for her. Anything that she'll let him, of course. Which clearly doesn't involve keeping her safe. He can't bear the thought of losing her. Of her going back to that monster she calls her father.

"I love you," she says, lifting her lips from his for a moment.

But it's a moment too long and he leans back in, wanting to be molded to her for eternity. Please, let this moment never end.

She lifts a foot from the ground and entwines her leg around his and he presses into her, unable to believe it's possible to feel like this.

"Wren!" he gasps, the urge to join with her overtaking all his senses. If they don't stop now, he's not going to be able to control himself. "We can't. Not out here."

"Then where?" She pulls him closer. "Nobody's here. I want you, Dex."

These words are his undoing and he lets out a moan as his hand slides further down her body, drawn to the most sacred parts of her like some kind of magnet.

This is all the encouragement Wren needs and before he can figure out what she's doing, she's adjusted their clothing and has practically climbed up his body. Now he's doing more than just touching her.

He's one with her. United. Together. Soaring toward a place that only she can take him.

"Wren." His voice breaks under the strain of emotion as he notices her eyes are wet with tears. "Are you okay?"

She bites down on her lip and nods. "I'm just happy. So happy."

He buries his face into the nape of her neck and closes his eyes as he moves against her.

"I love you," he says, just as it all gets too much.

They gasp into each other's mouths reveling in an intense

wave of feeling, holding each other tight as their passion sends them soaring.

And now his own eyes are wet with tears. Tears of love and worry. Tears of joy and sadness. Tears of knowing that soon he'll have to say goodbye.

Their bodies still and he kisses her gently, worrying that he'd just made a terrible mistake. He loves Wren. Respects her. He doesn't want her to feel used or objectified.

Gently lowering her to the ground, he glances around. It's quiet out here but far from private. Anyone could have seen them if they wandered from camp.

"There's nobody here." Wren laughs. "You look scared to death."

He grins as he returns his clothes to a more respectable position. "I don't want to be giving Luca any lessons he's not ready for yet. We'll leave that job to Kian and Nova."

"Hey, Dex," she says, her face serious as she buttons up her shirt. "I'm so glad you were the one to find me in the ocean."

"Why?" He smiles warmly at her. "Would you have done that with whoever happened to find you?"

But she doesn't return his smile. "I haven't done that with anyone else. I want you to know that."

"I know," he says, although the truth is that he hadn't been certain. He's glad to hear that what just happened was as new to her as it was to him.

He leans in for another kiss. "I wish you wouldn't go."

"I have to." She sighs deeply. "It makes the most sense. It's what I'd do if my heart wasn't flip-flopping all over the place thanks to you. If I stay here I'll only end up resenting you. I don't want that."

"I don't want that, either." He means it. If he clips this little bird's wings then she'll no longer be the girl he fell in love with. She'll be a shadow of herself. Which means not only will she resent him, but he'll resent himself.

"You need to trust me." She runs her fingers down his cheek. "I know Cy. I wouldn't go back if I thought he'd hurt me. I can handle him. There's far more I can do to help the situation from the inside than I can do from up here."

"You're not just trying to get away from your mother are you?" he asks, fully aware of how much she's struggling with their reunion.

"That's just an added bonus," she mumbles into his lips as she goes in for another kiss.

But this time he pulls back, wanting to have his say. It's been heartbreaking to watch the hurt look on Avis's face every time Wren takes steps to avoid her. "She seems pretty genuine. Are you sure you won't give her a chance?"

Wren slips out from under Dex's outstretched arms and paces. "Trust me, if I wasn't giving her a chance you'd all know about it. And I thought you'd said you'd back me up on this? However I wanted to react."

"I am backing you up!" He throws out his arms. "I haven't even mentioned it to you until now."

"Some wounds just don't heal with the click of a finger." She snaps her fingers to demonstrate, but her expression remains soft. She's not upset with him. She's just bubbling over with frustration at the reunion she never asked for. "Imagine how you'd feel if you found out who killed your mother. Would you forgive them?"

"That's not the same thing." He shakes his head. "Avis didn't kill anybody. She was the one who was almost killed."

"Dex, I'm getting there." She returns to him and tucks her face against his chest. "I'm not like Phoenix. He's always been faster to react. Faster to forgive. Faster to fall in love, too."

"You noticed that as well?" he laughs. "The way he and Felicia have been making eyes at each other?"

"It's making me want to vomit." She leans back so she can see his face. "Of all people! Bloody Felicia! I'd rather he made eyes at Dean."

"I don't know. They're kind of sweet together." He smiles, enjoying how cute Wren looks when she's annoyed. "Besides, she needs someone nice after what happened to Thom. Nova said that whole thing nearly destroyed her."

"Did you just call Phoenix *nice?*" Wren stifles a laugh.

"Don't quote me on it," he says. "I just meant that she could do worse. We know that Phoenix will take care of her."

"Did you say *will?*" Wren is aghast. "I think you mean *would.* As in he *would* take care of her if they were a thing. Which they're not. Definitely not. Phee flirts with everyone. You saw how he was with Nova."

"Speaking of which, we need to get back to the camp." Dex tugs on Wren's hand. "Before they get suspicious."

"Of what?" Wren winks at him.

"Of exactly what just happened." He leads her out of the trees, his heart heavy with the realization that this might be the last moment he has with her alone. Going back to the Oasis is beyond dangerous. But she's made up her mind. And when Wren decides on something, he's powerless to argue.

"Just for the record, I'm glad that what just happened… happened," she says. "With you."

"Me, too." He lets go of her hand to wrap his arm around her shoulders. "I'd like the chance to do it again one day if you wouldn't mind staying alive a bit longer."

"I'll see what I can arrange."

"I mean it, Wren. You need to be careful."

"I know." She loops her arm around his waist. "It's all going to be fine. I promise."

He closes his eyes for a moment as they walk.

It's all going to be fine, he repeats to himself.

Just fine.

WREN

*W*ren wakes before sunrise, determined to avoid an anguished goodbye with Dex.

She props herself up on an elbow and listens to the sound of his gentle breathing. It's a shame it's too dark to see his face. She'd love to drink in his features one more time before she leaves.

Blowing him a kiss, she creeps from the edge of the shelter and steps out into the light rain that's been falling ever since she left the forest with him. It's as if the sky is just as overcome with emotion as they were.

She yearns for the day they can do that all over again somewhere more private so they can take their time. Which is exactly why she has to go back to Cy. If any of them have any hope of living a life of freedom then they have to defeat him.

She blinks away the rain, grateful that Phoenix had shown up to help them build the shelters. These people have been through enough. Sleeping without shelter may have been the thing that finished them off. They need a strong army. Not a bunch of people with pneumonia.

Taking a few cautious steps, she's grateful to have escaped unnoticed.

But a noise behind her has Wren spinning back to see Luca's wide eyes in the moonlight. He's standing beside Kian who's sleeping on the ground, half his body shielded by a large leaf and the other by the edge of the shelter that's keeping Nova dry. With a bit of creativity everyone had been able to fit underneath some kind of roof. Except Kian who'd insisted he preferred to sleep outside.

"Shh!" Wren puts her index finger to her lips as she urges Luca to stay quiet, her heart beating rapidly.

The boy doesn't move so Wren continues, moving away from the camp as quickly and quietly as she can.

She jogs through the trees, heading downhill toward the Oasis, certain of her plan, but uncertain how it will play out.

Her best approach to get to Cy is to walk straight up to him.

No messages.

No middlemen.

And nobody there to provide an audience.

Cy has always behaved differently when it's just the two of them. He's still harsh. Still cruel. But without an audience, he's a little more muted.

And she needs the most muted version of him possible.

She stumbles on a tree branch and picks her way over it, trying to stick to the path that's been worn by the footsteps of generations of people heading up to the cliffs. The same path she walked with her father on a day not too long ago.

The same day he killed a mother deer and dragged Wren down the cliff.

It wasn't just the deer who died in that moment. All Wren's faith in her father had come to a stop along with that poor animal's heart.

Now she just has to hope that all his faith in her hasn't completely perished. Because she needs him to trust her again.

Not completely. Just enough so that she can find a way to get Magnus out.

Because if she fails to break him free, then Kian's going to enter the Oasis and try to do it himself. Which would be even more dangerous.

Pushing these thoughts from her mind, she continues on, making good time given she's walking alone.

But the walk is still long and by the time the ground levels out again, the sun has risen and flecks of golden light are breaking through the forest canopy. Birds are calling to each other as they hop between the branches, sending raindrops sliding off leaves and puddling on the ground.

If only her people back in the Outlands could see this. If only they knew what was possible, then maybe they'd fight a little harder to restore the land. It's hard to fight for something when you don't even know it exists.

The hulk of the Oasis looms ahead and Wren pushes forward, keen to get on with what she's come here to do. But with a chip that no longer works, she's going to need someone to let her onboard. She has no idea who that will be just yet.

Wren circles the ship to the gardens, seeing Zali standing alone tugging at her hair as she surveys her decimated crops, not seeming to notice the rain that's soaking through her clothes. Cy is no doubt pressuring her to do the impossible and feed the colony from what's left out here—row after row of broken stems, ravaged by selfishness and greed. Zali looks every bit as defeated as her poor garden. No amount of rain is going to bring this sorry state back to life.

"Hey!" Wren calls from the tree line.

Zali's head snaps up and she turns in the direction of Wren's voice.

"It's me! Wren."

Zali limps over to her and tilts her head. She has a dark circle under one eye and the other is black and purple. She's thinner than the last time Wren saw her and her shoulders are hunched forward.

"Holy hell," Wren breathes, realizing that things must be far worse than even she'd anticipated. It seems declaring allegiance to Cy had been no guarantee of a better life. The people in the lab had fared far better than Zali. Well, the ones who made it out, of course.

"What do you want?" asks Zali. Her tone is cold. Harsh. Almost cruel, which is surprising for someone who was once deemed to be amongst a group of the kindest people in Askala.

"Has he been hurting you?" Wren can't take her eyes off Zali's bruised face.

"I said *what do you want?*" Zali angles her face away from Wren.

"I need you to open the door for me." Wren wonders if she should approach someone else. It doesn't seem she's going to get anywhere here.

"Why should I do anything for you?" Zali crosses her arms across her boney chest. "You're *his* daughter."

"Which is why you need to let me in," says Wren. "Through the door that leads to the ballroom. Please, Zali. I want to make things right."

Zali turns her back on Wren. "Nothing can make this right."

Risking being seen, Wren darts out from the trees to grab Zali's arm. "It's not too late! We can still fix this. Please, let me through the door. That's all you have to do."

"Aren't you supposed to be dead?" Zali wrenches her arm away from Wren and rubs it.

"All the more reason to help me," Wren says gently. "You can't get in trouble for helping a ghost."

"We'll all be ghosts soon." Zali takes another step away.

"We have an army," Wren says without thinking. She hadn't intended to give that away. It could be their whole undoing. "We're going to bring the Commander down."

Zali blinks with something new in her tired eyes. It's only a glimmer but it's definitely hope that's shining from within. Unlike her garden, Zali's not dead yet. She can still recover from all that Cy's thrown at her.

"Come on, then." Zali changes direction and heads down the path that leads to the door Wren wants access to.

Glancing around to make sure nobody's seen them, Wren follows.

Zali doesn't say a word to her as they walk, like that would take energy she doesn't possess. And Wren doesn't push her, afraid she might say something that would make Zali change her mind.

Wren steps up to the door first and turns to Zali, waiting.

"Thank you." Wren smiles at her, not expecting anything in return, other than her wrist pressed to the sensor. Which is just as well, as that's all she gets.

Zali opens the door and scoots away with what must be the last reserves of her energy. Even the people who hid in the lab have had more to eat than she clearly has. Whether intentionally or not, Cy is starving these people to death.

Wren walks through the door and onto the stage of the ballroom.

It seems twice its size when empty. It's hard to believe this room was built for dancing and eating and whatever else they used to do in here. Wren's only known it as a place of misery. Is it possible that one day there could be the sound of laughter bouncing off these dusty chandeliers once more? Will Nova and Kian's child have the opportunity to run through this room daring Luca to catch him?

Feeling her father's eyes upon her, she looks over at the meeting room to see Cy standing in the doorway staring at her.

He doesn't look shocked. As he should.

He doesn't look angry. As she knows he is.

And he doesn't look happy. As she'd hoped he might be.

"Dad." She steps down from the stage and walks toward him, keeping her eyes on him.

Never break eye contact, little bird. It's a sign of weakness.

"You're alive." The tone of his voice betrays his true emotions and she realizes he's both shocked and angry. And very unhappy.

"I missed you." She blinks at him with a small smile.

Always play to your enemy's weakness, little bird. Reel them in.

He continues to stare at her and she falls silent as she stands before him, waiting for him to react.

Be patient, little bird. Let your enemy reveal their position fi—

His open palm comes out of nowhere and she has no chance to react before he brings it down across her cheek.

Searing pain slices through her face as she struggles to keep on her feet.

Never show you're in pain, little bird. Let your enemy think you're invincible.

"I deserved that," she lies. "Do it again if you need to."

Don't be afraid to call your enemy's bluff, little bird. They're probably more frightened than you are.

The second slap is worse than the first, the force of it knocking her to the floor. Hauling herself to her feet, her mind reels as she realizes her training is useless against a man who knows every one of her tricks, given he was the one who taught her.

She waits, trembling, as she prays he won't strike her again.

"I should have called you Phoenix," Cy sneers. "The little bird who rose from the ashes. How did you do it, Wren? Where have you been hiding? Who else got out with you?"

"I followed your training," she says. "Always have an escape route. Always. I dug a tunnel that led to the forest. I escaped alone. Those fools were too stupid to even think of getting out."

He stares at her for several long seconds, seeming to be

deciding if he believes her. She remains quiet, not wanting to dig herself into any holes she can't climb out of.

"Not even your stumpy boyfriend escaped with you?" He crosses his arms and Wren breathes out a sigh. He can't slap her when his arms are crossed. "Surely, you didn't leave him behind?"

She shakes her head. "I knew if I told him I was leaving, he'd tell the others. If we had too many people in the tunnel it might collapse. Always best to work alone. You taught me that."

He rubs at his chin and she catches the pride that's creeping across his face.

"And it's taken you all this time to come back to me?"

"I was so weak from all the smoke," she says. "I collapsed under a tree. I must've fallen unconscious as I only just woke up. I came straight here, even though I was scared you were going to be angry with me. I want to help. I need you. And you need me."

Cy studies her and she searches his eyes for a sign of affection, shocked to find it's absent. Could Dex have been right? Does her father really not love her? If so, then she's just made the biggest mistake of her life.

And the deadliest.

"Prove it." He spits out the words like a dare. Calling her bluff like she just called his.

"I'll do anything." She regrets these words instantly. Because she won't do anything. If he asks her to hurt someone she loves, then she's out.

Instantly.

And it will be the last thing she ever does.

"Give me your knife." Cy holds out his hand. She's not surprised he noticed it, despite how well hidden she'd kept it. His eyes are like x-ray machines when it comes to spotting a weapon. Or perhaps he just knew there's no way she'd walk back in here without one.

She reaches into the back of her waistband, withdraws the knife by the handle and places it in his hand. Hopefully he doesn't notice how much she's shaking. Because handing your enemy your weapon has got to be the closest thing to suicide she's ever done.

And more than anything right now, she doesn't want to die.

Cy makes no attempt to put the knife away, choosing instead to examine it, running his finger down the blunt edge of the blade. "Nice knife. If I didn't know better I'd say it might be the exact one that was used to kill Garbo on the upper deck."

Wren concentrates on keeping her expression neutral as his gaze bores into her. He knows exactly what she did. There's no point denying it. But she's not prepared to admit to it, either.

"You do realize I'd promised you to Garbo?" He raises his eyebrows.

"He was a little old for me, don't you think?" Wren tries to keep her tone light.

"No, I don't think." He tucks the knife into the front of his trousers, keeping the handle exposed near his navel. She knows it's a reminder for her. One that she doesn't need.

Resisting the urge to tap her foot, she waits. There's no way he's going to let her off with a slap across the face and her knife confiscated. There will be more. A public apology perhaps? She's not even sure he's figured it out himself. She hadn't given him time, which was another part of the reason for surprising him like this.

"I think I've decided I'll forgive you." He smiles at her, revealing his top row of teeth. She knows this smile. It's not genuine. Which means it isn't good. "I'm just going to need something from you first. So I know you really are sorry."

Wren swallows as she holds his gaze. He doesn't have to know how rapidly her heart is beating. How her stomach has turned so far inside out she doubts she'll ever keep a meal down again.

"What do you want?" she asks.

"A grandchild." He smiles. "A grandson to be more specific."

Wren gasps. This wasn't something she'd been expecting.

At all.

"I'm too young." She pulls her face into the most innocent expression she can muster. Everything is riding on this conversation. The entire rest of her life.

"Didn't stop that slut friend of yours from getting knocked up with the Maggot's grandchild," he sneers. "I reckon you can handle it."

She winces at his cruel words. That sounds nothing like Nova.

"What about Phoenix?" she asks, certain the experience of siring a grandchild would be far less traumatic for him than it would be for her. "He can provide you with an heir."

"He can." Cy scratches his chin. "But we'd never really know if he's the father, would we? Especially with the kind of girls he takes a liking to. No, I want it to be you. Then we know for certain the bloodline is pure."

This excuse seems a little flimsy to Wren, but she doesn't push it. Instead, she madly searches her mind for another way out of this.

"As long as I get to choose the father." She folds her arms and lifts her chin, trying to gain some impossible kind of power in this bargain.

"I thought you said Dex is dead?" He narrows his eyes at her.

"He is!" She knows she says this too quickly. In her haste to try to gain some power, she'd forgotten Dex is supposed to be dead. She needs to be more careful. But she hadn't mentioned Dex specifically... "I've had my eye on someone else."

Cy tips back his head and laughs. "Just as well. I don't want a one-armed grandchild!"

"That's not how it works." Wren grits her teeth. "I was

thinking of Kian. Imagine how much that would upset Magnus if your own daughter were to bear his grandchild."

This is the best idea she could come up with. Kian wouldn't touch her, of course. And it would buy her some time.

Cy is laughing so hard now that tears spring from his eyes. "Now *he* I know is dead. I killed him myself."

Wren internally curses. Cy has really thrown her off guard here. How could she have forgotten that, too? Cy had left Kian for dead in the ballroom. Wren had been the one to help him!

"Of course," she whispers.

"Do you know something?" Cy narrows his eyes at her. "Don't tell me the mini-maggot survived!"

"I forgot." She falls silent, deciding that perhaps she can do less damage that way.

"He'd better not be alive," Cy sneers. "Not that I'd have agreed to that, anyway. I have someone else in mind. One of my men. He's good stock."

Wren's shoulders sag, not the least bit interested in any of Cy's men's stock. Or anything else they have to offer.

"Don't move a muscle." He walks away from her before waiting to see if she'll comply. Of course, she will. Mainly because she doesn't have a choice.

He goes to the door of the ballroom and calls over one of his men.

Wren waits as he whispers some orders and the guard nods his head. Putting her hand on her stomach she hopes that somehow it's possible she's already pregnant. She's not ready to have a baby—not with Dex and not with anyone—but if she's being forced to then there's only one choice as to who it needs to be with. The idea of having anyone else's child growing inside her makes her want to throw up.

Cy returns, grinning at her in a way that sends a shiver running the length of her spine.

"Want to know who I chose for you?" he asks.

She shakes her head. It doesn't matter who he chose. She doesn't want any of them. They're all oafs. And none of them are Dex. Her only hope is that she can win back Cy's affections enough that they can overthrow him and she'll be released from any promises he may have made on her behalf.

"Let's make it a surprise then." Cy loops his arm around Wren's shoulders and leads her into the boardroom. "And there's another surprise we need to talk about."

She looks around at the splintered furniture, the result of Cy's violent temper. But the table's still standing, as well as a couple of chairs.

Cy pulls one out and gestures for her to sit down.

She does as she's told and he looms from behind her.

"Put your hand on the table," he instructs.

"My hand?" She tries to turn back to look at him, but he places his fingers on the top of her head and faces her forward again. "I don't have any other weapons!"

"Your hand," he says. "Put it on the table."

She slides her right hand onto the table, trying hard to disguise the way it's shaking. What could he possibly be thinking?

"Not that one!" His grip on her head tightens and she winces. "The other one!"

She pulls back and slides her left palm onto the table. "Dad? What are you doing? What's happening here?"

"We need a present for your new man," he hisses into her ear. "Something that will show him you're Bound to him. Proof of your loyalty. Any ideas?"

She tries to draw back, but he releases her head to clamp her wrist to the table.

"Don't fight me, little bird. You said you'd do anything, and this is what I want."

"You want my hand?" She can scarcely believe it. Dex had

been right. So right. She should never have come back here. Cy isn't stable right now. Perhaps he never has been.

"I don't want your hand." He laughs as he pulls at her fingers, folding them back so that only her ring finger is extended. "I want your finger."

"Cy! Dad! No!" She tries to pull away, but his grip is firm. "Don't do this! Please!"

"Keep still!" he screams into her ear as he releases his grip.

Instinctively, her hand flies back and she clutches it to her chest.

"I'm giving you a choice here." Spit flies from his mouth and lands on her cheek as he shouts. "I either take a finger or I take your whole hand. If you don't like those options, then I'll be happy to take your head. Now, put your hand back on the table. Your choice."

Wren's whole body is shaking as bile climbs up the back of her throat. She remembers how brave she'd been when she'd put her hand in that awful machine after the Proving. She'd accepted the potential loss of her finger back then, so why is it so difficult to accept it now?

Is it because it's definite? Or is it because it's her father who's doing it? For no reason other than to satisfy his own evil desires.

"I'm waiting," Cy says.

Wren holds out her left hand. With a little difficulty she tucks her other fingers into a fist, leaving her ring finger extended. She looks down at it. Surely, he's not really going to do this?

Cy likes to play mind games. He's just trying to scare her as part of his revenge.

"Please, don't," she begs as she places her hand on the table. "It's not necessary. You can trust me. I promise you can. I'll never leave your side again."

"We both know that's not true, don't we?" His voice is calm. Too calm. It's not the voice of a man about to disfigure his daughter. "I need you to know that betraying me has consequences. I want you to remember that every time you look down at your hand. Just like the Unbound had to when the Maggot sent them the message that they weren't good enough."

"That's not why he did it." She winces as Cy withdraws the knife from his waistband with the unmistakable sound of metal sliding across leather.

"I taught you to be brave, Wren." He wipes the blade on his pants and holds it up. "And loyal. Hold still and prove to me that you're both those things."

She keeps her hand on the table and squeezes her eyes closed.

"Open your eyes!" Cy commands.

She opens them just in time to see the knife swinging down, the blade catching the light as it sweeps through the air.

The noise as it slices through her bone and hits the table is a blur in her ears. The pain takes a second to register and in that one blissful moment she tries to tell herself that he missed.

But it's unmistakable.

The agonizing pain.

The flood of blood.

The sight of her finger sitting on the ancient table like a fat grub dug up from the garden. Still twitching as the nerves come to grips with the fact they're no longer attached to her hand.

She whimpers, not caring what Cy thinks of her as she brings her hand to her shoulder, trying to keep it raised in the hope of stemming the bleeding. She doesn't like her chances with the violent way her heart is thumping.

Is this how Nova felt when she pulled her hand from the machine? At least she'd been given some kind of anesthetic. And the wound had been cauterized so that it didn't bleed like this.

The knife is stuck in the table, standing upright and Cy leaves it there as he steps back to survey his work.

"Pick it up, little bird."

She reaches for the knife, surprised he'd let her take it. It seems too good to be true. Because she knows exactly what she's going to do with it.

She's going to slice his belly right open and let his guts fall out onto the floor.

"Not the knife!" he shouts. "The finger. It's your gift, remember? We need to take it to your new man so you can get started on my grandson."

She weighs up her chances of being able to get the knife free from the table in time to slam it into his chest before he realizes what's happening.

It's too risky. The knife is stuck deep and if she struggles with it, even for just a second, it will cost her far too dearly.

So, instead, she picks up her finger with her right hand, her damaged hand still in far too much agony to do anything except cling to her shoulder as it trickles blood down her shirt.

The finger is warm and sticky. It's hard to believe it was ever a part of her body. She wonders how something that was once so familiar can suddenly feel so foreign.

Cy forces the knife from the table and tucks it back in his waistband. "Come on. Your man is waiting. And don't go thinking that something like a missing finger will put him off. He'll be just as keen to get started on this grandchild as I am."

Wren stands, but her legs are wobbling too much and she falls back into the chair. Her head is spinning and the room is covered in dark spots.

Knowing she's going to faint, she closes her eyes and leans forward, trying her best to stay conscious. Who knows what Cy will do to her if she loses control. He's already done so much more than she believed he was capable of.

Letting out a deep sigh of annoyance, Cy hoists her into the air, cradling her in his arms like he used to do when she was a child.

Except when she was a child, she'd enjoyed it. She'd felt safe in his arms.

How foolish she'd been.

He carries her out to the ballroom and she has no choice but to let him. She can't fight him now. She has no strength. No fight left in the body that was trained to fight.

He's crushed her.

Destroyed her.

She no longer feels like Wren. She's a broken shell, holding onto her even more damaged soul.

The blood is still seeping from her hand and she tries to wrap it in her shirt, but even that's too much effort, so she closes her eyes and rests her head against the chest of the man she despises.

"Good girl, Wren," he coos. "You did well. Now, just do this one more thing for me and everything can go back to how it was."

She wouldn't answer him even if she had the strength. Because nothing will ever go back to how it was.

If she manages to survive this, then she's going to kill Cy.

Only one of them is going to get out of this alive.

They arrive at a door and Cy thumps on it. "Open the door for your Commander!"

Wren keeps her eyes closed, not being able to bear to see the man who will do even worse to her than what her father's already done.

"Commander," a gruff voice bellows.

Cy walks into the room and lowers Wren onto the bed. "Here's your woman. You know what to do with her. Are you capable of putting my grandson inside her belly?"

"Yes, Commander. Long live the Commander."

Wren hates the man's voice. And she hates the man it belongs to. She will never willingly give him what he's been ordered to take. If he wants to put a child in her belly then he's going to have to do it by force. Because Wren would rather die than submit to him.

"She's bleeding, Commander," the man says.

"Just a minor wound to her hand." Cy's voice is coming from the door now and Wren can only hope he's leaving. "But don't worry. All the bits you need still work."

"Excellent," the man sneers. "I look forward to finding out just what kind of order this one's in. Been waiting years to find out."

"She has a present for you," says Cy. "Don't forget to ask for it."

"She's a present enough," he says. "Thank you, Commander."

There's the sliding of the door and Wren curls herself into a ball, her eyes still closed, and her hand still throbbing.

The man is standing beside the bed. She can feel his presence like a storm cloud. Threatening. Ominous. Set to destroy what little hope she has left.

"What's in your hand?" he asks. "Is this my present?"

Wren opens her hand and her finger rolls out onto the bed.

She hears a gasp and then her left hand is pulled out from under her and the man quickly wraps it in something.

"We need to stop the blood," he says, sitting down beside her.

It's then that Wren's eyes spring open.

"Jagger?"

It's the guard who helped them escape the lab. The same one who'd sworn he was on their side.

He gives her a gentle smile and winks at her. "Don't worry. I'm not going to hurt you. It seems your father's done a good enough job of that."

And for the first time since she set foot back on the Oasis, Wren's heart slows down and she lets out a long breath.

Jagger is the one guard she hadn't even dared to hope her father had chosen for her.

Luck is on her side. Which means she's going to live.

It also means one other very important thing...Cy is going to die.

NOVA

Knowing Kian needs to go and being okay with Kian going are two different things. Nova squints even though the sun is barely cresting over the top of the trees. Staying strong as she watches him leave feels like too much.

She chews on her lip as she watches Kian give Luca a fierce hug. Luca goes to pull away only to grip him again, whispering something in Kian's ear.

Kian swallows then nods, and the smile Nova wasn't expecting is blinding. Luca grins before running off, a skip in his step.

For the briefest moment, the tightness around Nova's chest loosens. Luca's determination that everything is going to turn out fine is a ray of sunshine in these dark times.

Kian straightens and walks over to Nova, slipping his arms around her. She cups his face, wishing she didn't have to let go. "What was that about?"

"Remember how we told him he'd be an amazing big brother? Well, he just told me that when I get back, he's going to tell everyone he's found a family."

Nova blinks. "That kid works fast."

Kian grins as he shrugs. "He's grown up in an uncertain world. I suppose he's learned to grab happiness when he sees it." He brushes a strand of hair from Nova's face. "And you have a special bond with him."

Leaning into his warm palm, Nova smiles. "So do you. He's protective of me but follows you like a shadow."

"Which is why I told him to look out for you while I'm gone. Otherwise, there was going to be an argument about whether he should come."

While Kian's gone...

Nova chews on her lip so it doesn't tremble. She traces his mouth with her fingers. "Be careful, okay?"

"I'm coming back, Nova." Kian's face is tight with determination. "With my father."

He's the beacon of hope we need. Kian's said that several times, now.

Nova nods even though she's not sure she agrees. Kian is who these people turn to. Dex is the one they smile for. Wren is the strength these people know they can depend on. And Nova has comforted every one of them.

"You'd better. It seems we're a family even before this one is born." She clasps her stomach, conscious it's starting to curve outward.

Kian's hand covers hers. "We belonged together long before any of this, Nova. We've proven we'll always return to each other."

His kiss is hot and intense. A fiery promise. A fierce vow.

And then he's gone.

Nova works hard to keep the tears at bay. Tears imply grieving. That she doesn't have faith he'll be back.

And although that's her greatest fear, she knows why Kian is doing this. Dean never turned up. They haven't heard from

Wren. And Kian believes his people need Magnus's strong leadership. His faith in Askala.

Kian needs Magnus to help him believe.

A hand falls on Nova's arm and she turns to find her mother standing behind her, her eyes soft with understanding. "Avis and I are going to collect sap and scout for food. Did you want to join us?"

Nova nods gratefully. Keeping busy is just what she needs right now. And the truth is, they have people to feed and care for.

They haven't moved far from the scattered shelters when Luca appears out of nowhere, his hands on his hips. "Kian said you might try to sneak off."

Nova suppresses an eye roll. Kian would've told Luca that so he kept an extra close eye on her. "We're going to get sap, maybe see if we can find some food. Do you want to come?"

Luca slips in beside her. "Of course I'm coming."

Nova ruffles his hair. Being surrounded by people who love her will make it easier to cope while Kian's gone. While she has no idea what's happening to him...

They head toward the edge of the forest only to stop as Dex appears from the trees, dragging several large branches behind him. It seems Nova's not the only one keeping busy while two of their loved ones are away.

He nods at them as he passes. "Morning."

Flick appears behind him, carrying two smaller branches. "We're getting ready for when Phee arrives."

Phee? "Of course," says Nova, deciding not to comment. "Good thinking."

Luca puffs out his little chest. "If Phoenix gets here before I'm back, tell him I won't be long."

Flick pauses, her eyes on Nova. "Are you going out?"

"Not far," Nova assures. "We're just going to get some sap.

Maybe some food if we can find it. You stay here and help Dex and the others."

"Are you sure? I could come."

Despite her words, Flick's face looks like that's the last thing she wants to do. Nova's glad. Flick wanting to work with Phoenix is a good thing. It means she's choosing to live again.

"I'm sure. We need more shelters just as much as we need sap and food."

"Exactly what I was thinking," says Flick with a nod.

Luca shakes his head as she walks away. "That's not what she was thinking."

Nova pushes him to start walking again. "Shush. She's still working as hard as any of us."

There's a quiet sigh from her mother as they enter the forest. "She's learned connections are what count in times like these."

Avis strides a few feet ahead. "And she figured it out before it's too late."

Nova and her mother glance at each other. Wren's absence is weighing heavily on Avis's mind.

She stops a few feet in then turns to them, all business. "Now, the first thing we're going to need is a branch. Find one about as wide as your thumb and as straight as possible."

Luca jumps up and down. "Yippee! We're making spears."

"We're not making spears," Avis admonishes. "We're making...scratching sticks."

But Luca isn't listening. He darts to the nearest tree, clambering up a few branches before finding what he's looking for. "Watch out below!"

They all step back as a branch crashes to the ground. A second one lands a moment later. Luca shimmies back down. "No more than two from any tree. If you choose a dry one, they snap off easily."

Before Nova can tell him how proud Kian would be that he

remembered, Luca ducks up the next tree. A moment later, two more branches hit the forest floor.

Luca grins. "Now, we make a spear."

Avis sighs. "A scratching stick."

They set about stripping the smaller branches from the main length of wood, and within a short space of time, they're all holding a sturdy, straight stick.

Avis looks around. "Now we have to sharpen it."

"My favorite bit!" Luca announces.

Nova can't help but smile. "You've done this before."

Avis shakes her head. "It's the most effective way we found to collect sap considering we had so few knives."

Luca's eyes glow. "Dharma could spear rabbits with them."

Nova shakes her head, wishing she didn't have to disappoint him. "Which we won't be doing today. It's not safe to go that far into the forest, plus we'd need a whole bunch to feed all the people we have here."

But Luca just shrugs before skipping away. "Sure thing, Nova."

Nova watches him. "He doesn't intend on listening to me, does he?"

Avis comes to stand beside her, a fond smile gracing her face. "He's how I imagined Wren would have been at his age."

Luca finds a small boulder protruding not far away and squats beside it. His brow furrowed in concentration, he starts to file the tip.

Thea places a hand on Avis's shoulder. "She'll come around. It'll just take some time."

"The one thing we don't have right now," says Avis, worry laced through her voice.

Because Wren has gone straight back to Ronan.

"Wren's tough," says Nova. "Like you, she's a survivor."

Avis glances at Nova, the scars on her face looking foreboding in the shadows of the forest. "But she believes Cy will want to forgive her. That he has the ability to forgive."

"Are you guys gonna make your spea—scratching sticks—or what?" Luca demands from beside the rocks.

They all jolt into motion, probably needing to keep busy just as much as the others. Nova lets Luca show her how to press down and rub the end of her stick against the rock, twisting it regularly. Slowly but surely, a point forms on the tip.

As she straightens, Nova's back objects to being hunched so long. She stretches it, and then her stomach complains about the lack of breakfast. She didn't tell Kian that the flatbread and roasted cockroaches were all finished last night.

But Wren has already left, risking so much and putting this plan into motion. Having Kian worry about them is the last thing he needs right now. Worse, he would've chosen to stay, putting aside his drive to free his father.

Which leaves them with little food but a full day to find more. Her stomach is going to have to wait.

Avis is looking around. "The larger trees produce the most sap. It would be better if we can go a little further in."

Luca grins and dashes forward.

"Not too far in!" Nova calls after him.

He stops beside a wide trunk several feet ahead. "This one?"

He waits for them to join him and Avis nods. "You always were a quick learner. Yes, this is a good one."

Nova's mother moves closer. "So now you scratch away the bark?"

Avis smiles. "I'll show you."

Luca seems content to stand back beside Nova and watch as Avis takes them through the steps. As Avis hacks away the rough bark, Nova's struck by the memory of watching her daughter do the same thing, up here at the cliffs.

It was during the Proving that Wren showed Nova how to collect the sap. Avis's motions are almost identical, yet Wren couldn't possibly have learned it from her. Removing the bark to expose the sap wood. Changing her grip on the stick so she can chip away a deep vee-shaped notch.

Thea's wide-eyed gasp as the thick sap starts to flow is just like Nova's reaction as she'd watched Wren.

The older generation are playing out history.

Thea glances around frantically. "We need something to catch it."

Wren had suggested Nova use her hands, but back then, they'd needed to use it immediately. Right now, no one wants to be walking around with a handful of sticky tar indefinitely.

But just like her daughter, Avis is resourceful. She bends over, rustling in the layers of netting draped around her body. Pulling away several ready-cut strips she presses them together between her hands. "Enough sheets and it's practically waterproof."

Thea shakes her head in wonder. "That stuff is amazing."

And Avis's body must be swathed with layers of it, all probably varying in size. She could have an entire parachute wrapped around her for all they know.

Nova glances down at Luca, raising her brow. "Maybe we should get Kian to tell Thea the story of when he first came into contact with that amazing netting."

Luca giggles. "You should've seen his face!"

Poor Kian. His introduction to Fairbanks included a leap from a beam so high up it would make Nova's heart jump into her throat just looking at it.

Avis bunches the compressed layers beneath the sap. "I did see his face. It was quite...memorable."

Nova's mother's face lights up with humor. "I think this is a story I need to hear."

"Should we?" Nova asks Luca.

Luca's shoulders slump. "But I was gonna see if I could find rabbits."

Nova's about to launch into the story, pointing out that Luca's the hero of this one, when a sound has them all freezing.

Her mother's hand flies to her throat. "Was that—"

Another growl, low and menacing, creeps through the trees like an ominous mist. Nova clutches Luca to her side, glancing around frantically.

The question is answered sooner than she'd like. A polar grizzly, dirty white and earthy brown, appears between the trees to their left. The sheer size of it tells her it's a male.

Nova's heart stalls as the bear lifts its nose, no doubt having followed their scent here. They never expected to see one so close. His massive head swings toward them, pinning them with a feral gaze.

Shoving Luca behind her, Nova sidesteps closer to her mother and Avis.

The bear watches her movements, its muzzle twitching enough to reveal a flash of white teeth. Nova's mother whimpers, grasping Nova's hand.

What did Kian tell her all those months ago when she was trapped, facing a polar grizzly, cornered and terrified?

Nova, hold your hands up in the air...talk to me, show him you're human...don't look directly at the bear.

"Hold your hands up in the air. Slowly, it'll make us look bigger," Nova says calmly. "And don't look directly at him. Just past the head. We don't want to be a threat, or prey."

Four sets of hands creep up, Nova's mother's hands trembling like branches in a storm. Luca has pressed himself against Nova's side. Her heart is like thunder in her chest. Three women and a child. Far enough in the forest to be alone.

Facing a massive polar grizzly.

"That's fine as long as he's not hungry," says Avis lightly, trying to keep the tension out of her voice but failing.

It's then that Nova looks a little more closely. The bear's skin looks too big for its body, its snout marred by scars. Nova gasps. One eye is opaque and desiccated.

Memories of that day come rushing back. Wren's hands moving lightning fast, pelting the bear with stone after stone. The bear roaring and turning around. Two more rocks hitting it in the eyes. The bear retreating, Nova falling into Kian's arms, relieved.

Could it be the same one? Now blinded in one eye? And starving as a result...

The grizzly pushes up onto his hind legs, looking just as colossal as he did then. But now, the skin hangs off his massive bones like the layers of Avis's netting. He roars his intent, the sound sending waves of terror through Nova.

"Up the tree! Now!" she shouts. She shoves Luca toward the trunk and he shimmies up, even managing to hold his stick despite the swift movements. Avis is next, leaping for a low branch and hauling herself up.

Nova's mother is frozen, staring at the predator that just returned to all fours.

"Thea!" Avis is leaning down, hand extended.

Nova shoves her mother, snapping her out of her paralysis. She heaves her up as Avis and Luca pull.

Nova can hear the bear's paws thunder over the soil as he runs toward her. Its pure hunger closing in on her. Using the adrenaline spiking through her veins, she follows the others, clambering up the fastest she ever has.

The bear slams into the tree, the pine needles shuddering with the impact.

"Keep going up!" Nova screams.

The bear has to be at least eight feet tall. They need to get higher than that.

The bark scratches Nova's palms as she helps her mother, glad Luca's frightened face is progressively moving higher into the boughs. Below, the bear roars his frustration and Nova slams her eyes shut. She's never heard anything more terrifying.

She looks down as a massive paw swipes the air. It hits a branch, smashing it to splinters.

But it doesn't reach them.

"Nova," her mother whimpers. "Bears can climb."

As if it were just given permission, the bear wraps its massive arms around the trunk. A tree that looked so big only an hour ago suddenly shrinks as its claws *clack* as they touch on the other side.

Nova looks up. "Luca, I need your stick!"

His young features panicked, Luca passes her the spear he was hoping to use against a rabbit. Bracing herself against the trunk, Nova wildly jabs it below her. The first time it misses, but the second time it hits something solid.

The grizzly roars with rage but releases the mangrove pine, its claws scraping down the bark.

"Please give up, please give up," Nova's mother pleads under her breath. They all hold still, the three words a litany amongst the branches.

Maybe it's a prayer.

But it works. The bear turns away, but not the way it came. It pauses, angling its head as its senses sample the air. It turns its body more fully, suddenly focused.

"No," Nova moans.

The bear has smelled the encampment. Its head rises higher, its shoulders quivering. Nova's heart goes from frenzied to frozen.

It's trembling with anticipation.

Now that it's discovered a feast far bigger, the grizzly turns away as if it's forgotten they exist. It lumbers toward the refugees who are about to become a smorgasbord.

Nova's heart cries the denial she wants to scream. The bear can't reach the Askalans!

But there's no Wren and her slingshot. No Dex to tell her to be brave. No Kian to be brave for her.

Gripping the spear, Nova makes a split decision. She's going to have to make them proud.

She's not going to let this happen without a fight.

Nova leaps, the sound of her mother's scream piercing the air. She feels a hand brush her arm but it's too late. She lands on the ground at the base of the tree.

"Nova!" This time it's Luca's frightened shout.

She wishes she could comfort him. Tell him one more time that he would make a wonderful big brother.

"Hey!" she calls to the bear. "I'm over here."

The bear stops, glancing back. Nova flexes her shoulders, drawing strength from the trunk pressed against her back. "Come on! Come and get me."

"What are you doing?" Avis asks, panic hiking her voice high.

But Nova doesn't take her eyes off the bear. It needs to turn away.

It needs to run at her.

The bear eyes Nova, its body still. Weighing up its options.

"Come on!" she screams. "What are you waiting for?"

Except the grizzly turns away, taking another step toward the encampment.

"No! This way!"

But the bear has found a better offer. More bodies. More meals. It begins to walk away.

There was one instruction Kian didn't say that day she was cornered. He knew it wasn't going to be needed. It was something Magnus had repeated so many times that they used to quote it along with him.

Never run from a bear. It'll trigger its predatory instinct.

Sweet Terra, she's going to have to run.

Nova picks up a rock and throws it. "You want food?" Nova screams. "Come and get it."

The stone bounces off the bear's back, making it spin around with an angry growl. Her pulse a tsunami crashing through her, Nova turns and flees.

The effect is instantaneous. A glance over her shoulder shows the bear's massive body leaping into action. It launches forward, white-brown skin rippling as its eye locks on her.

"Nova!" It's her mother, wailing a denial.

But it's too late. The bear has found its prey.

Ducking around a tree, Nova's breath is harsh in her ears. Her legs can't seem to work fast enough. Her breath isn't keeping up with her suddenly starving lungs. A quick glance yanks a whimper from her throat.

The bear is catching up faster than she expected. The thunder of paws on the ground rumbles through Nova. The bear roars and Nova instinctively ducks. It's a sound of pure violence. A bay for blood.

Knowing that timing will be the difference between life and death for herself and her baby, Nova slams into a tree, her momentum crashing to a halt.

She spins around to find the bear hasn't stopped. It launches itself at her, jaws open wide, hungry eyes anticipating the kill.

Everything slows. It's like Father Time wants these last moments branded in her memory.

Nova slams her back against the rough bark, her hand gripping the stick. It feels too fragile, too small.

So does she.

The bear sails through the air. Dark claws glinting in the muted light. White teeth shiny with saliva. It roars its fury.

Nova raises the spear and jams the end into the tree. She screams her defiance.

The bear's momentum is what impales it, the spear piercing its hide just below its chin and slicing upward. A strange grunt jerks from the bear as its body slams into Nova and pain explodes as she's crushed. For long moments, black dots pulse behind her eyelids. The suffocating scent of grimy fur fills her lungs.

The bear twitches, spurring Nova into action. She shoves her hands into the pelt surrounding her, finding it slick with blood, and pushes. A few thrusts and she's out.

As fresh air assaults her, Nova looks around. The forest is quiet. The bear's dead.

And she's alive.

"Nova!" A small body launches at her and Nova clasps Luca to her. Her knees collapse as the adrenaline drains from her body.

The tears prick when Nova feels her mother's arms wrap around her. Silently, she holds Nova, her tears cool in her hair.

Luca pulls back, eyes alight. Nova almost smiles despite it all. Of course, Luca would be the first to recover. "That was awesome!"

Nova looks up to find Avis has come to stand beside them. She hikes her hands on her hips. "Well, looks like we're having bear for dinner."

KIAN

*K*ian stands at the edge of the forest, watching the Oasis. In the early morning light, everything is still. Silent.

Dead.

The home he grew up in would've been alive with movement by now. People heading to the garden. Others to the water treatment. Some to the forest or the lake or the beach. But today, nothing moves.

There's no one.

Kian's chest aches. What else has happened in there to change things so much? What's happened to the people who swore allegiance to Ronan?

And how is he going to get in there so his father can help them make this right again?

It's been two days since Wren left for the Oasis and so far there's been no sign of Magnus. What's more, Dean didn't arrive. Without reinforcements, it's even more important he frees his father when Wren's been unable.

Kian jogs around to the beach, staying within the tree line.

At least the ladder that climbs up the side of the ship is more hidden than arriving up the gangplank.

The moment Kian leaves the trees he feels exposed. He sprints for the beach, plastering himself against the side of the Oasis. Listening for any shouts or signs he's been seen, he works hard to keep his breathing under control, but there's nothing.

He's hoping Ronan and his men are still asleep, complacent because they believe there's no threat. Kian's jaw tightens. It's only a matter of time before they find out otherwise. He climbs the rusted old ladder.

Below him is the beach where Nova and he succumbed to the strength of their feelings. That moment conceived their child.

A child who proves Bound and Unbound divisions were wrong. The new Askala will be stronger and better for what they've learned.

Once Ronan is gone.

Peeking over the edge of the handrail, Kian holds his breath. His heart thumping like a drum makes it hard to hear, but there's still nothing. Leaping over, he keeps low as he runs to the door.

A quick scan of his wrist and it whooshes open. He freezes when he sees a man sitting on the other side. Kian raises his fists, realizing too late he should've waited for a lesson or two from Phoenix.

But the man doesn't move. A moment later, a soft snore fills the corridor. Kian's hands drop as the strong stench of fermented berries rises from him like fumes. Gingerly, he steps over him, freezing when a breeze gusts through the open door.

The man snuffles and rubs his nose. Keeping his spread legs still, Kian reaches over and swipes to close the door, cutting off the light and fresh air.

The snoring resumes and Kian silently slips away, knowing

he probably just used up what little luck he has. It seems Ronan still has men posted.

Voices somewhere to his left have Kian instinctively turning right. It's the wrong direction to the brig, but he needs a way to distract the guards. Right now, he has no idea how he's going to do that.

Moving as swiftly and quietly as he can, he navigates the corridors he played in as a child. He hears the odd shuffle behind doors as people begin to wake, but he doesn't stop. Who knows who's still loyal to Ronan.

And who's too scared not to be.

Without conscious thought, Kian finds himself at the stair-well that goes up to the pod deck. He pauses, knowing this is probably the riskiest place to be.

But it's also the most likely place to find the one person he trusts. Kian glances around but he doesn't know why he both-ers. There's nothing he'll be able to use as a weapon. Askala wasn't designed for that.

It was created to care and nurture people, even if that care was biased.

Scanning his hand over the sensor, Kian plasters himself against the wall, staying out of sight of the now open door. Pulse thrumming, he waits.

When he hears a sound, his breath evaporates. But it's not a suspicious grunt. Or a growl of anger.

It's his younger sister, Willow. "We're almost finished, Mom."

Not believing his ears, Kian peeks around the door jamb. Willow is walking down the length of the pod pool, drawing a scoop through the water. Their mother approaches her, holding out a large bucket.

"There's more again today," she says sadly.

Kian steps out. "Mom?"

The bucket slaps to the ground as his mother lifts shocked eyes to his. She mouths his name but no sound comes out.

A quick glance tells Kian they're alone. It's all the permission he needs as he strides toward her. They clasp tightly, Willow wrapping her arms around both as she smiles the biggest smile he's ever seen.

His mother, on the other hand, cries on his shoulder. Great, wretched sobs and Kian can't tell if they're relief or grief.

Probably both.

Finally, she pulls back, cupping his face. "You're back."

Kian nods, his throat thick with emotion.

"And Nova?" Willow asks, her features still pinched as she's not sure whether she can celebrate yet.

"I found her. She and Felicia came back with me. The baby's fine."

Willow's eyes widen with happiness. "That's"—her face crumples—"really good news."

Kian releases his mother so he can crouch down and give her a proper hug. "It really is."

His mother's hand falls onto his shoulder, the tension in it telling him she has bad news. "Those who defied Ronan. They died in the lab fire."

Kian stands. "Some did, but we got back just in time. Most of them escaped. They're in the forest, by the cliffs."

His mother claps her hand to her mouth, more good news being too overwhelming. Glancing around, Kian leads them toward the wall. They need to talk, but standing out here feels too vulnerable.

Willow clamps onto his hand, hanging on like he might evaporate any moment. Kian squeezes her palm. His younger sister has discovered how unpredictable the world is.

And how fragile.

"How are Holly and Jasper?"

His mother's shoulders sag. "Hungry. Scared. Like we all are." She tries to pull up a smile. "But safe."

For now.

"And Dad?"

"I haven't…" Her lip trembles as she looks away. "I haven't seen or spoken to him. Ronan assures me he's where he belongs."

Please let that be the brig.

"What are you doing here, Kian?" his mother asks, eyes suddenly darting around as she realizes how dangerous this is.

"He's why I'm here. I want to get Dad out."

Willow gasps, her clasped hands flying to her chest. "You're going to free him?"

Kian squats down. "I'm going to take him to the forest. It's not safe for him here."

His younger sister frowns as she digests this. "Because he's going to help free everyone."

"Yeah, he will." His hands tighten on her young shoulders. He's not sure if he should feel proud or sad that she's accepted this so readily.

Pushing up, he faces his mother. "Once we have a plan, we'll be back. Ronan won't be allowed to get away with this."

His mother bites her lip. "The guards still patrol—Ronan's getting paranoid. Especially around the brig." She looks away. "I've tried to get to Magnus several times, as have others."

"Ronan knows Dad is the foundation of Askala."

Willow pushes between them. "Which is why it's so important you get him out."

His mother straightens her shoulders. "What do you need?"

Seeing the glimmer of hope in his mother's eyes tells Kian exactly how vital his father is to this fight. He glances around. "I'm going to need a distraction. Something that will get the guards away from the brig."

Stepping past him, his mother scans the pod pool. Kian follows her gaze, for the first time taking it in properly. He takes a few steps away from the wall as if needing to get closer to believe what he's seeing.

What used to be a thriving ecosystem now looks more like the desecrated ocean not far away.

Kian frowns as he takes a few more steps. "The phytoplankton..."

His mother walks past him, kneeling beside the pool. "The guards, the others...they come and take pods whenever they want. The constant breaking of the surface has fractured the phytoplankton islands too many times. They're not recovering."

Willow picks up the scoop she was holding when Kian first arrived. "The pods that are left are starving."

Drawing it through the water, she pulls it up, revealing several gray pteropods in the bottom. She tips their lifeless bodies into the bucket she's standing beside and Kian's stomach clenches as he sees that it's almost half full.

"You do this every morning?"

"Yes," his mother says. "Otherwise the water quality would drop."

It wouldn't just drop. The pool would turn into a stagnant pod graveyard.

She hikes her hands to her hips. "But right now, you need a distraction." Her eyes alight on the bucket. "Willow, pass me that."

Willow lifts it, her arms looking like fragile twigs. Kian frowns. All the more reason to get his father out.

His mother takes the bucket, and before Kian can ask what she has planned, she tips the slippery dead pods back into the pool.

He looks at her in shock. "You're going to kill the pods?"

"They're dying already, Kian. But no, I'm not going to kill them. Just reduce the water quality."

Several of the more decayed pods bob to the surface, gently glistening with slime. Kian has to look away. He grew up caring for these fragile, vital animals. They kept their colony healthy and thriving.

"So, now we wait?"

His mother shakes her head. "Ronan knows how important the pods are. He's been coming more and more often to check how they're doing."

Not sure what she's saying, Kian follows her back to the door. "And you've told him they need to leave the pool alone?"

"Ronan only hears what he wants to." She lifts her hand. "Maybe this will make him listen."

She places her palm on the red button that Kian had forgotten was there. In all his life, they've never had to use it. "I press this, they come running."

"What? No! Ronan will be furious." There's no way Kian is going to let her put herself in that kind of danger.

His mother looks away. "We have no choice."

Kian leaps forward. "No! We'll find another—"

But it's too late. She slams her hand down and a blaring siren pierces the air. His mother pulls in a deep breath. "You need to hide." She points to some barrels beside her. "And get ready to run when you can."

The sound of the siren wails over Kian's eardrums. It's the sound of panic. A sound that's guaranteed to have Ronan and his guards here within minutes.

His mother kneels in front of Willow. "I want you to go look after Holly and Jasper. I'll be there shortly."

Eyes wide and frightened, Willow dashes through the door.

Kian stands rooted to the floor. This isn't what he had in mind. His mother just placed herself in the firing line.

"Now, Kian!" His mother runs to the pool, her dark braid jolting down her back. "You can't be found!"

Kian jumps behind the barrels as the sound of boots pounds through the walls. A second later, the door slides open.

Ronan barrels through, men pouring out behind him. "What's happened?"

Peeking around, he sees his mother beside the pool, holding the scoop in a white-knuckled grip. "It's the pods, Cy."

Ronan storms to the edge, taking in the dead bodies floating on the surface. He roars in anger. "How did this happen?" He spins back to glare at Kian's mother. "You know I've made the order to kill anyone who endangers the pods."

Kian grits his teeth as he ducks down. Ronan is the biggest threat the pods have ever seen. And yet his mother is the one risking herself.

His mother's head tucks between her shoulders. "I'm sorry, I clean out the dead ones every morning. I've just been so tired...I slept in..."

"You stupid bitch!" Ronan screams. His hand whips out, striking her across the face. "Don't you know how important the pods are?"

His mother tumbles to the ground, the trickle of blood from her lip apparent even at a distance.

Kian clenches his throat around the objection screaming through him. He has to lock every muscle in place to stop himself from leaping out.

Ronan's men fan out around him, forming an intimidating semi-circle around his mother. Kian trembles, wanting to go to her.

His mother slowly stands, wiping the edge of her mouth. "You won't hurt me. You need me."

She's saying those words for Kian's benefit. Although it shreds him to do it, he needs to leave.

He needs to get to his father.

Ronan's hands clench and unclench by his side. How can Kian leave, though, when another hit like that could kill his mother?

A small body separates from the shadows beside the door, taking a cautious step forward. For a second Kian thinks Willow came back, and his muscles contract, ready to leap.

Except the short dark hair that steps toward Ronan isn't Willow. Kian blinks as if to double check as Wren slips beside her father.

Standing in the background isn't something he's ever associated with Wren, let alone the wary way she's stepping. It's like she's become a half version of herself. What in sweet Terra has Ronan done to her?

Ronan turns to his daughter, his eyes alight. "Maybe I should do to Amity what I did to you."

Wren winces, avoiding Ronan's gaze.

Uneasiness is winding through Kian like a serpent. Something's happened to Wren, and it's not good. He's never known her to be so compliant. So silent. She's nothing like the feisty girl who demanded she go back to the Oasis to win back her father's trust.

"What do we need to do?" Ronan sneers as he turns back to Kian's mother.

His mother avoids Ronan's gaze, just as cowed as Wren. "We need to scoop the dead ones out as quickly as possible so they don't spoil the water. That's why I called you all here."

"Are you waiting for an invitation, Wren?" Ronan shoves her roughly. "Get to work so you can get back to making me that grandson you promised me."

Wren stumbles as she takes the scoop from Kian's mother's hands. Kian's eyes widen, but not because of the rough way Ronan just treated Wren... It's her left hand.

The butchered stump, the garish gap.

Sweet Terra, Ronan exacted his revenge.

She starts to scoop as the others watch and Kian uses that moment to slip out the door. His stomach churns as he sprints down the hall, heading straight for the brig.

He needs to get his father out.

They need to save Askala.

He turns a corner, relieved to see a clear path ahead. Running on, he reaches the brig.

There are no guards, meaning his mother's distraction worked perfectly. Kian scans his hand on the sensor, slipping in and closing the door behind him. He pauses, allowing his eyes to adjust to the gloom, and the smell assaults his nostrils. Stale sweat and unwashed body.

Taking a step, Kian knows he came just in time. Before him, his father lays on the cot tucked in the corner of his room, his back to the door.

His father curls around himself more fully. "I don't want your food."

Falling to his knees beside him, Kian reaches out. "Dad, it's me. Kian."

His father spins around and Kian has to stop himself from reeling back. His father's face is scruffy with beard, his hair a wild mane around his head. His face is gaunt and dirty, his clothes hanging off him.

"Kian?"

Kian embraces him, and they hold each other for long seconds. "I'm here."

Things are going to be okay.

He draws back, hiding the shock at how much weight his father has lost. If he'd known, he would've brought something for him to eat.

Ronan is going to have a lot to answer for.

"How did you get here?" His father frowns. "Where's—"

"I snuck in to free you. There are others, in the forest. We're going to make this right."

His father jerks back. "Make this right?"

"Quick. I'll explain later." Kian stands, holding out his hand. "We don't have much time."

His father stares at him, then down at his hand, and Kian wonders if the isolation and deprivation have taken a toll. Dark brows bunched low, his father withdraws. "But you turned your back on Askala."

Kian's hand drops. "What? No! I left so I could save it."

"You left to find your precious Nova," his father spits. "Your Unbound mistress."

Kian shakes off the shock of those words. He's not sure what's going on, but he knows they don't have time for this. They can argue about the fact he disagreed with his father's decisions when they get to the forest.

He walks to the door. "We'll figure it out. Right now, Askala needs you."

Except his father shakes his head. "I'm not going."

"What?" Kian spins around. "It's okay, Mom knows. She's going to wait for us to come back. We're going to overthrow Ronan."

But his father is already turning his head away. "There's no point."

Feeling like the timer for a bomb was tripped the moment he stepped onto the Oasis, Kian jams his hands into his hair. "How much have you been given to eat? Drink? You'll think more clearly once you've got something in your stomach."

His father snorts. "They bring food every day." His eyes blaze. "And I send it back."

"You what?"

"I tried, Kian. You know I did." His back curves in defeat. "But my own son turned away from everything I built. It made me realize something..."

Kian takes a step back only to slam into the door. Whatever his father says next is going to be inescapable.

"I realized I could never have won. Humans are selfish. Greedy. That can't be bred out of them."

"What are you saying?" whispers Kian.

His father raises his gaze, his eyes calm with conviction. "Ronan will do what needs to be done."

"You're just going to...let him?"

"I'm going to let nature run its course. Human extinction is the best thing that can happen to planet Earth."

Kian shakes his head, although he can't shake the bitterness those words have branded on his tongue. "It's the isolation, the hopelessness that's talking. Come with me, I'll show you what we're fighting for."

The love his father feels for his mother. His children. The same love Kian has for Nova, that Dex and Wren share, that drove Avis to face her fear and return. The same bonds that can care for the Earth as much as each other.

His father stands, his face now dark with anger. "It's only because I'm everything I feared—selfish and greedy—that I haven't called the guards." He points to the door. "Leave now before I do the right thing."

And give his son to the enemy? To be killed?

Kian opens the door and stumbles out.

Blindly, he navigates the corridors that will take him out of the ship he called home his entire life. He trips twice on his way to the forest. Each time he picks himself up, not caring about the scrapes on his palms.

His chest feels cracked.

His foundations are shattered.

And now, somehow, he has to convince the others they still have hope.

DEX

*D*ex waits for Kian's return by pacing the edges of the camp. But after several long minutes his legs get tired and he wonders how Wren manages to fit so much pacing into her day.

It's so hard not knowing what's happening on board the Oasis. Two of the people he loves most in this world are there.

And neither of them are safe.

Walking into the forest, he goes to the tree where Wren had taken his breath away and changed him as a person forever. He leans against the trunk and closes his eyes, remembering the feel of her. The touch. The taste.

Why had he let her go back? This is the question that keeps swirling in his mind, despite being very clear about the answer.

He'd had no choice.

She'd made up her mind and nothing he said was going to change it. That was why she'd left when he'd still been asleep. He wasn't upset with her for that. He'd sort of expected it. Someone as smart as Wren would have known he'd try to stop her. Which would only have broken their hearts even more.

And now Kian's been gone for hours. Almost the whole day has passed. How long could it possibly take?

Pushing away from the tree, Dex kicks at a pile of leaves, furious he'd agreed to this fool's mission. Getting Magnus out isn't really that important in the grand scheme of things. Not more important than Wren and Kian's safety.

"Hey, dude. Go easy on those innocent leaves!"

Dex turns to see Phoenix grinning at him. His arms are folded across his bare chest and he has three purple flowers tucked behind his ear.

"You're looking very pretty today." Dex points at the flowers.

Phoenix grins. "Why, thank you."

"Have you seen Wr—"

"Attack!" There's a flurry of movement and Luca leaps from the bushes waving his spear in the air and growling.

Dex throws up his arms above his head. "I surrender!"

Phoenix follows his lead and stands beside Dex, arms raised. "Please, don't hurt us, fierce warrior."

"Back to camp," Luca instructs in a deep voice. "You're my prisoners now."

Dex and Phoenix allow themselves to be led from the trees, back to the encampment.

"Luca!" says Nova when she sees them. "Get over here, you little mischief maker."

Luca giggles and dashes over to her. She ruffles his hair and Dex smiles to see this budding relationship. He'd never doubted that Nova would make a wonderful mother. He just hadn't expected it to happen so...instantly.

"Hey, little mate," Phoenix calls over to Luca. "How many of those spears do you think you can make?"

"As many as you want." Luca's face lights up.

"One for each person here?"

Luca looks up at Nova for approval, and seeing that she's smiling, he nods back to Phoenix.

"Excellent," says Phoenix. "Gather a team and get started as soon as you can."

"Good idea," says Dex, more convinced than ever that it's time to get serious about training these peace-loving people to fight.

Luca runs straight up to Bea and Vern as his first recruits. They smile fondly as he dashes off to find his next volunteer. Dex has no doubt he'll gather a small army in record time. His innocent face is hard to say no to—unless you're Felicia, who politely declines in favor of approaching Phoenix.

Phoenix removes one of the flowers from behind his ear, bows and holds it out to her. "Something beautiful for someone beautiful."

Dex rolls his eyes as Felicia takes the flower, her face flushing a similar shade to Phoenix's hair as she holds it to her nose. It's a shame Wren isn't here to see this. Her nose would crinkle in her adorably grumpy face to see this budding relationship refuse to shrivel and die like she hoped it would.

Phoenix holds out another flower toward his mother.

"Thanks, Phee," says Avis, clearly pleased with the attention.

Which leaves Phoenix with one last flower. He removes it and twirls between his fingers. "Where's Wren?"

"What do you mean?" Dex puts his hand to his chest as his heart picks up a faster rhythm. He'd been about to ask Phoenix the same thing.

"Wren," says Phoenix, oblivious to Dex's distress. "You know the one. Short, stubborn, strong little thing. Makes goo-goo eyes at dudes with one hand."

"She went back to your father to beg forgiveness." Dex's words come out in a tumble and Phoenix's face turns gray. "Haven't you seen her?"

Phoenix shakes his head. "When? How long ago?"

"Two days." Dex's stomach churns. This is even worse than he feared.

"Cy's said nothing about this. Not a word. And I know she hasn't been in her cabin because I've been sleeping in there. Maybe she didn't make it back to the Oasis?"

"She must've made it." Dex pulls at his hair, trying to come up with a reasonable explanation for why Phoenix hadn't seen her. "Where else would she be?"

"Kian's gone after her." Nova steps forward. "To see if he can release Magnus."

"That's not possible," says Phoenix. "The brig's heavily guarded. I thought of doing it myself, but it's too dangerous."

Dex's legs threaten to buckle. "What's he done to her? Where is she?"

"You need to help her." Avis clutches Phoenix's wrist. "Help your sister. Please! I can't lose her again."

Phoenix nods. But the fear in his eyes betrays how much help he believes he's going to be. He knows better than anyone what Ronan is capable of. Except perhaps Avis.

Kian bursts through the trees and Dex scans for Wren, praying to see her leap out from behind him.

But there's no Wren. And no Magnus.

"She's not with me," says Kian, noticing his anguish. "Nor is my father."

Dex's father rushes over at these words. They wait as Nova throws her arms around Kian and they embrace like they'd thought they were never going to see each other again.

"Are you okay?" Nova asks, running her fingers down Kian's back.

But Dex doesn't want to wait for his answer. Kian's alive which makes him okay. It's Wren he's worried about.

Kian releases Nova to look at her. "I'm o—"

"Where's Wren?" Dex asks. "Did you see her?"

"I saw her with Ronan. She's alive," says Kian, his eyes filling with anguish. Then he notices Phoenix standing beside Felicia. "But I didn't see you there."

Dex sighs with relief. But before he can ask after her health Phoenix lets out a series of curses.

"Why the hell didn't Cy tell me she was there?"

"Maybe he doesn't trust you," says Kian.

"I need to go back." Phoenix shuffles his feet as his concern builds. "I don't care if he trusts me or not."

"You should stay here with us," Felicia suggests. "You might be safer."

"I'm not leaving Wren alone with him." Phoenix clenches a fist, his cheeks pink with rage.

"What did she look like?" Dex asks Kian, desperate for more information on her. "Was she okay?"

Kian holds his gaze, agonizing over his words, and Dex steps toward him. "Kian, tell us. What did you see? What did she look like?"

His cousin's face breaks under the strain of the words he's trying to find. "She…it…well…." Kian takes two steps away, claws at his hair and spins back. "She's not good. Ronan cut off her finger."

Nova's gasp echoes around the camp as they struggle to take in what Kian just told them.

"I'm going to kill that bastard!" Phoenix has both fists clenched now, and he strikes at the air.

"My poor baby girl," sobs Avis, leaning into Thea who's wrapped a firm arm around her new friend's shoulders.

Dex blinks at Kian, struggling to accept this. It can't be true! Not Wren. If Ronan's taken her finger what else has he done to her?

"It gets worse," says Kian, confirming his fears. "Ronan said something about her needing to make him a grandson. I'm worried that—"

"I have to go to her!" Rage builds in the pit of Dex's stomach. He knows he won't be the father Ronan has in mind for his grandson. Which can only mean one thing. "I have to get her out."

But as he tries to take another step, Kian grips him by the arm. "You're not going anywhere near there. It's too dangerous. It's a miracle I got myself out of there alive."

"Let go of me." Dex tries to squirm away but Kian's grip is tight.

"Kian's right." Dex's father takes hold of his other arm. "It's not safe. We'll get her back, but we need to be smart about it."

Before he can protest, Phoenix turns and runs back into the trees. He's fast. Faster than Dex could ever hope to be.

"Where's he going?" Felicia asks, seeming genuinely surprised.

"To help Wren, obviously." Dex rolls his eyes.

Avis turns to Thea and buries her face in her shoulder, shuddering with grief. Both her children are in danger now.

"Phoenix can do more than you can," Kian says, letting go of Dex. "Let him handle it."

"Who says he can do more than me?" Dex straightens his back and glares at his cousin. "Sometimes brains count for more than muscle."

"Not in this case." Dex's father keeps hold of his arm as he turns to Kian. "Brute strength seems to be Ronan's preferred language. We need to come up with a plan if we're going to be smart."

Dex scowls, hating the truth in these words.

"What happened to Magnus?" his father asks Kian. "Did you get to him?"

Dex relaxes against his father's grip. This is an answer he wants to hear. It's the whole reason both Wren and Kian risked their lives. He can only hope it hadn't been for nothing.

"I found him." Kian looks above their heads as he talks, not seeming to want to make eye contact. "We decided it's best he stays where he is for now. There'd be too much suspicion if he disappeared."

There's something that's not ringing true. It's not so much what he's saying, it's the tone. Dex has grown up beside Kian. He can spot one of his rare lies at ten paces. And he's certain this is one of them. The other thing he knows about Kian is that he wouldn't lie unless he needed to. But it's not the time to call him out on it.

However, it seems his father disagrees. He lets go of Dex to step up to Kian. "What really happened?"

Kian glances around, checking to see who's in earshot. With most of the camp being ordered around by Luca to collect sticks or busy preparing the polar grizzly carcass for tonight's feast, he seems to decide it's safe enough to talk.

"He refused to come with me," Kian says in a low voice.

"He what?" Dex's father stumbles back. "It was Amity wasn't it? He refused to leave her."

That makes sense and Dex nods as if answering for Kian.

But Kian shakes his head. "He's not thinking straight. He's been refusing food. He's wasting away in the brig. I think he's lost his mind."

"If it wasn't Amity"—Nova puts a hand on Kian's back—"then what was it?"

Kian's eyes prick with tears and Dex's stomach lurches. Whatever he's about to tell them, it's not going to be good.

"He said he's going to let nature run its course." Kian swallows, the words not coming out easily. "That human extinction is the best thing that can happen to the planet."

"He hasn't lost his mind," Dex's father sneers. "He's found it. That's the true Magnus talking. The one I grew up with. He always thought of the planet first and the people second. *Always*. Why do you think we clashed so much?"

"You clashed because you were in love with my mother,"

Kian shoots back, his voice strained. "That wasn't my father talking. He'd never put anything else before his family."

"Are you sure about that?" Veins are protruding from Dex's father's forehead as he spits out his words. "Because it looks like he just did."

"You're just jealous of him." Kian's face is aflame, his fists clenched. "You always have been."

"Enough, Kian." Nova shifts her hand from his back to his arm, but he's too caught up in his emotion to listen.

"It's true! My father isn't like that!"

Dex's father opens his mouth to respond, but this time it's Dex who takes hold of him.

"Dad! Stop it. This isn't helping." He pulls him away from Kian. "Let's go for a walk. Everyone needs to calm down."

"Good idea," says Nova, keeping a hold of Kian. "We could all use a little space."

Dex drags his father away from the group and into the trees. When he feels like his father is prepared to follow willingly, he lets go and they walk into the forest, taking the path that leads down away from the cliffs.

"Where are we going?" his father asks. "We can't go to the Oasis."

"We're not going to the Oasis." Dex strides forward, the energy he'd seemed to lack earlier in the day now surging through his muscles. "We're going to the beach."

His father doesn't ask why. It's obvious. They can't stay in the forest unarmed after what happened to Nova and they can't stay at the cliffs. The beach will be deserted. It's somewhere safe they can sit and let their tempers cool.

They continue down the path and Dex turns over everything that just happened in his mind, his thoughts remaining with Wren. He needs to get to her. Urgently. But in the smartest way possible.

His father is seething beside him as they walk, although Dex knows it isn't Wren he has on his mind.

"I'm not jealous of him," his father says after a long silence. "I used to be. I'll admit that. When it all happened, I was consumed by it. But not now. Amity was always better suited to Magnus. I couldn't have made her happy in the way he did."

Dex nods to show he's listening but doesn't reply. He can't bring himself to care about his father's love life when his own has been cut so abruptly short.

"Your mother made me happy, Dex. I admit that I didn't quite love her in the same way she loved me. But I did love her."

"I know." Dex sighs, struggling to show interest in a conversation he feels he's had before. It's Wren they need to be talking about.

"Even though I felt betrayed by our father for choosing Magnus to lead Askala, I came to peace with that," his father continues, oblivious to Dex's frustration. "Being the leader isn't always a desirable position."

"Tell me about it." Dex remembers the feeling of joy when Kian had returned and he'd been able to hand back the leadership. He's always been a lot more comfortable being the spare than the heir. It seems his father had come to the same conclusion. Except... "But you became leader of the league who planned to overthrow Magnus. If that had worked, you'd have become leader."

His father doesn't reply for a long time. Could he be more ambitious than he'd let on?

"Sometimes we don't get a choice," he finally says. "Kian's the leader now and I'm happy for that. He has all of his father's good qualities and none of his bad. He's doing a fine job."

Having reached the bottom of the hill, they step out onto the sand and a warm breeze caresses Dex's face. Checking that they're truly alone, they walk toward the water's edge.

"This is where I first saw Wren." Dex looks out at the dark

clouds gathering on the horizon, remembering seeing her struggling in the water, a leatherskin having decided she'd make a tasty meal. If he'd known at the time what she'd end up meaning to him, instead of standing by and watching her fight a beast several times her size, he'd have run into the ocean's acidic depths and helped her.

Not that she'd needed his help.

But she definitely needs it now.

There's no denying that this is one of the reasons he'd brought his father here. It wasn't just the need to cool off. It was his need to feel close to Wren.

"I know you love her," his father says. "We'll find a way to get her out of there. But I'm glad you listened and didn't run off. It would break my heart to lose you. You're all I've got."

Dex shifts his gaze to his father, surprised to hear him express himself like this. But pleased the conversation has finally shifted away from Magnus.

"I'm proud of you, son." His father drapes an arm around his shoulders. "I should never have doubted you'd be a true Bound."

"I didn't know you did." Dex raises his eyebrows.

"I did." His father's voice breaks. "I admit I did. I was worried that having an Unbound mother would harm your chances. I was a fool. If anything, it was having me for a father that might've done that. But it didn't. You're smart and you're kind, Dex. You're the best person I've ever known. I'm so sorry. Please, forgive me."

"Forgive you for what?" Dex puts his arm around him, trying to soothe the sobs that are now wracking his father's thin frame. "You did your best to be a good father."

"I was a terrible father. I'm sorry. So sorry."

Dex pats his father on the back. It seems Magnus isn't the only one losing his mind out here. This situation is bringing up all kinds of emotions in people.

"Where did this come from Dad?" Dex gently breaks away,

surprised at this sudden outburst. "I thought you were doing okay?"

"Because it's no use! Can't you see that? It was obvious to me when Kian returned empty-handed that this was all over. There's nothing else we can do. Ronan's won."

"He hasn't won!" This is the last thing Dex needs to hear right now. Ronan can't have won. Because that means they've lost, and there's no way he's going to accept that. "We need to stay strong. We can't win this if we all fall apart."

"How can we win?" His father clenches his fists. "Ronan has the strength. And the flamethrowers."

"But we have the determination. And the brains." But even as Dex says the words, he wonders if that's going to be enough.

"If only we had the strength."

Dex nods, shifting his gaze back out to the horizon where the clouds have parted to let through a golden ray of sunlight. The sun will set soon. They don't have long before they'll need to get back to camp.

Maybe his father's right. Maybe Ronan *has* won. Because it seems every time they turn a corner there's an obstacle in their path. And even when they manage to climb over the top, there's another one waiting for them—bigger and more threatening.

And now Wren's in danger and Magnus is refusing to leave the brig. Even Kian lost his cool back there and that never happens. It's so hard to stay positive when negativity is screaming at you from every possible angle.

"Look!" His father points out at the water.

"It's beautiful, isn't it?" Dex hasn't ever known his father to get so excited over a sunset. He's more of a dramatic thunderstorm kind of guy.

"No! Look!" His father jumps up and down. "They're coming! It's Dean and his Remnants! It has to be!"

Dex peers out, his heart pumping when he sees what his

father's looking at. A raft is approaching. It's hard to tell from this distance, but it seems to be loaded with people.

Could this be the army they'd given up waiting for? Is it possible that Dean has come good on his word and actually decided to do something useful for once?

"I think you're right, Dad," he says, hope lighting in his chest, as the waves surge the raft forward and he's certain he spots someone with bright red hair standing at the front.

Now they can add strength to their determination and brains.

Now, they have a chance. A real one.

Wren's face fills his mind.

"I'm coming," he whispers to her. "I'm going to get you out. Just hold on."

WREN

*W*ren lies on the bed with Jagger snoring beside her. It's impossible to sleep with his cacophony of bodily functions, not all of them coming from his mouth. But she dares not complain. He might be annoying but he's safe. True to his word, he hasn't laid a finger on her, except for show when Cy's been around.

He might be twice her age and more than twice her size, but he's a gentle giant. She looks at him now with his chest rising and falling in a restless rhythm. People are vulnerable when they sleep. She could suffocate him and he'd never know what happened. Jagger is trusting her just as much as she's been forced to trust him.

The chip he wears on a string is nestled in the hairs on his chest and she tries not to think too much about where it came from. Despite the fog she's walking around in, it's been impossible not to notice the bandaged left hands of a number of the former Bound. Cy said he'd find a way to get around the Oasis and it seems like he has.

It's only early evening. Too early to sleep under normal

circumstances. But with not much else to do to fill their days, the people have taken to sleeping at all kinds of strange hours.

Wren lifts up her hand to inspect her missing digit. It's easier to look at in the dim light after sunset. She looks like Nova now, which is helping to dull the shock of her disfigurement. It's not completely foreign for her to look at a hand with four fingers. Or an arm without a hand.

A scab is forming around the wound and the weeping has subsided. But the stinging is still raw. A throbbing ache that doesn't want to leave her alone, the discomfort matched only by the gaping emptiness in her stomach. It's been an age since she had anything to eat. There just isn't any food around for that. But Jagger's been bringing her water, insisting she keep her fluids up.

Slowly, her body seems to be replenishing all the blood she lost. Although, she's well aware her mind is going to take far longer to repair.

It wasn't just her finger that Cy took. He robbed her of her ability to trust her own judgment. And that's what's thrown her most of all.

She really had thought she'd be able to win Cy over. But he's made it more than clear that's not going to happen. He's moved on, wanting a grandson to replace her. Even if she managed to produce him one of those, that wouldn't help her cause. He'd get rid of her in the same way he got rid of her own mother once she'd fulfilled her purpose.

Perhaps she'd been too quick to judge her mother's abandonment of them? Because Wren is no longer just disappointed with Cy. She's afraid of him. As surely her mother must've been all those years ago.

There's a quiet knocking at the cabin door and Wren creeps out of bed, hoping it's Phoenix.

"Come in," she says at the door, quiet enough not to wake

Jagger but hopefully loud enough for her visitor to hear. She really wishes Dex hadn't canceled her chip.

The door slides back and Amity is standing there clutching a jar with one hand, her other pressed to the sensor.

Wren's eyes fly open. Amity is risking her life leaving the pool deck like this. Especially when the pods are in such a bad state.

"Here." Amity holds out the jar. "I brought you some pods. You need the strength."

Wren shakes her head. "We all do. You eat them."

"I already had my share." Amity jiggles the jar, the dark circles under her eyes betraying her lie. There's no way this woman has been eating. "Take them. Please. We need you strong."

Too hungry to complain, Wren takes the jar and puts the two pods in her mouth, swallowing them down quickly and handing the jar back. It's best if there's no evidence of Amity's visit left behind.

"Thank you." Wren's stomach groans at the unexpected work it now has to do to extract the goodness from some food at last.

"Is Kian in there?" Amity asks, peering over Wren's shoulder.

"Kian?" Wren steps into the hallway. "Have you seen him here?"

Amity nods, keeping her voice low. "He came to the pool. We created a distraction so he could get Magnus out. But…Magnus is still in the brig and I haven't seen Kian since. I'm worried about him."

Wren shakes her head. "So, that's what that commotion was all about. Smart. But no, I haven't seen him. I didn't even know he was here. Could he have talked to Magnus and left?"

Amity shakes her head. "But Magnus is still imprisoned. That doesn't make sense. I thought you'd know something. That's why I came here."

"I'm sorry if you wasted the pods on me." Wren wipes her mouth.

"I didn't waste them." Amity's eyes burn with determination. "Kian trusts you. Which means so do I. We have to keep the good people strong."

Wren nods. "I feel a little better already. Thank you."

"Is he hurting you?" Amity inclines her head toward the cabin.

"No." Wren gives her a small smile. "Some of the good people are well disguised."

"I'll see if I can bring him a pod later." Amity straightens her back, clutching the empty jar in her hand until her knuckles are white.

Wren's about to tell her not to put herself at further risk when she realizes there's more to Amity's deliveries than just the pods themselves. It's giving her purpose. It's the one thing she can do when everything else seems hopeless.

Amity gives Wren one last sad smile then turns back down the corridor. Wren watches her disappear, trying to reconcile that hunched-over figure with the strong woman who'd proudly hung onto the arm of the leader of Askala, confident their future was assured.

But it seems the world can change without warning. And sometimes the new normal can be a shock to the system. Which leaves two choices...

Accept it.

Or fight.

The sound of footsteps pounding down the corridor has Wren retreating inside, again wishing she was able to close the door.

She leans against the wall, heart pounding and sweat beading on her forehead.

Cy.

Those sounded like Cy's footsteps.

She doesn't want to see him. Not now and not ever.

It's only then that she remembers her choice was to fight. When Cy took her finger, she swore to herself that she'd kill him. She can't do that if she's afraid of him.

It's time to woman up and get her act together.

She has two pods in her belly. Nine working fingers. And a shipload of people on her side.

Peeling herself off the wall, she turns and waits for Cy, determined to look him in the eye.

The flash of red hair and muscled chest that barrels toward her might look like her father, but she soon realizes it isn't him. It's a man worth a hundred versions of Cy.

"Phee!" Wren extends her arms and Phoenix flies into them, lifting her from the ground as he plants his feet and squeezes her tight.

"Are you okay?" he asks.

"Yes." She nods into his shoulder.

He lowers her to the floor and reaches straight for her hand, groaning as he inspects her missing finger.

"I can't believe it." Pain is streaking across her twin's face. "I just found out. That bastard."

"I'm okay," she says again. "It's healing. It could've been worse."

"I hate him, Wren." He lifts her hand to his lips and kisses it. "I hate him."

"Shh! Talk like that is dangerous out here." She leads him into the cabin where at least some of his traitorous talk will be muffled by the walls. Phoenix uses the chip hanging around his neck to close the door.

"What's going on?" Jagger sits up in bed, eyes wide with confusion.

"I should be the one asking you that," Phoenix roars back.

"What the hell are you doing here with my sister? I don't care what Cy's ordered you to do."

"Stop, Phee!" Wren quickly steps between the two men. "He hasn't hurt me. I swear it. He's been helping me, just like he helped us get out of the lab."

Phoenix unclenches his fists and lets out a deep breath, swinging his gaze between Wren and Jagger until he's satisfied she's telling the truth.

"I'm going to leave you two to catch up." Jagger hauls himself out of bed and rubs at his eyes. "I'll see what the Commander's up to."

"Sorry about...that." Phoenix extends his hand and Jagger shakes it firmly. "I let my anger get the better of me. Thanks for looking after her."

"It's a lot to take in. I damn near lost the plot when I first saw what he did to her." Jagger edges his way past Phoenix's large frame and uses his chip to open the door, disappearing as it slides closed again.

"Who told you?" Wren turns to Phoenix. "About my hand, I mean."

"Kian."

"What?" Wren sits down on the bed and leans against the headboard. "I heard he came back, but I didn't see him."

"He saw you."

She nods, wondering where he'd been hiding. "Did he get to Magnus?"

Phoenix shrugs. "I didn't stick around long enough to find out. Although, he returned to camp alone, so I'd say not."

His gaze keeps coming back to her hand and Wren crosses her arms to obstruct his view, remembering how Dex had a habit of doing the same thing when she'd first met him. She'd been the one to convince him to stop hiding what made him different. But now she understands a whole lot better why he used to do it. And she admires him all the more for the way he was able to let that habit go.

"It's not as bad as it looks," she says. "It barely hurts."

He lifts a brow at her.

There's no point lying to Phoenix. There never has been.

"It's a bit sore."

He lifts the other brow, still staring at her hand.

"Okay. It hurts like a bitch."

But instead of laughing, like she'd thought he would, he paces the room punching the air and cursing. "You should never have come back! Why, Wren? What possessed you?"

"I underestimated him." She clutches her hand to her chest. "And I overestimated what I mean to him."

"He doesn't give a crap about anyone but himself! You should know that!" He takes a deep breath and stops his pacing to sit on the bed beside her. "Our mother is the only one who ever cared about us. Yet, instead of accepting her, you ran straight back to the person who's done nothing but hurt us since the day we were born."

Wren hangs her head. Why does accepting their mother seem so much harder than turning her back on the man who hurt them? "I'll try harder to forgive her."

Phoenix lets out a long sigh. "You really don't get it. She's done nothing wrong for you to have to forgive. She was scared of him, Wren. Petrified. You saw what he did to her face. It's a hundred times worse than what he did to your hand."

Wren swallows, fighting the shame that's rising within. It's true. Every word of it. She'd been so scared of Cy after he hurt her. She can't even imagine how their mother must've felt.

"Then I won't try harder to forgive her. I'll just...try harder to let my resentment go." Shuffling over to Phoenix, she wraps her arms around him and buries her face in the comfort of his chest. After several long seconds he returns the embrace and holds her tight, dropping a kiss on the top of her head.

"Love you, little bird."

"Please don't call me that anymore." She blinks up at him. "Cy ruined that name."

"Nah." He ruffles her hair. "He stole that name from me, not the other way around. Don't listen to him. You'll always be my little bird."

The door to the cabin slides open and Jagger appears, his face lined with concern.

"The Commander's asking for you." He's looking directly at Wren. "I think you'd better go. You know how he gets if he's kept waiting."

Wren drags herself off the bed.

Phoenix is right beside her. "You're not going anywhere near him without me."

"Don't Phee." She pushes him away. "There's no point in us both endangering ourselves."

"She's right," says Jagger. "Seeing you with her being all protective will only inflame him, putting her more at risk. You stay here. Get some rest. I'll look after her."

"I didn't come back here to wait in a cabin!" Phoenix takes a step toward the door, but Jagger is blocking it.

"No, Phoenix. You can't come. Not this time."

"Go back to the camp," Wren urges. "Teach them how to fight. It's time we acted."

Phoenix rakes at his hair. "But I came back for you."

"And you saw that I'm okay. Go and look after the others. They need you more than I do. Our mother needs you. And..." She swallows, trying to push out the next words that she knows will tip him over the edge. "And Felicia needs you."

She watches as her twin puffs out his chest, the idea of rescuing a damsel in distress filling him with new determination.

He nods. "As long as you're okay."

145

She puts her uninjured hand on his arm. "I wasn't okay. But I swear I am now. Jagger will take care of me."

"We need to move." Jagger steps back out into the hallway. "The longer he waits, the more aggressive he gets."

"Say hello to…" Wren hesitates. Saying hello to Dex isn't nearly enough. "Tell Dex I love him, all right?"

Phoenix rolls his eyes. "Do I have to?"

"You do." She pushes up on her toes and brushes her lips across her brother's cheek before leaving him to follow Jagger down the corridor.

"Look after her!" Phoenix calls after them.

Jagger raises a hand to show he heard but doesn't turn back.

As soon as they round the corner, he puts a possessive hand on Wren's shoulder.

"Gotta show Cy that—"

"I know why you're doing it."

She's surprised when Jagger doesn't lead her to the ballroom. She'd just assumed that's where Cy would be. Instead, they head up the stairs, climbing higher and higher.

"The party deck?" she asks.

"I'm afraid so." Jagger rolls his eyes.

They exit the stairwell and the sound of drums fills Wren's ears. "He's celebrating a bit too soon, don't you think?"

But Jagger doesn't hear her over the noise.

They continue down the corridor, right to the end where it opens out into the large expanse the Unbound once used to hold their infamous parties. At first, the scene before Wren doesn't look a whole lot different. There are people in various states of undress gyrating to the sound of the drums with the bulk of Cy's frame in the middle of them, enjoying the attention several women are giving him.

Then Wren looks closer and sees it's nothing like the party deck used to be. The smiles are missing from the people's faces. Their movements are forced. Almost robotic in their lack of energy. The berry wine must have dried up. These people aren't drunk. They're starving.

And every one of them is scared.

Cy sees Wren and signals for the drummers to cut the beat they're pumping into the room. Their obedience is instant, and the silence draws Wren and Jagger forward.

Wren keeps her gaze on Cy, not trusting him for a moment. Those days are long gone.

He approaches them and tears Wren from Jagger's grasp, landing a wet kiss on her cheek.

"My daughter!" He smiles broadly at the crowd. "My daughter who's been busy making me a grandson. A boy who'll grow to rule over all of you one day."

The crowd nod their heads approvingly, although Wren knows this is the last thing they want.

"But that's not why I brought her here." Cy's smile shifts to a frown in that way he has of changing moods faster than Wren can blink. "I wanted to show you something."

He grips Wren's left wrist and hoists her arm into the air, her missing finger visible to all. A murmur ripples across the room. These people are used to seeing missing fingers. But not a newly missing digit on the hand of their leader's daughter.

"That's right," says Cy. "My sweet daughter tried to run away from me. She wasn't loyal like you lot. So, I cut off her finger to remind her why that wasn't such a good idea. If she does it again, then I'll take her middle finger next. Then her index finger. Then this cute little one here. And then I'll take her thumb."

The crowd are finding it hard to smile now as they tuck their own hands behind their backs or in their pockets, not knowing where Cy's going to take this next. Wren tries her best not to squirm, hoping this is as far as Cy's showing off is going to go. Surely, he doesn't think she's betrayed him again? She's barely left Jagger's cabin.

"And if that doesn't teach my willful daughter, I'm going to have to take her hand." There are a few stifled gasps in the crowd. "Then her arm. Then lucky for me she has a whole other hand where I can start again. You get the picture..."

Wren stands as still as she can, trying not to let her fear show on her face. Fear will do nothing to help these terrified people.

"Has anyone else here betrayed me?" Cy scans the crowd. "Anyone who's walking around with more fingers than they deserve?"

The people shake their heads and Wren bites down on her tongue to stop herself from fighting back.

"Oh, don't look so shocked." Cy tuts. "Magnus took more fingers in one day than I have in a lifetime. Who's your real enemy?"

Surely, he can't think that these people are going to believe that? Magnus's methods may not have been perfect, but there's no question that life in Askala under his rule was far preferable to how it is now. And he did it for reasons other than his own selfish power. He was trying to build a better world.

"Now, let's get back to the party!" Cy lets go of Wren's wrist to pump his own fist in the air as the drummers pick up their rhythm again.

The people shuffle their feet and plaster on their smiles, dancing out of a fear that's just as palpable as Cy's evil.

Wren gasps as she's grabbed roughly around the waist, relieved to find it's Jagger, who's pressing himself against her as he stomps to the rhythm. If she didn't know better, she'd think he was enjoying himself. But she can see the hint of sorrow in his eyes as he forces a kiss on her lips.

Trying her best not to pull away, Wren closes her eyes and focuses on the beat of the drums in her chest.

They're marking the seconds that are passing.

Which will soon turn to minutes.

Then hours.

Then days.

Time is marching forward. Soon, Cy's time will be done.

The crowd cheers at something and Wren pulls away from Jagger to raise her fist in the air.

Bring it on, Cy.

Bring. It. On.

NOVA

*L*uca watches the meat sizzle on the fire with wide eyes. "I've never had bear meat before."

Nova strokes his hair back from his forehead, smiling. The night surrounds the many small fires dotted in the encampment, the flames illuminating the anticipation on everyone's faces. They're about to have a feast. "It has a strong...bear taste."

"Kinda like cockroaches have a strong bug taste?"

"Something like that," Nova chuckles. "But less crunchy."

Luca looks up at her. "You should've seen yourself, Nova. You were awesome!"

"I was more scared than I've ever been in my life." Nova doubts she'll ever forget the sight of those dagger-like teeth aimed at her throat. "It's not something I'd choose to repeat."

The smell of roasting meat has Luca's stomach grumbling and he grins. "Well, everyone's pretty glad you did!" He grips her hand. "You were so brave."

Coming from Luca, the boy who jumps from beams spearing into the sky, the boy who swims toward a raft in an acidic ocean...when he doesn't know how to swim, that's high praise.

An arm slides around Nova's shoulder. "She sure was."

Nova leans into Kian, feeling both the tension and the tenderness in his hold. Kian's proud of how she faced the bear. The story also terrified him.

She nudges him with her shoulder. "I think you wish I was still the timid Nova who would've stayed up the tree."

Kian shakes his head. "I'm less likely to die of a heart attack, but no, I don't want that."

That's not far from the truth. When Kian heard what happened with the bear, he looked like he'd forgotten to breathe. Nova had stepped in close, wondering if he was about to faint.

He presses his lips to her hair. "You've always had the heart of a lioness, Nova. It was Askala that had you believing otherwise."

Nova wraps her arms around his waist. That's not an easy thing for Kian to acknowledge. There's been something about him since he returned. A melancholy air that seems more than just disappointment that his father isn't by his side.

It's like Kian's struggling to find hope.

"Is it ready?" asks Luca.

Nova withdraws the strip of meat, the fat sizzling and sparking over the flames. "I think it might be."

The sound of voices has Nova freezing. They're male voices. Voices coming from the forest.

More than just the voices of Dex and Callix, who they're expecting will return any moment.

Kian is instantly on high alert. He straightens, subtly stepping in front of Nova. But Nova isn't having any of that. She slips around, standing by his side as they stare into the night. A brush against her leg and she finds Luca beside her, the little spear he hasn't let go of clenched in his fist.

The voices suddenly stop and Nova's pulse escalates. Has

Ronan found them? Did the smell of the meat bring him here? She gasps. Have Dex and Callix been hurt?

Kian draws in a short, sharp breath and Nova sees what sparked it a second later. Sweet Terra, that was a flash of red hair!

Shadows break away from the tree line, all large and lumbering. Men. At least ten of them.

A smaller one steps forward. "Aw man, that smells good."

"Dex?" Nova asks in disbelief.

"Please tell me there's some left. If Luca's eaten the whole bear, I ain't going to be happy."

He's joking as always. But he's surrounded by men. Is he their captive? Are their people in danger?

Callix appears beside his son. "We arrived at the beach just in time to be a welcoming committee."

Dean steps up on Dex's other side, his red hair glinting in the firelight. "Although I like this one much better. They didn't even have a pod on them."

Kian's body slackens. "Dean," he murmurs in disbelief. "And he brought people from the Outlands."

Dean slaps the shoulder of the man beside him. "See, Cain? I told you there'd be food."

Nova blinks. Dean came? And he brought reinforcements?

She steps forward, hope blooming in her chest. "Welcome. There's enough for—"

The words die as the men enter the pool of light. The man Dean called Cain.

She knows him.

Nova has to suppress the whimper that climbs up her throat. He can't be...

"Nova?" Kian's voice is full of concern. "Is something wrong?"

"We don't have anything. We told you that."

"We could take your clothes," Cain had suggested, his eyes glinting.

"But...we need our clothes."

His grin had been slow and deliberate. "Nah, they're only going to get in the way when you pay for the first cup."

Somehow, Nova chokes out two words. "I'm fine."

The same fear that had gripped her throat is trying to strangle her again. This is the man she needs to align herself with?

Kian looks back toward the men. "Hey, I know you. You were in the village."

Cain steps forward, his eyes flicking to Nova but giving nothing away. "I see you found her. Glad I could help."

From what Kian told her, Cain had provided very little information for an exorbitant price. If it weren't for the baby Shiloh helped deliver, Kian never would've found her. But Nova hasn't told him how Cain and his friend threatened them.

That Cain's friend killed Thom over a spilled pot of watery broth.

Or the price he would've demanded if Avis hadn't helped them escape.

Kian turns to Dean, his jaw clenched. This is the army that Dean brought? Exactly how trustworthy are they going to be?

Nova pulls Luca closer to her, studying the men. All dirty and frowning. All strong and hardened.

She senses the people of Askala assemble behind them. Curious, as naïve as she was when she first arrived in the Outlands, they wait to see what sort of welcome this will be. None of them look as if they're ready to defend themselves against these intruders.

She doubts it even occurred to them.

Resisting the urge to step closer to Kian, Nova lifts her chin.

Kian nods, eyeing the new recruits. "Thank you for coming, I know the voyage isn't without danger. Please, join us. There's plenty of meat."

He's realized it, too. They need these men. They can't win the fight against Ronan without them.

Nova straightens her shoulders. Cain met a desperate girl who didn't know her own strength. That girl no longer exists. "And there's water, and a safe place to rest."

The men break into small groups, dispersing among the fires roasting the meat. Their eyes glint with hunger and Nova hopes it's only for food. Cain's gaze holds hers for longer than it should as he stalks past, but Nova doesn't look away.

If she can face a bear and defeat it, she can do what it takes to save Askala. Even if it includes fighting alongside a man like Cain.

Kian's brow is creased as he turns to Nova. "Is everything okay?" he asks quietly.

"It was just the surprise," she assures him. "It made me think of the Outlands."

Kian studies her for long moments, no doubt recognizing the half-truth she just told him. She jumps in before he can ask any more questions. She'll tell him the whole story when this is all over. "This is the boost we needed, Kian."

His jaw works. "We can't trust them."

"We didn't think we could trust Jagger. And we couldn't have saved Dex and the others without him."

Kian's eyes close, his face strained and tight. Wren seems to have discovered her father isn't who she thought he was. Kian has learned the same painful truth. "I just don't know anymore, Nova."

Nova waits for him to open his eyes before shaking her head as she holds his gaze. "You do, Kian. The right path has always been in your heart. Askala had you believing otherwise."

Breath whooshing out, he rests his forehead against Nova's. "Together."

Nova smiles. "We never realized the diversity that word

would encompass." She cups his face. "It's a good thing they came."

They don't need Magnus to believe in this. They need Kian to.

Kian pulls back, his face settling into the determined lines that are now becoming familiar. "I'm going to go talk to them."

Nova nods, squeezing his arm. "We feed them, they fight for us. It's a good deal."

Dean watches Kian approach, his chin jutted at a cocky angle. Nova wonders if he delayed his arrival by a few days on purpose, just to show Kian how much he needed him. Kian reaches out a hand and Dean shakes it, looking a little surprised.

It seems Dean hasn't learned that Kian would never put his own pride above his people.

Nova's about to ensure there's more meat put on the fire when Flick sidles up to her, eyeing the men warily. "I don't like having them here," she hisses.

Glancing at her, Nova wonders if Flick remembers Cain. "They're here to help us."

"Those men in the village sure as hell didn't help Thom."

It seems she doesn't remember. Considering she was barely semi-conscious for most of their time there, then dazed with shock after Thom was killed, Nova isn't surprised.

And Cain wasn't the one who killed Thom. His friend was. And what if Cain is the father of Jagger, the man who helped save all these people's lives? Could he be someone who, away from the violence and desperation of the Outlands, would make the same choice Jagger did?

Nova doesn't have the liberty to decide whether Cain deserves a second chance. There's no choice. They need him.

"That same ferocity that makes you nervous is what will give us the advantage when we attack the Oasis, Flick. It's a good thing they've arrived."

Nova wonders how many times she'll have to say that before she believes it.

Flick wraps her arms around herself despite the warmth of the fire. "I still don't feel safe with them here."

A warm voice reaches from behind her. "Will this help?"

Phoenix materializes from the shadows, dropping an arm around Flick's shoulders. Her startled face melts into joy. "Phee!"

He glances over at the new members, eyeing the way they're shoveling meat into their mouth as quickly as they can grab it. "Well, it seems like a lack of table manners must run in the family. Dean eats like my father."

Avis rushes over, clasping Phoenix in an embrace. "You're back early!"

Phoenix hugs his mother, watching Dex approach now that he's noticed the commotion. "I couldn't stay. Not after what Cy's done."

Dex's jaw looks like it could crack any second. "What's the news?"

Phoenix holds Dex's gaze. "It's true. Cy cut off Wren's finger."

Dex's hand clenches and unclenches. "And the expectation for a grandson?"

"She was lucky, Cy paired her with Jagger. He's keeping her safe." Phoenix sighs. "Cy's a fool. He harmed the one person who believed there was good in him."

"And he doesn't realize she's not alone."

They hold each other's gaze, some silent promise passing between them. They've gone from believing they were rivals for Wren's love, to being united by their love for Wren.

Phoenix's lips twitch. "She sent a message." He looks away, his face puckering. "Said she loves you."

Dex blinks, those words the first to draw a reaction from him. He turns to Kian. "When do we attack?"

156

Phoenix comes to stand beside him. "The longer we leave it, the greater the chance Cy will figure something is up."

And the longer Wren is forced to live under his oppression alongside the people of Askala.

Nova holds her breath. They're talking of war. Of a fight they can't afford to lose. She wishes this choice never had to arrive.

She knows it just did.

Kian glances at the people around him. This is not the army any of them would've chosen, but it's the one they'll fight with. The people who will put their lives at risk to free Askala.

"Tomorrow, we prepare and train. We become one." Kian throws back his shoulders. "The day after, we strike before dawn."

Nova stands tall beside him.

Who knows what the price will be, but they can't afford to lose.

KIAN

*W*hen Kian wakes, the air is black with night, but he can sense it's not long till dawn. Not that it matters, the moment he wakes, he knows he won't be going back to sleep.

The countdown has begun.

Moving as quietly as possible, he extricates himself from Nova. Each night, they've held each other tight. At first, it was because they'd just reunited and touch was so much more precious.

Now, a war hangs over them. A battle that will come at a price. Now, they cling to each other because time is precious.

Nova sighs in her sleep as Kian slips away, but she doesn't wake. He's glad. She'd ensured the Remnants arriving last night had food for as long as they wanted, ignoring any suggestions of rest. The longer she can sleep now, the better.

Climbing out of the shelter, Kian decides he'll make sure all the fires are out. Meat would've been left to cook above each one, ensuring there's plenty of food for everyone to eat their fill. They're all going to need their strength.

Except as Kian walks around the camp, he finds all the fires have already had dirt kicked on them. The odd curl of smoke climbs through the pre-dawn air, but that's it. It seems he's not the only one up early.

He heads to the trees, figuring if he's going to pace, he should do it somewhere he won't disturb the others. He's just reached the first tree when someone startles beside a trunk.

"Whoa, Kian!" Dex half-whispers, half-shouts. "If we can all walk as silently as you, then we'll certainly have the element of surprise with tomorrow's attack."

Kian's brows shoot up. "Hey. I suppose that's what happens when you grow up with my father."

They'd spend hours out in the forest. The more silently they moved, the less of an observer they became. They melded with the trees, became a part of their environment. His father believed that's the way it should be. They're some of the most special memories Kian has from his childhood.

Dex sighs. "I'm so sorry. Magnus is someone we all looked up to."

Kian's glad the darkness hides his wince. "He wasn't thinking straight. He'll see he was wrong when we get there."

"Sure."

Dex's tone holds little certainty and Kian can't blame him. But surely his father can't have been serious. Surely, he can't want to see humanity extinct.

There's the snap of a branch somewhere behind them. "You won't like me saying this," comes Phoenix's voice. "But I bet Wren said she could talk our dad around before she left here."

Kian stiffens, not liking the parallel Phoenix just made. He opens his mouth, only to stop. Arguing will bring attention to his father's loss of faith, and no one needs to hear that right now.

Especially Kian.

Phoenix is panting as he comes to stand beside them, meaning he's already been for a run this morning.

"Couldn't sleep either, huh?" asks Kian.

"And I'm the one used to sleeping on the ground," he replies.

Dex crosses his arms. "I won't sleep until Wren is away from that bastard."

Kian reaches out and squeezes his cousin's shoulder. "Tomorrow we get her back. But first, we need a plan."

The first glow of dawn illuminates the determined faces of Dex and Phoenix. Kian draws in a breath as if he's trying to suck in their resolve. Every person on the Oasis is depending on them.

"Attacking before dawn will give us the element of surprise," says Kian. "We want to find where he is and overpower him before he knows what hit him. The quicker and more efficiently we do that, the less blood will be shed."

Dex is staring thoughtfully at the trees. "It's too bad we can't open all the doors remotely. It would mean everyone has easy access, including the people from the Outlands."

"We can."

They spin around at Callix's voice. He approaches from the camp, joining their small group. "The laptop will be able to access the mainframe once we're a little closer."

Dex shakes his head. "When I came to you about freeing Magnus, you said it wasn't possible now that the lab has burned down."

Callix's gaze flicks to Kian. "Risking everything to get Magnus out wasn't smart. We need every element of surprise we can get."

"You lied?" Kian steps forward, the shock quickly shattered by fury. "We could've got him out!"

Dex is by his side in an instant. "Wren left because you said we can't. She could've been killed!"

Phoenix flanks Dex's other side, his scowl ferocious. "My sister lost a finger."

But Callix is unfazed. "I didn't expect you to go anyway." He crosses his arms. "And I was right. Magnus turned his back on us."

Controlling the anger takes effort. They don't need division right now. They need unity. Kian takes a step back. "So, we can open the doors?"

Callix nods. "We just need to be a bit closer and I'll be able to open them all from the laptop."

Phoenix cracks his knuckles. "The rest is straightforward. We go in, tell Cy it's over, and if he wants to fight about it, then he's welcome to."

"Ronan won't want to chat about it over tea," Dex states flatly. "Nor will he hand over Askala on a silver platter."

And that's where the issue is. Ronan is a violent, greedy man.

Phoenix throws back his shoulders. "We have spears and numbers."

"And the League," adds Callix.

The Unbound who were plotting to overthrow Askala all along. Kian's father probably knows about them by now—Ronan would've enjoyed telling Magnus all about the people who were planning to be rid of him. People who didn't believe in what Magnus was fighting for.

Reinforcing his father's belief that humans are inherently selfish.

Dex rubs his chin. "That's true. The people under Ronan's rule will be happy for an opportunity to overthrow him."

"Except for the ones who are too scared," cautions Phoenix. "That's how my father became the Commander in the first place. He rules with fear."

Kian clenches his fists. "Then it's important we go in strong. Show them this is worth the fight. We need to move fast, and we need to show strength."

Footsteps crunch over the rustling sounds of the camp waking up. They turn to find Dean strolling over, his cocky gaze aimed directly at Kian.

"I'd recommend the fighters from the Outlands go in first, then. Your people are best as backup."

Frowning, Kian stares back. "We should go in together."

"Then you'll be slower and weaker. My brother will thank you."

Phoenix steps forward, looking so much like his uncle, yet everything about him is so different. The glint in his eye doesn't make Kian nervous. "I say we spend the day training, then decide."

He's right. There's only one way for them to find out how the people of Askala are going to be able to fight this battle.

Back at the camp, Kian sees Nova emerge from their shelter, Luca already rushing to her side. He turns to the others. "We'll train, then tonight we finalize the plan. Does everyone agree?"

They all nod, faces solemn and hard. All except Dean, who gives Kian a jaunty salute. "Breakfast, then the fun begins."

He spins on his heel and heads back to where Cain stands beside the dying coals of one of the fires. He passes Dean a strip of meat and they both eat as if last night's feast never happened.

Dex shakes his head. "You know you're desperate when they're your salvation."

Callix shrugs. "They'll eat more food than they've ever seen, and we'll be rid of Ronan. It's a win-win scenario."

Kian walks back to Nova, drawn to her as those words stick in his mind like they've grown burrs. His father never would've thought this was a win-win situation. And yet, he turned his back on all of them, including those he says he loves.

And where does that leave Kian? Leading a battle he's deeply uncomfortable with. Fighting, when all he's ever believed in is peace. Asking his people to die for this.

Nova's brow furrows as he approaches. She knows something isn't right and Kian doesn't bother hiding it from her. There's no point. Some days, he's not sure where his soul ends and hers begins.

They embrace and Kian pulls back. "Training starts after breakfast. Tonight, we'll decide the order of attack."

"Makes sense. We'll need the strongest at the front."

Kian sighs, his hands tightening around her waist. "I wish that didn't include you."

The meat they're all eating is thanks to Nova's courage and determination. But it's not just that. There's a fierceness to Nova's heart, a grace that they'll need.

That he needs.

Nova rests her forehead on his chest. "I know you do. You want to protect me just as much as everyone else here." She looks up, her gaze steady. "Which is why you're finding this so hard. You wanted a new Askala, but you didn't expect to have to lead us into battle to have it."

His eyes flutter closed, trying to keep these emotions at bay. "How do I know this is the right thing to do?" he chokes.

Nova presses her palm against his chest. "What does your heart say, Kian?"

"That we're fighting for more than one thing." His eyes open, propelled by the truth pulsing within him. "Not just humanity. Not just Earth. But the place where both meet."

The words tumble out without thought, with such conviction that Kian blinks for a few seconds.

Nova smiles softly. "I think that's worth fighting for. That it's worth the price this will ask of us."

Kian rests his forehead against hers. "I love you, Nova."

She presses a kiss to his lips. "I know. And I love you more because this is so hard for you to do, Kian. We're fighting for a future." Taking his hand, she curves his palm around her growing belly. "For all of us."

Kian jumps when something jabs into the back of his thigh. He spins around, rubbing the spot.

"Sorry," says Luca, not sounding particularly apologetic as he stabs his spear into the ground. "But you looked like you were about to kiss again."

"And that's a problem?" asks Kian.

"It is if Thea asked me to give this to Nova." Luca holds out a piece of bear meat on a stick. He scrunches up his nose. "I prefer cockroaches."

Nova smiles as she takes the meat. "You guys are going to make me fat."

Luca grins. "Thea said that's the plan."

Kian ruffles his hair. "Now that, I'd like to see." He glances around, seeing that everyone is standing around, finishing their breakfast, too. "We'd best get started. Luca, can you tell everyone who will be coming tomorrow that we're about to start?"

A handful of people—those too old, too sick, or those needed to care for the children—will be staying back.

Everyone else is expected to fight.

Luca scampers off, always keen to help. Kian knows they're going to have the conversation that Luca needs to stay with the women. This is one expedition he won't be able to talk himself into going on.

Kian walks to the clearing beside the encampment that they decided will be their training ground. It doesn't take long for them all to arrive. It's not far to walk...and there's not that many of them.

Fifty or so people look expectantly at Kian. The people of Askala are the majority, shuffling and arms crossed as if it's cold. The people of the Outlands stand a little to the side, frowning and bouncing on the balls of their feet. Cain turns his head and spits before resuming chewing on a piece of bear meat.

A weight settles in Kian's chest. The words he's about to speak will cement this course of action. He pulls in a deep breath, making room for it.

This is worth fighting for.

He scans the waiting faces. "War shouldn't be chosen lightly. And only when the alternative is greater suffering than the battle itself. This is the situation we find ourselves in now. The people on the Oasis are hurting. They're being desecrated along with everything we've built."

Dex is standing at the front and his chin lifts. He's thinking of Wren. Of the price she paid when she returned. That she's already started fighting for this.

Kian raises his fist. "And we're their only hope. Today, we learn how to fight. Tomorrow, we make this right."

A roar lifts from the people of Askala.

"Tomorrow, we defeat Ronan."

This time, the voices of the Remnants add to the bay for victory. For the first time, Kian's heart lifts. Freed from its cell of uncertainty thanks to Nova's words, the conviction and determination of the faces around him raises it. Fills it with hope.

Has him believing.

He extends his arm to Phoenix. "Phoenix will be leading the training."

Phoenix steps into the center of the clearing. "Right, I want you to form groups of three. One person from the Outlands, two from Askala."

People glance at each other, already nervous, but they comply. Cain grins as he makes a beeline for Shiloh. Kian frowns, about to join them, only to find Nova beats him to it. She slips an arm through Shiloh's, whispering something to her.

Kian watches for a few more seconds. Nova doesn't like Cain, although she hasn't told him why. But she's not letting that get in the way of supporting Shiloh.

"Excellent," Phoenix calls out. "We're going to start with defensive techniques. Blocks, sidestepping, that sort of thing. Follow my lead."

Phoenix starts walking everyone through the moves, his strong body well accustomed to the motions.

"Looks like we're the last two." Kian turns to find Dean standing beside him.

Kian glances around, noting that no one has chosen to team up with Dean. "Of course we are," he mutters.

"Right," Phoenix calls out. "Now, holding the spear with both hands, I want you to block like this." He juts out his spear over and over at different angles. "I want your partners to see if they can get past it. Slowly and gently to start with. Stop before spears touch skin."

Kian's barely turned toward Dean when he jabs at him. Kian jumps back, using his own stick to knock it out of the way, looking at him incredulously.

Dean shrugs one shoulder. "Ronan's men aren't going to wait for you to be ready."

Kian blocks the next lunge, but the spear tip still scrapes down his side. He glares at Dean. "I appreciate you taking my welfare so seriously."

Dean grins and lunges again. This time, Kian blocks so hard Dean's spear is almost knocked out of his hands.

Dean slaps it back into his palm, gripping it so hard Kian wonders how it doesn't snap. His gaze flicks around before centering on Kian's chest. "The funny thing is, you're probably the best fighter among your beloved Bound."

The sounds of sticks hitting sticks crack around them. Kian glances at those surrounding him. Frowning faces focus on the crude weapons and lunging attacks coming at them.

The tip of Dean's spear whizzes past Kian's nose and he jerks his head back.

Dean's gaze glitters with triumph. "Let's hope you're more focused tomorrow."

Kian narrows his eyes. "My turn."

For the next hour, they thrust and parry, jab and block. The cracking of wood on wood fills the clearing as they practice. Whenever they swap, Kian takes the chance to check on his people. Despite what Dean predicts, he sees them all working hard.

Dex leaping and deflecting, comfortably making up for the fact he's only holding his spear with one hand.

Nova looking at Cain with the same expression Kian imagined she would've used when facing the polar grizzly.

Shiloh. Thea. Callix. All determined to defend.

His sense of confidence grows, and he relaxes into the sparring with Dean. Phoenix is a good teacher. And his students are keen to learn.

It's only after lunch, when they begin the offensive strategies, that Kian realizes he was buoyed by a false sense of faith. Defending yourself is instinctive. Blocking a punch, getting out of the way of a spear, all those the Askalans can learn and apply.

But attacking someone...that goes against everything they'd been bred for.

After Phoenix walks them through some basic strikes, Kian circles the clearing, wishing Dean didn't decide to join him in his pacing. The people from the Outlands jump into the exercise with relish. Their spears aim for the throats, the hearts, the stomachs of their would-be opponents.

Kian watches as the Askalans eyes widen with every strike that stops inches from their skin. When it's their turn, their advances are muted, their strikes faltering. They don't want to hurt...or be hurt. One or two Remnants curl their lips in disdain, swatting away the spears.

When a fourth length of wood clatters to the ground, Dean shakes his head. "Ronan's going to run away screaming in fear."

Kian keeps his gaze straight ahead. "Bound or Unbound, these people have grown up believing in the right to life. This doesn't come easy to them."

"You're lucky I came, then. We barely stand a chance as it is."

They both spin around when Thea cries out as the Remnant she's facing blocks her attack and snatches her spear off her.

Dean shakes his head again. "Like I said, the Remnants should go in first."

Clenching his teeth, Kian wishes it were that simple. "They have no ties to Askala. We can't ask that of them."

Dean does a double take. "That's what's holding you back? You think it's not fair on the poor little Remnants?"

Before Kian can respond, Shiloh shouts a battle cry. She leaps at Cain, her spear aiming for his gut. Cain sidesteps as if this was choreographed, sweeping Shiloh's feet from beneath her and she falls flat on her back. In a blink, he pounces on her, straddling her hips as he presses the length of his spear across her throat. He leers with victory. "Nice try, beautiful."

Kian steps forward as Shiloh lays frozen, eyes wide and unblinking. Cain's actions were unnecessary.

Except the tip of a spear appears beneath Cain's chin. He stills and looks up, finding Nova standing above him. "Get off her."

Cain's smile drops as he pushes himself upright. "Well, well, well. There is a spark in there."

Silently, Kian moves to Nova's side. She steps back and drops her spear. Holding her hand out, she helps Shiloh up.

Cheeks flushed, Shiloh creates some space between herself and Cain. Around them, everyone has stopped, and is watching. "Thank you," she murmurs to Nova.

Nova nods. "Our strength is in our unity," she says loudly and clearly.

Phoenix comes up beside her. "She's right," he says, turning to talk to everyone. "Your power will come from working together. Cy's men can't defeat several of you at once."

A few nods circulate around them before everyone returns to practicing. Nova is one of them. If she can do it, they can, too.

Nova pulls in a deep breath, letting it out slowly as if she's steadying herself. Kian grasps her hand, asking silently if she's okay. She looks up at him, eyes steady as she tries to smile. But he sees the way her lip trembles just a fraction, the way her breathing hasn't slowed.

He opens his mouth but Nova shakes her head. "This isn't easy for any of us," she whispers. "We need to show strength."

Phoenix leans in. "Right again, Blondie." He turns to Kian. "I don't care how many of them face Cy's men, these people aren't going to stand a chance if they don't think they've got this."

They step back as Thea walks past with a young man. He's holding his hand against his chest as he frowns with pain. Thea smiles almost apologetically. "He tripped and cut his hand on his spear, but a bit of sap will fix it."

Dex approaches them, chest heaving from the training as they watch Thea take her patient away.

He jams his spear into the ground. "The training isn't going gangbusters, is it?"

Phoenix shakes his head. "I'd need six months to get these people ready to fight."

Kian rubs his forehead. His body feels like it's just doubled in weight. "We'll need to send the Remnants in first."

Dean raises a brow. "You really think they don't want to be the first line of attack?"

As they watch, one of them roars as he runs at an Askalan. The woman retreats, holding her hands up to protect herself, her spear forgotten. The Remnant pushes her out of the way and turns to Callix, the third person in their trio, and jabs his spear at his throat. Callix tries to block, but the weapon's already gone. If the Remnant had followed through, Callix would be dead.

The Remnant laughs, turning to his mate beside him and they fist pump.

Kian's shoulders sag. "Phoenix, Dean, Dex, Nova, Callix, and I will lead the Outlanders in the initial ambush. The others will wait outside the Oasis, capturing anyone who tries to escape."

Dex nods. Nova's face settles into resolute lines.

Dean grins.

Kian turns away, preparing to join in the training that's too little, too late.

When they send in the Remnants first, violence will be inevitable.

It's a given that lives will be lost.

The only unknown is how many and who.

DEX

The Oasis looks eerie in the moonlight, despite it being the only home Dex has ever known. It's strange to think that this ancient hulk of metal once floated on the ocean. He's heard stories about their ancestors who set sail in it, only to find themselves being hurtled through the air and landing right where the ship sits now.

He'd love to know more about them. Surely, they must all have had stories of their own. Battles they had to fight, and barriers they had to break. How had they decided who would set foot on the Oasis and who stayed behind to take their chances in the Outlands? Magnus once told him that the ship had been owned by an eccentric billionaire who filled it with young people he'd deemed to be worthy of a future, with his methods evolving into the Askala Dex had grown up in.

Dex has never really given his faceless, nameless ancestors much thought before. But now that he's standing outside the Oasis, readying himself to shape the ship's future once again, he feels close to them somehow. Like they have more in common than just the blood that's pumping through his veins.

His actions today will shape the lives of his children. And his children's children. Including whether or not he'll live long enough for them to even exist.

"Are you okay?" asks Nova, her spear clutched firmly in her hand. It's the same spear she used to kill the bear. *Her lucky spear*, he'd heard her tell Luca as she'd left him in the care of Avis.

He nods. "Just taking a moment. It's pretty big, isn't it?"

"The ship?"

"No, what we're about to do."

"Oh. Yeah, huge." Nova's voice is full of awe. Or perhaps that's fear. It's hard to tell without being able to study her face.

"Got it," says Dex's dad from the ground beside him. "Just say the word, Kian, and all the doors will open."

"Do it as soon as I open the door at the top of the gang-plank." Kian takes a step toward the ship. "And stay hidden. We need you safe."

Dex knows his father isn't happy about being left outside, but he's the best person to operate the laptop. Having all the doors open at once will mean they can move quickly around the ship. There'll be nowhere for anyone to hide.

Including Ronan.

Kian holds up his hand in the dim light. All eyes are on him.

"Let's do it."

Three simple words that couldn't be more complicated.

Or dangerous.

Kian leads the way up the gangplank, closely followed by Dean and his men. Dex and Nova are behind them with Phoenix at the very back.

Nova hadn't wanted to be separated from Kian, but he'd insisted on it, saying she was safer in the middle of the pack, and she'd reluctantly agreed.

When they reach the top of the gangplank, Kian opens the door and walks straight through without so much as a pause.

He's ready. They're all ready.

And Dex is certain Wren is, too.

There's noise up ahead. A cry and a bang, followed by raised voices as the people in front of Dex surge forward.

Dex braces himself as he steps through the door. They'd thought they'd be sneaking up on a sleeping ship, but it seems someone must've been awake and keeping guard.

Phoenix is pressed up behind Dex, urging him to clear the doorway, itching for the fight that lies ahead in a way Dex will never be able to understand.

There's so much shouting and movement ahead, it's hard to tell what's happening in the dim light.

They march forward and Dex tries to angle himself to keep in front of Nova. He knows she's strong—she's more than proven that—but she's also pregnant.

Kian's cry reverberates around the corridor and Dex isn't sure if it's because his voice is familiar or because it's especially loud.

"Kian!" Nova calls out over the noise of grunting and shouting as they try to fight their way through the wall of men in front of them.

They break through just in time to see Kian's spear clutched tightly in his hand as he slices it through the air, heading straight for the throat of one of Ronan's guards who's been pinned to the ground by Dean.

Kian's face is contorted, and Dex knows this is possibly the hardest thing he's ever done. Kian is all about love and kindness, not death and punishment. But he also knows if they don't win this fight, the lives of all his people will be filled with nothing but pain and suffering. And if he wants Dean's men to follow him into this battle, he needs to prove his worth.

Dex winces as Kian's spear finds its mark. The sound of the weapon puncturing the guard's neck and piercing the floor is one he'll never forget. Blood spurts from the guard's body, sending crimson splatters across the faces of Dean's cheering men.

But their victory is short-lived as two more guards come rushing at them from down the corridor, their flamethrowers held in front like shields.

Dean's men don't give the guards a chance to get their fingers to the trigger, knocking them out of their hands with their spears. Phoenix growls as he throws himself on top of one of the men and Dex decides to take this moment of distraction to look for Wren.

He takes off down the corridor, seeing nothing but frightened faces in the doorways of the open cabin doors. And not one of them is Wren's.

"Stay where you are," he tells them as he moves further down the hallway. "We're taking back Askala."

"About time!" someone calls after him.

"Dex!"

He spins around to see Nova chasing after him.

"Go back to Kian," he tells her, knowing he can't keep her safe by himself.

"Not without you." Her eyes are wide and serious. "We agreed to stick together. Come with me."

He shakes his head, his footsteps coming to a reluctant stop. "I need to find Wren."

"She could be anywhere." Nova stops beside him, takes a step back and then another forward, clearly torn about which direction she should be going. He knows she can't leave him alone like this. But she can't leave Kian, either.

It's different for him. His heart is being pulled in one direction only.

"Go, Nova," he pleads. "Go back to Kian. I'm fine."

Nova stares at him for what feels like an hour but can't be more than a few seconds.

"Go!" he says again. "Please, Nova. Kian needs you. I'll be right behind you."

She nods. Turns. And runs back down the corridor. Sweet Nova. The girl who puts everyone else before herself. The girl whose genes were deemed unworthy, no matter how much she's continued to prove herself.

He swivels and continues down the corridor only to run straight into a tattooed wall of flesh.

Another guard!

"What the hell do you think you're doing with that spear!" the guard roars. "You could take someone's eye out. Or their finger…"

Dex weighs up his options as the guard laughs at his own joke. He can turn and run in the direction Nova went. Although, this guard is likely to be faster than he is. He can try to dart around him, but that presents the same problem.

He doesn't give himself time to think about the third option before he puts it into motion, swinging his spear up without warning, aiming straight for the guard's throat. He knows now why Kian did what he did. He had to set the example. He had to instill in them the belief that they could do this, too. Askala was never going to be won back with a tea party.

But this guard isn't being pinned to the ground. He has two free hands and, as it turns out, lightning fast reflexes.

He grabs Dex's spear and slams him against the wall. Flipping it horizontal, he presses the weapon against Dex's throat.

Dex squirms as he claws at the spear, trying to pry it away.

He. Can't. Breathe.

He can't even think.

With his heart racing and his feet kicking, he fights the pain that's tearing through his body as his lungs beg for oxygen.

The guard smiles at him, increasing the pressure on his throat. "Nice try."

Blackness is starting to close in and Dex is glad Nova had

the sense to leave him. The only thing that could make this worse would be knowing he'd put her in danger, too.

"Not long now," the man soothes as if he's talking to a baby. "Soon your purple face will turn a nice shade of blue."

Dex feels the moment the fight leaves his body. He's powerless to stop this guy. To stop the fate that's sweeping him away with the same force as the tornado when it took hold of this ship.

He lets his eyes close, the effort of keeping them open far too much. This can't be it. It can't!

But it certainly feels like it is.

He can feel the guard's breath on his cheek as he increases the pressure yet again. "I'll be damned if I was going to let myself be killed by a one-armed freak like you."

"How about a girl, then?"

Dex's eyes spring open just in time to see Wren raise a knife in the air and slam it into the guard's back.

Hard. Fast. No hesitation.

The pressure in Dex's throat releases and Wren hauls the guard away from him, throwing him to the ground like he's made from rags.

Dex drags in lungful after lungful of air in loud, rasping gasps as he watches a pool of blood expand around the man who came so close to killing him.

"Never liked him anyway." Wren wipes the small knife on the guard's trousers and sticks it in the back of her waistband.

"Wren," Dex chokes out, unsure if he's ever going to be able to speak properly again.

She turns to him and smiles. "Did you come to save me?"

He'd laugh if he could. But instead he reaches out and she flies into his arms.

He holds her tight and she molds herself into his chest like she was born to fit right there.

He revels in her closeness, drawing in her scent along with

more glorious air. He'd tried to save her and once again she'd saved him. He's starting to lose count of the amount of times they've rescued each other.

"What are you doing here?" she asks, breaking away.

"We're all here," he says. "We're taking Askala back."

"Who's we?" Her brows spring up and she glances around.

"Kian, Nova, Phoenix..." He winces, finding talking a struggle with his throat so bruised and aching. "Dean's here, too, with an army he brought back from the Outlands."

Wren nods, her eyes lighting with a fury he's seen before. It's a fury they need right now. The same fury that just saved his life.

Then remembering what Phoenix told him, he looks down at her hand, pain stabbing at his heart when he sees the glaring gap between her fingers.

"It's nothing," she says, not bringing her hand closer but not drawing it away. "Besides, I've still got four more fingers than you."

He smiles, knowing she's trying to make light of something that can never be made light of. And she's not only doing it for him. Just like Nova had walked around in a daze when it happened to her, Wren's just not able to deal with it herself just yet.

They spring apart at what sounds like a thousand footsteps and Kian appears from around the corner with his army behind him.

Dex bends to pick up his spear before it gets trampled, deciding to be more careful to keep it in his hand from now on.

"Dex! Wren!" Kian's eyes are wide as he runs at them, taking in the body on the ground and the spear in Dex's hand. "You okay?"

"It was Wr—"

"He was amazing!" says Wren, nudging Dex. "He killed him with one blow."

Dex nods, knowing they don't have time for explanations right now.

"Where's Ronan?" Kian asks.

Wren clenches her fists. "The party deck."

"At this hour?" Kian tilts his head.

"He's been going all night. But, Kian…" Wren grabs him on the arm and clamps her gaze on him. "He's mine, okay? I'm the one who's going to kill him. Promise me that."

Kian stares at Wren for three beats before nodding. For once, Dex isn't certain what he's thinking. It's the first time, and perhaps the last, that Kian will hand out permission for a life to be taken. Dex doubts even Kian knows how he feels about that.

"Lead the way." Kian holds out his hand and waits for Wren to pass him by.

Dex sticks close to Wren's side, not wanting to be separated from her again. He's made that mistake far too many times already.

Dean and his men are right behind them, brandishing their newly acquired flamethrowers as they head for the stairwell.

"Don't use those things inside," Phoenix warns. "This whole ship could go up."

"Metal doesn't burn," one of the men retorts.

Dex rolls his eyes, unable to help himself from turning to reply. "Yeah, it melts. So much better."

"Stop being a smart ass," Dean hisses.

"Hey, we're a team," Kian reminds them. "Everyone's together on this. Got it?"

"Room for one new member?"

Dex turns to see his father has joined them.

"Callix, I asked you to wait outside!" Kian rakes his hair as he shakes his head.

"I'm more help to you in here," his father says and Kian nods, seeming to decide to let it go. They really do need every man they can get right now.

"Come on, then." Wren leads the way into the stairwell and they march their way up, taking the stairs two at a time.

The familiar sound of beating drums greets them at the top landing and Wren looks at Dex as they step out into the hallway. She doesn't say anything. She doesn't need to. They both know exactly how each other feels. Everything they needed to say has already been said. That makes him feel incredibly lucky, because who knows how much time they have left.

Phoenix pushes his way past Dean's men. "Best if I walk in first with Wren."

Dex hesitates, taking in Phoenix's muscular frame and the flamethrower strapped around his broad shoulders, and nods. They need to think with their heads here, not their hearts. That's what got them into this trouble in the first place.

"I'm right behind you," Dex says to Wren.

"You always have been." She shoots him a smile. It's true. He's always supported her, just as she's supported him. That's never going to change. Especially now.

Dex's father stands beside him and a raw churning starts inside Dex's stomach as they walk forward, his heart seeming to take up the intensity of the beating drums with each step he takes.

"I'll protect you," his father says.

"Maybe I'll be the one protecting you," he shoots back.

"Maybe."

They walk on toward the open door of the party room and Dex can feel the group behind him taking a collective deep breath. This isn't going to be pretty...

The drums are loud but there are fewer people partying than normal. Perhaps it's because of the early hour. Or perhaps they've become weary of Ronan's ways. The people who are dancing aren't looking especially enthusiastic about it.

Ronan is propped up on a mattress in the middle of the room with a flask in one hand and three women draped across him. He's wearing a crown made from vines and the dark circles under his eyes betray how long it's been since he actually slept. He looks every bit the evil ruler. Dex fights a feeling he's never felt before.

Hate.

This man has destroyed their lives. He's sadistic and relentless. Willing to hurt or maim anyone in his path to get his own way, including his own daughter. And Dex can't wait to watch him fall.

All heads turn to Wren and Phoenix as they stride across the room with their army behind them, and the look on Ronan's face is possibly the best thing Dex ever remembers seeing in his life.

He's shocked. He's confused. And he's more than a little bit afraid.

Scanning the room for his guards, he clicks his fingers and two of them approach. One of them is Jagger and Dex can only hope that Dean's men don't try to hurt him.

Ronan hauls himself to his feet and the women scatter from the mattress, backing as far away from this situation as they can manage.

"My beloved children," Ronan says, adjusting the flamethrower strapped around his shoulders. "Have you brought me an army to fight with?"

"It's over, Cy." Phoenix is trying to angle himself in front of Wren, but she's not having any of it. "It ends now."

"Tell your guards to step away." Kian walks forward.

Ronan's eyes widen at the sight of him. Then he scans the rest of the army, seeing Dex and Callix. It's like he's looking at the army of the living dead.

"I knew it," he seethes.

"It's time to choose a side," Kian says to Ronan's guards. "Join us and we'll let you live."

Jagger is the first to move, going to Kian and standing beside him, raising his flamethrower in Ronan's direction. The other guard freezes, his eyes wide with surprise.

"Stay with Cy and I'll kill you myself," Wren adds. Dex has to suppress a smile at her gall. She's as far away from being a little bird as a person can get. And he loves her all the more for it.

The guard scuttles over to stand beside Jagger while Dean removes his flamethrower and hands it to one of his men.

Kian looks around, taking in the frightened faces of the people pressing themselves against the walls.

"Leave now!" he calls out to them. "If you don't need to be here then return to your cabins. You'll be safe there."

"Do *not* leave," shouts Ronan. "Anybody who leaves will be killed as a traitor."

The people look between Kian and Ronan for several long moments. Then one by one, they leave the room. It's obvious who's in charge here and nobody wants to be present the moment Ronan realizes it, too.

"Stop!" roars Ronan. "Don't leave! You'll regret it if you do!"

But nobody listens and with each plea that Ronan delivers, his voice fills with more and more desperation.

"Who stands with Ronan?" Kian asks.

Dex scans the room but it remains silent.

"Wren." Ronan's eyes fill with tears. "Phee. My children. I've always loved you. I was hard on you because I wanted you to be strong. I did it out of love. You know that, don't you? I'm your father. You can't abandon your own father in the same way your mother abandoned you. I'm the one who's always been h—"

"Enough!" Wren holds up her hand. "She didn't abandon us. You drove her away, just like you drove us away. You don't love us, you didn't love our mother, and you sure as hell didn't love Mercy. You know how I know that?"

Ronan blinks at Wren, but she doesn't wait for him to respond before she continues.

"I know that because you're not capable of love. You like the

181

idea of it. You like the power it can bring. But your heart isn't capable of feeling it. Not now. Not ever. I'm ashamed to be your daughter."

Dex clutches his spear, trying to stop himself from going to Wren. She's been hurt so badly by this monster. He just wants to make it all better, but he knows he can't. This is something Wren needs to deal with herself. And he's so proud of her for the way she's handling herself.

Ronan drops to his knees, leaving his flamethrower swinging idly at his back as he raises his palms. This is the moment.

Surrender.

He knows this fight is over. He's been outplayed at his own game.

"Don't hurt me!" he begs. "Please. I didn't mean it. I'll try harder. I'll be the father you always wanted."

Phoenix steps forward now. "You know, we didn't really want a father. It was a mother we wanted. And you took her from us."

"Please." Ronan looks up at his children. "Don't hurt me. I love you. I do."

Wren withdraws the knife she has tucked in her waistband and Dex holds his breath, not sure if he believes she's going to kill him. She wants to, he's certain of that. But will she be able to? It's one thing to kill a man who's about to take someone else's life, but it's another to kill a man standing with his hands in the air begging for forgiveness.

Especially, when it's the man who raised her...

Wren looks at the knife and tilts her head as she studies her father.

"Make no mistake about it," she says. "I *am* going to kill you. But you don't deserve to die so fast. I want you to see what Askala becomes first. I want you to see how badly you failed."

Phoenix twitches behind her, seeming torn between wanting

182

to exact his revenge and needing to support his sister. Especially when it's so unclear if this is what she really wants or if she's just too kindhearted to carry out her true wishes.

"Kian is our leader now," says Wren, taking a step back. "The son of Magnus. And he's the best leader Askala has ever seen."

Dex lets out a long sigh, both disappointed and proud of Wren that she couldn't go through with killing her father, as he lets the sweet truth of her words flow through his body.

They did it! They stood up to Ronan, refusing to accept his tyranny. They assembled an army, took control and brought Ronan and his ruthless guards down. Now, with Kian in charge, they have a chance of rebuilding Askala into the place it was always meant to be.

A place of peace. A place where a future is possible.

There's a blur of movement as a flamethrower is waved in the air. "Actually, that's not exactly how things are going to play out here."

Every set of eyes in the room turns, seeking out the owner of the voice.

Dean.

Dex curses under his breath. Of course, it's Dean. They should've known they couldn't trust him. And here he is strutting forward like some kind of demented raven.

Fighting the urge to step forward and punch this slime ball in the nose, Dex clenches his spear and grits his teeth, ready to back up Kian the moment he needs it.

"Step back, Dean," says Kian, his voice stern and full of warning.

"I don't think so." Dean motions for his men to come and stand by his side.

They flank him, their flamethrowers held out and their sneers speaking for them. That especially awful one who Nova seems to dislike is right by Dean's side. The ugliest army Dex could ever dream up, because all their hearts are made from spite.

This must've been Dean's plan all along. To take Askala for himself...how could they have missed this?

"One team." Kian's voice is full of warning. "We're all on the same side here."

"That's right." Dean grins, looking eerily similar to his brother kneeling on the ground before them. "Except we never discussed the leader. Given I'm the one who supplied the army here today, I say it should be me."

Dean's men grunt in agreement and Dex works even harder to stay where he is. Dean can't be allowed to get away with this!

"Brother," says Ronan, pulling himself to a stand. "I'm so glad to see you."

"I'm not your brother," Dean spits back at him. "I'm the leader now and you are nothing to me."

Dex bursts forward, unable to contain his frustration for another moment. "This is madness! Dean, get back behind Kian! You have no idea what you're doing here. Kian is the leader we need. He's the leader we all want. Not...you."

Dean bursts into a raucous laugh. "Who the hell do you think you are, Dex?"

"It doesn't matter who I am." Dex grits his teeth. "All that matters are the decisions we make from here on. And choosing Kian as our leader is what's best."

Kian puts a hand on his arm, trying to urge him back, but Dean mutters something that grabs Dex's attention even harder.

"What did you just say?" Dex shakes off Kian and marches over to Dean putting his face right in front of his. His head is spinning and his stomach is clenching into tight knots. Surely, Dean didn't just say what he thought he said?

"You heard me," says Dean, grinning.

"Say it again," Dex demands, needing to be certain.

"I said, I should have killed you while I had the chance."

Dean lifts his chin and looks to his men for support. They jostle and nudge each other.

"And when was that, Dean?" Dex is practically growling now as all the pieces to the puzzle he never wanted to fit together slam into place. "When should you have killed me?"

"At the same time I killed your stupid mother." Dean pulls back his shoulders. "Instead of cutting off your hand, I should have taken off your head."

Dex lifts his spear, not thinking, not hesitating, not even knowing what he's about to do. But he's shaking so hard that it falls from his hand and he's left standing in front of the man who ruined his life.

Speechless. Defenseless. Unable to function.

"Why?" he asks, his voice little more than a hoarse whisper. "Why?"

Dean curls his lip, keeping his head high and his shoulders back. "Because your father offered me twenty pods. That's why."

Dex turns to look at his father, desperate to see the same shock and denial that's slicing him through to the core.

But that's not what he sees.

His father is looking at him, his eyes filled with undeniable shame.

And in that one look, Dex's whole world falls apart.

WREN

*D*ex!

Wren has to go to Dex. He's still standing there in front of Dean with his spear at his feet, frozen in time. Her entire being is flooded with grief. She wants to run to him and wrap him in her arms and make his pain go away.

And after she's done with that, she wants to kill Dean.

And maybe Callix.

But who's she kidding? She didn't even have the guts to kill her father.

Then several things happen at once.

First, Callix runs from the room. Then, Dex breaks free of his shock and chases after him. Wren tries to follow but both Kian and Phoenix take hold of her and root her to the spot.

"Let them sort it out," says Kian, gently but firmly. "You can't help him this time. They need to talk."

She opens her mouth to protest but her attention is immediately stolen by Cy. He's making a noise that she can only describe as...*keening*. It's a horrible wail that's escaping his lips and winding through the room as he presses his palms to his cheeks.

"Is he crying?" Phoenix loosens his grip on Wren. "Or is he having a seizure?"

Wren shrugs, still wanting to follow Dex but now equally as concerned about what's unfolding before them. She's never heard a sound like this before.

Cy's face is changing colors from purple to pink to a cool alabaster as he continues to make that godawful sound, his hands still stuck to his cheeks.

"Is he singing?" asks Phoenix. "No, I think he really is crying."

"What the hell is wrong with you?" Dean struts over to Cy and shoves him hard in the chest.

The noise coming from Cy extinguishes immediately as he lifts his gaze to Dean with a murderous glint in his eyes.

Both Wren and Phoenix gasp. They may not have heard that noise before, but this is a look they're very familiar with. And never once when they've seen it has it ended well for the person on the receiving end.

Phoenix lurches forward and Kian lets go of Wren to take him by the arm and force him back.

"Stay back," he hisses.

"He's right," says Wren. "One less asshole for us to have to sort out."

There's no way Wren can go after Dex now. She just has to hope he can handle his father. Kian's probably right. She can't fight all of Dex's battles. Sometimes there are demons we need to fight with our own bare hands.

Dean shoves Cy again. "I asked what the hell is wrong with you? I'm your leader now. Answer me when I ask a question."

"You killed Mercy." Cy speaks slowly, his voice filled with equal measures of anger and hate. "My own brother killed the woman I love."

"Pretty sure your daughter explained earlier that you didn't actually love her." Dean smirks, enjoying his own cleverness.

"Leave me out of this," Wren growls, not wanting anything to do with the man who's not just trying to steal Askala but is responsible for such a brutal act against Dex and his mother.

"You. Killed. Mercy." Cy is talking through gritted teeth now, his nostrils flaring as crimson rushes to his cheeks.

"Look, that was an accident," says Dean, holding his footing but leaning just slightly back. "She shouldn't have got in the way."

Wren draws in a sharp breath at the look on Cy's face.

"You. Killed. Mercy," he repeats.

"I just told you that was an accident," Dean continues, oblivious to the danger he's in. "Callix asked me to cut off his son's finger. Sick bastard. But Dex wasn't any smarter back then than he is now. He woke up and started crying just as I was about to make the cut."

"He was only a baby!" Wren surges toward Dean, but Phoenix clamps his arm around her waist, scooping her up.

Dean turns to Wren. "A stupid baby who didn't know what was good for him."

She kicks out at Phoenix but he's holding her far too tightly. She might be brave and she might be angry but she's no match for her twin when it comes to strength.

With Dean's attention diverted, Cy reaches for the flamethrower strapped to his back and brings it to his chest. "You. Killed. Mercy."

"She got in the way!" Dean turns back, his eyes widening to see Cy's weapon so close to his face and he reaches for his own. "The bitch practically asked for it."

Wren stills in Phoenix's arms and he sets her down. This is going to get ugly very fast.

Cy's mouth flaps open at the same time he raises his flamethrower and clamps his finger on the trigger.

"Don't!" cries Kian. "You'll burn us all alive if you set that thing off in here."

Dean goes to put his own finger on the trigger of his weapon, but Cy sends out a short burst of flame aimed directly at him.

"What the hell!" Dean leaps back, shaking his burned hand as he turns to his men. "Do something!"

Cy lets out another flame in the direction of Dean's men. They fiddle in a panic with their flamethrowers, clearly having no idea how to operate them.

"You're going down, Ronan," shouts Dean.

"You'd need a real army for that," laughs Cy. "Not this bunch of little girls you've brought with you."

Dean scowls at his men, and for once Wren agrees with Cy. Dean's army isn't exactly being very effective right now.

"These men would protect me with their life!" Dean shouts, trying to regain control.

The men nod and sneer, but not at all convincingly. This group of skinny men could all be bought with the promise of a good feed and a warm bed. Not one of them would lay down their life for a snake like Dean. They don't know the meaning of the word loyalty.

Dean's scowl deepens. This scenario clearly isn't playing out the way he imagined.

"You're going down, Ronan," he says again, although there's hesitation in his voice this time. "I'm your Commander now."

Cy turns purple at these words, the veins on his forehead protruding like they're going to burst. Dean's words have hit him where it hurts. Nobody lays claim to Cy's position as Commander.

Wren winces as she waits for his response.

"If I go down, we all go down." Cy marches forward, this time with fire spewing from the end of his flamethrower.

Dean doesn't pause. He runs as fast as he can straight to the door. Cy follows, the flames falling just short of roasting Dean.

Wren's mouth drops open. She hadn't expected Dean to give

up this easily. But then again she should've known he was a coward. A coward who attacks innocent babies asleep in their cribs. It's a shame Cy's flames hadn't reached him...

Cy turns back when Dean disappears down the hallway, his eyes fixed on Dean's men, flames continuing to pour from his weapon.

The men look at each other, and scatter.

Not knowing which direction to turn, Cy swings his flamethrower in an arc as he marches forward. A few of the men make it out the door, some with the back of their shirt alight. But more have been cornered by Cy and are holding their spears up as if that's going to offer them some protection.

"Stop, now!" shouts Kian, shielding his face from the heat as he tries to get close enough to Cy to overpower him. "Dean's gone. Enough, before you burn the ship down."

Cy turns his flamethrower in Kian's direction, not reducing the strength of the molten flare shooting from his weapon and forcing him back. The men dash from the corner of the room, making it to the door and disappearing down the hallway.

Wren looks at the few who remain. Apart from Phoenix, Kian and Nova, there's only Jagger. Cy's other guard escaped with the rest of Dean's men.

Kian scrambles back, positioning himself in front of Nova who's quickly backing away.

"I'll kill you all!" Cy growls, as the threadbare carpet catches alight. "Starting with the son of the great almighty Maggot. Only this time I'll kill him properly!"

"Get out of here!" Wren screams. "He won't stop. You need to leave! Go and help the others."

Jagger runs to the door, seeming to realize there's more he can do to help outside this room than within it.

"Come with us, Wren." Kian shuffles Nova back a few more steps as Cy closes the gap with equal measure.

The flames are consuming the carpet now, spreading at a

frightening rate as they head for the walls and turn the plaster to black, then scarlet. Ribbons of fire twine their way up to the ceiling.

Wren looks at Phoenix and they both know in one glance that neither of them are going to go anywhere. They need to see this out. And that means making sure the man who sired them perishes in this fire he seems determined to start.

Cy is distracted by the flames now, hypnotized by the power he's wielding. He's always been fascinated with fire. It's been his weapon of choice from the very start.

He raises his flamethrower above his head, laughing as it licks at the ceiling. With his twisted crown of vines upon his head and the torch held high in his right hand, he looks like a photo Wren once saw of a giant copper statue that had been famous before it sank beneath the ocean's depths. Only that statue hadn't looked so evil. But hopefully it's an omen for Cy's fate.

"Go!" Wren shouts again. "Now! We're right behind you. Get everyone off this ship."

Kian and Nova take two more steps but seem as reluctant as Wren and Phoenix are to leave this monster unattended in this doomed vessel.

Smoke is filling the room now and Wren holds up her arm, putting her elbow across her nose and mouth.

"Kian! Nova!" cries a small voice from the hallway. "Kian! Nova!"

They spin around to see Luca standing there, his eyes wide and small face crumpled with fear.

"Go!" Wren urges, but her plea wasn't needed this time. Kian and Nova are racing toward Luca, disappearing as a thick wall of smoke envelopes them.

"Put it down, Cy!" Phoenix shouts. "It's over!"

"Where's the son of the Maggot?" Cy cries out. "And my bastard brother! I'm going to kill them both."

Wren winces. Why hadn't she killed Cy when she had the chance? She could have stopped all of this happening. She'd been far too weak. Never again. She has to set this right.

"He's getting away!" cries Phoenix.

It's hard to see with all the smoke, but Phoenix is right.

Cy's made his way to the door and is tearing off down the hallway, lighting the carpet on fire behind him as he moves toward the stairwell.

But thankfully after so many years of use, the ancient carpet has more holes than it does threads. Picking their way across the patchwork of flames, Wren and Phoenix move slower than Cy and are about halfway to the stairwell when the leg of Wren's trousers catches fire. She leans over and beats it out, cursing as she remembers just how flammable hemp cloth is.

Seeing the danger she's in, Phoenix runs back to her, his leather pants shielding him from the flames as he scoops her up and throws her over his shoulder.

For once, she's happy to accept his help.

They get to the stairwell and Phoenix lowers Wren back to the ground.

"Did he go up or down?" she asks, keen to keep moving.

"I didn't see. But he'll have gone up."

"How do you know?"

"Rats always head for higher ground," he sneers.

They pound up the stairs and Wren can't help but think this is a bad idea. This isn't a flood they're escaping from. It's a fire. And flames and smoke only head in one direction—the exact same one they're heading.

The door to the deck is open and they scramble out, breathing in the fresh air as they look around for any sign of Cy. It's early morning and the sun has just started to rise as if it, too, wanted to see what all the commotion is about.

Smoke is billowing out the door behind them as it fills the stairwell. It's too late to save the Oasis now. This ship is doomed to go up in a ball of Cy's vengeful flames. Hopefully Kian and Nova have managed to raise the alarm and will be able to get everyone off in time while they make sure Cy's reign of destruction ends right here.

Right now.

"He's at the ladder!" Phoenix grabs Wren by the hand and they rush over toward Cy's hunched frame.

Wren's not sure if she's relieved or worried to have found Cy here. If he manages to get himself off this ship and down that ladder who knows how many people he could kill. But at least they've found him.

"Get off the ladder!" Cy shouts down. "Now!"

"Don't get too close," warns Phoenix, aware that Cy could spin around at any moment and incinerate them both.

Phoenix leans over the railing a few yards down, straining his neck to see who's on the ladder and what they're dealing with here. "It's the people from the camp! They're trying to get on board."

Wren's desperate to see what's going on but each time she goes to lean out, that sick feeling returns as she becomes aware of just how high up they are. Cy forcing her down that cliff hadn't cured her fear of heights. Somehow it's only made it worse. Now she knows just how frightening the reality of plummeting to the bottom can be.

Cy lets out a cry of frustration and powers up his flamethrower again, aiming it directly over the edge.

This time Wren leans out. Phoenix instinctively grabs the back of her shirt to keep her steady and she steps closer to him.

Bea and Vern are at the top of the ladder, using their spears to try to knock Cy over so they can get onboard the Oasis. There's a stream of people behind them, all the way to the ground.

"Go back down!" Wren shouts. "The ship is on fire!"

Can't they see the smoke and the flames? Don't they realize there's no use in climbing aboard this ship of certain death?

"Out of my way!" Cy shoots out a flame and Wren screams as Vern tumbles from the ladder, his clothing a ball of blistering fire.

Bea's cry echoes across Askala and Wren feels the tears fall from her own eyes as she watches Bea leap from the ladder, choosing death over a life spent without the man she loves.

People are scrambling down the ladder now, some climbing on top of others who are moving too slow in their desperation to get down.

But Cy doesn't let up his flame, burning on and on until the top of the ladder breaks away from the ship. It peels back as gravity takes hold, pulling it to the ground along with anyone unlucky enough to still be hanging onto it.

The sound of the screams as people are crushed and fall is too much for Phoenix. He pushes himself back from the railings and storms toward Cy.

"Phee!" Wren is right behind, grabbing at him to stop, but he shakes her off like she's an annoying cricket.

Cy is far too dangerous to get close to right now. Phoenix is going to end up like a polar grizzly on a barbecue.

"Stop, Phee!"

"He's the one who needs to stop!" Phoenix takes hold of Cy by placing a hand on each of his shoulders and forcing him away from the edge.

"No!" Wren cries as Cy turns around and points the flamethrower directly in her twin's face. "Don't do it! He's your son!"

Cy clamps his finger down on the trigger and the three of them freeze as there's the sound of a click.

But no flame.

Wren lets out a long breath. It's out of fuel. But Cy has proven that he was prepared to kill his own son, just like he'd left her to die in the burning lab. His weapon may have run out of fuel, but his evil is a limitless force. The only thing that will stop him is death.

Wren extracts the knife from her waistband and launches herself at him.

Except Cy is too fast. The man who taught her every move she knows can't be taken by surprise.

He knocks the knife from Wren's hand with his flamethrower, sending both weapons scuttling across the deck.

Wren brings up her fist, ready to connect with Cy's nose but he deflects that, too.

Phoenix forces his way in and pummels Cy in the stomach, the chest, the side of his head. His blows are brutal, each one landing with force built from a lifetime of pent up anger. If anyone else were on the receiving end, Wren would feel sorry for them.

But not Cy.

Never Cy.

She watches as her father staggers, swinging his fists and landing one right in Phoenix's ribs, sending him stumbling backward.

Anger and fear surge through Wren's body, winding and tangling through her veins until they land in the pit of her stomach. She steps in and throws the next punch, connecting with Cy's nose. Normally she'd follow this up with a left hook but her maimed hand is still too sore, so she slams her knee into his groin instead.

Cy reaches for her, sliding his fingers into her cropped hair and pulling down hard. She screams as hair tears from her scalp and Phoenix launches himself between them, sending another punch to Cy's jaw. It cracks, hanging down at an awkward angle as Cy roars in agony.

Wren rubs at her head, enjoying the sound of Cy's pain.

But Phoenix isn't prepared to give him the same relief.

Without even taking a breath, he slams Cy again, this time the impact landing on the side of his face. Blood spurts as a tooth flies from his mouth.

Cy spits out a few more teeth and takes a step back. He raises his fists, his eyes losing their focus but not the hatred that's pouring from them as he realizes he's been outmatched by his own children.

"Is that all you got?" His words are slurred but enough to show he's still got fight left in him. "You're pathetic. A total disappointment."

Phoenix charges him again, his fist connecting with the side of his head, sending Cy flying several feet backward and he falls to the ground.

Wren dashes over to her knife and picks it up. She throws herself toward Cy, determined to do what she'd failed at earlier.

It's time to end this.

She lands on top of Cy, the knife held firmly in her fist, and she plunges it into his chest.

He looks up at her, his words muffled by the blood that's seeping from his mouth.

She locks her gaze on him as she twists her knife, wanting her face to be the last thing he ever sees.

"I could have been so much more than your daughter," she says. "I could have been your greatest ally."

But, instead, he chose to drive her to this. And she refuses to feel any guilt.

Cy's head flops to the side and Phoenix pulls Wren off him.

"It's over," he says. "It's over."

She can't believe it. She actually did it. She killed Cy. The man responsible for both giving her life and trying to take it away.

It was a fitting end for a man who caused so much pain and destruction. Maybe now Askala has a chance to heal.

She throws her arms around her twin and they hold each

other for a few precious moments before a loud bang from the level below has them tearing apart.

The fire has really taken hold now. They don't have much time.

"We need to find a way off this thing." Phoenix grips Wren by the hand.

They go to the door but there's thick smoke pouring from it now. It would be suicide to go through there. And with no ladder to climb down, they're running out of options.

"We'll have to scale our way down the side of the ship," says Phoenix.

Wren shakes her head. "No, Phee. No, I can't."

"You can." He practically drags her to the opening in the railings where the ladder once was. "You have to!"

"You go." She swallows, knowing she can't do this. Cy always said her fear of heights was her weakness and it seems he was right. Her phobia could be the very thing that ends up killing her.

"I'm not leaving you here." Phoenix drags her closer to the edge. "I'll carry you if I have to."

They look down to the ground below. There's pure chaos. Screaming. Crying. Injured people being carried to safety along with the bodies of those who weren't so lucky. Everyone wants to get as far away from this ship as they can before it turns into a total fireball. It's not safe to be near.

But there's one set of dark eyes staring up at them. One face that is upturned. Two hands outstretched.

Their mother.

The woman who is too frightened to sit beside a campfire is standing beside this inferno searching for the children she lost once before and is determined never to lose again.

She cries out when she sees them and immediately starts to fiddle with the strange netting she wears as a skirt.

"What's she doing?" Phoenix asks, but it soon becomes very clear.

She's unwinding yard after yard of fabric.

There's a scream and Felicia rushes up to their mother's side, her distress at seeing Phoenix trapped on board the ship obvious. She already lost Thom. Wren knows she'll be determined not to lose Phoenix, too.

Felicia helps their mother and the last of the fabric comes free, leaving her wearing a pair of brown trousers.

The two women take an end each and stretch it out, calling behind them for help. Aarov runs over with another man and the four of them hold a corner each.

"That clever woman." Phoenix shakes his head. "She's made a net."

Wren's heart pounds as she realizes what this means.

Her mother has faced her fear of fire to rescue them. Which means that if Wren wants to survive this, then she also needs to face her fear.

She needs to jump.

"I can't do it." She clutches Phoenix's arm.

"You don't have a choice, Wren." Phoenix steps back, motioning for her to go first. "It's time for this little bird to fly."

Knowing that Phoenix will never jump without her, Wren steps up to the edge and looks down. If she doesn't do this then it won't just be her who will burn alive on this ship. Phoenix will, too. And she can't let that happen.

But it's...so far down.

There's another explosion from below the deck and she knows she doesn't have time to hesitate.

"Trust me, Wren," her mother calls up.

Wren looks at her, wanting to trust her, but fighting a lifetime of resentment. She'd been raised to believe this woman was her enemy. She left Wren when she'd needed her most.

"Come on, Wren," Phoenix urges.

Wren looks at him and nods. Then needing to see the body of the man who'd betrayed them one last time she looks across at Cy.

Except he's not there. She must be confused with all the smoke. There's so much going on up here.

"We don't have time," says Phoenix. "We need to hurry!"

Wren looks back down at her mother whose eyes have never left her this whole time and she realizes that she hadn't left when Wren needed her most. Right now is when she needs her.

And she's right here.

Wren draws in a deep breath and leaps from the edge of the ship, sailing through the air with her eyes squeezed tightly closed.

Her mother is here. She put aside her fears and came for her. And now, like it or not, Wren is coming for her, too.

She hits the netting and feels it stretch around her body as relief slides through her.

She did it! And it wasn't that bad.

Except, the netting is springing up and she feels her direction change as she's thrown up into the air again.

"No!" she cries, arms flailing and feet kicking as she fights the grip of the momentum.

Her stomach flips over as she falls again, but this fall is softer and when she's thrown up, she doesn't fly nearly as high. When she lands, this time she stays put as the netting is lowered to the ground.

She scrambles off and looks back up to the top of the burning ship to see Phoenix readying himself to jump.

There's no time for a happy reunion with her mother just now. They need to get Phoenix to safety. The heat from the ship is intense and parts of it have started to crumble away. Smoke is pouring from the upper deck now, making it hard to see clearly.

With the net in position once more, Wren cries out for Phoenix to jump.

But just as he's about to launch himself off the edge, some-thing pulls him from behind and he disappears back into the cloud of smoke.

"What happened?" screeches Felicia. "Where is he?"

"He's there," shouts Aarov. "Look!"

"Phoenix!" Wren cries when she sees it's true. He's standing on the edge once more. "Jump!"

He flies off the edge and Wren can only hope the four people who hold his life in their hands are strong enough to catch him.

But just before he hits the net, Wren sees her mother release her corner, letting it fall slack.

Phoenix crashes to the ground with a horrible thud. There's no bouncing back up. No falling gently back to Earth. Every one of his bones must be broken. Including his shattered skull.

"What the hell did you do?" Wren screams, rushing at her mother. "You killed him!"

But Aarov is pulling Wren away from her mother and she can't get her hands around her throat. She'd trusted her! She'd jumped and put her faith in this woman only to be let down once again.

"It's not Phoenix," her mother is saying. "It's not him."

"Of course, it is." Wren is letting her tears fall freely now, trying to imagine a world without Phoenix. It's not a world she's ever known, and nor does she want to. "You killed him. How could you?"

"It's not Phoenix," her mother says again. "It's Cy."

Aarov releases Wren and she goes to the crumpled body and turns it over to see a large black tattoo staring back at her.

Mercy.

It's Cy. Her mother's right. It's Cy who fell. Not Phoenix. And this time he's undoubtedly one hundred percent most certainly dead.

Looking back up to the top of the ship, she sees her twin waving for their attention.

Aarov helps her drag Cy's body out of the way and the net is stretched out once again.

Her mother's face is determined. Focused on saving her son. It was this focus that had helped her to see exactly who had jumped the last time.

Amongst the smoke and mayhem, Phoenix may have looked like his father to everyone else, including Wren, but not to his own mother. She knew the difference. And she'd been very clear on who deserved to live and who deserved to die.

"Go!" Felicia cries and Phoenix leaps from the edge of the Oasis just as a huge fireball explodes behind him, lighting up the early morning sky in a brilliant display of vermillion terror.

He lands on the net and flies back up. They catch him again and Wren bites down on her lip so hard she draws blood.

He's okay. Phoenix is okay. Somehow they got off this deathtrap alive, all thanks to their mother and not one ounce of thanks to their father.

Phoenix lands on the net twice more before he sticks and is lowered to the ground.

Wren launches herself on top of him.

"I thought you were dead," she says over and over.

"Rising from the dead must run in the family." He glances at Cy's mangled body.

"I should have checked his pulse." Wren plants another kiss on the middle of his forehead and he wipes it away. "I was sure he was dead."

"Well, he is now."

Felicia is beside them a moment later and Phoenix wraps his arms around her. "You saved me."

"I did." Felicia pushes back her curls and presses her lips to Phoenix's. "Which means now you're mine."

"Fine by me." Phoenix's words are muffled by Felicia and Wren gets to her feet, not needing to witness something so revolting at such close proximity. Besides, there's someone else she needs to talk to.

Her mother is waiting patiently, giving Wren the time that she's been demanding from her ever since she returned.

But she's had enough time. The first moment of the rest of their lives has already begun.

"Mom." Wren approaches her, aware this is the first time she's called her by this name.

"Wren." Her mother swallows, her arms twitching by her side. "My beautiful, brave daughter."

Wren shakes her head as she slips her arms around the very person responsible for making her so brave.

Her mother holds her tight, in a way only a mother can and for just one moment, the chaos around them slips into pause, and they're the only two people on the planet who exist.

"Mom," Wren says again, liking the sound of that on her lips. "You came for me."

"Oh, my darling." Her mom kisses the top of her head. "I never, ever left."

NOVA

*N*ova grabs Luca to her, not stopping as they race down the hall. "Luca! You were supposed to stay at camp!"

His small body trembles in her arms as he clings to her. "Everything's on fire, Nova."

"This way," calls Kian. He ushers them down the first flight of stairs they come across and down the corridor, the sound of Ronan's boots echoing behind them. Slipping into the first open door they pass, Nova finds they're in one of the cabins.

They press themselves against the wall, breathing hard. But there's no clomping, no shouted threats.

Kian waits a few more strained seconds. "He must've given up."

Nova holds her breath, but there's still nothing.

"Avis doesn't like fire," whimpers Luca against her neck.

"Shh," Nova soothes, brushing his bangs back from his eyes. "I'm sure she's fine."

Kian glances outside the open door, confirming they're the only ones here. Ronan's gone, and everyone else scattered the moment he began his manic use of the flamethrower. "Avis is probably outside, which is a much safer place to be."

He steps out into the corridor, looking one way and then the other.

Nova joins him, Luca gripping her as an ashen haze fills the hallway. "At least the doors are open," she says to Kian. People will be able to navigate their way out...as long as the exit they choose is safe.

Kian frowns as he moves closer to them. "Except it means there's no way to contain the fire."

As if to prove his words, a crash resounds above them. Nova instinctively wraps herself around Luca, cradling him to her as he shivers. Screams seep through the walls, one or two abruptly cut off.

Nova's eyes widen with horror. "We have to get everyone out."

Kian glances down at Luca. "You need to get him to safety."

"What? No! We stick together."

Luca's arms cinch tighter around Nova. "I'm staying with you, Nova. We're family."

Kian's face twists. "We can't take him further in."

Another crash above them has Nova's stomach plummeting. Kian's right. They need to get Luca off the Oasis.

They stare at each other, the haze thickening as the air heats. They can't have come this far only to separate. For Kian to go into the bowels of an inferno and Nova to try and escape it.

But Luca is a child. One who's depending on them.

A single tear trickles down Nova's cheek. Dex is dealing with a betrayal that forever changed him. Wren's making sure Ronan's insanity ends.

And now Nova has to leave Kian. They were supposed to be together. That's how they were going to conquer this.

Kian reaches out to wipe the tear away, his own soulful gaze a pool of pain. "I'll meet you outside," he promises, even though Nova knows he can't assure that. "Quick, you need to go."

Who knows how long they have before this dried out, decaying hulk consumes itself.

Nova tightens her hold on Luca. After she's got him to safety—

"Promise me you won't come back in, Nova." She's about to object when Kian presses his hand to her stomach. "Our child deserves a chance, just like Luca."

He's right. By the time she takes Luca to safety and returns, trying to find Kian in this burning maze would be impossible.

Something splinters in Nova's chest. When she woke in the pre-dawn she'd thought of a name. She hasn't even had a chance to tell him.

There's a flash of movement to their left. "Nova! Kian! Thank goodness I found you!"

Nova's mother rushes toward them, her skin pale beneath a layer of gray ash. She grabs them both in a fierce hug. "Quick. The fire is growing fast. We don't have much time."

"Thea? What are you doing here?" asks Kian.

"A few have managed to escape. Shiloh and I are helping as many as we can." She pauses, looking at her daughter. "I couldn't lose you again."

More screams echo through the thin walls, this time from somewhere on their right. Nova's mother's face pales. "How many more are there?"

Nova doesn't give herself time to think. She pushes Luca toward her mother. "Take him. We'll get the others out."

Her mother's already shaking her head, but it's Luca who screams the denial. "No! I'm not leaving you."

"Please," Nova pleads quietly. She knows the growing sounds of destruction around them would swallow the word, but her mother is frozen, her stricken eyes telling Nova she heard.

They need to get Luca out of here. But Nova belongs with Kian. They're the ones who need to finish what their Proving ignited.

And her mother knows that. Even if it means letting her go.

With a short nod, her mother reaches for Luca. As he realizes what's happening, Luca tightens his arms around Nova's neck. "No, Nova! I'm staying with you."

But her mother peels him off, turns and runs. Luca twists and struggles, but the arms that have him have held down patients fighting pain. He won't be able to escape her mother's steel grip.

Nova watches as he reaches out as if he's drowning and she's the only one who can save him. "Family stay together," he screams as he's carried around the corner.

She turns to Kian. There's no time to acknowledge how much it hurt to see Luca's devastated face. "We need to keep moving."

Kian pauses for precious seconds. He wants her to stay as much as her mother does. But then he nods. "Ronan started on the upper decks. We need to head down and use one of the exits there."

Nova heads in the opposite direction her mother just left, gripping Kian's hand. Luca's safe and they're together. They need to help the others. "At least the doors leading out will be open." Just like the internal ones, Callix overrode the system so they could move quickly and freely.

The same way the fire is now.

They start running toward the nearest staircase and Nova gasps when she grabs the handrail. She jerks her hand back. "It's hot."

Kian's frown is the deepest she's seen it. "Stay away from the walls, too."

Nova glances at the one beside her, then to the other side. It feels like they're walking around in a bomb.

As they reach the bottom of the stairs, the smoke thins a little. But the screams only become louder. Cries for help echo from all directions, making it hard to identify where they're coming from.

A young man dashes past them, running up the stairs before they can stop him. They're just about to go after him when a child barrels at them, crashing into Kian's legs. He picks up the little girl and she curls into his arms like she wants to crawl into his chest.

"Cara, come back!" The panicked cry comes from their left and they hurry down the hall. A woman, tears soaking her cheeks, sees them and lets out a sob. "Cara!"

Kian passes the girl over and the mother clutches her with shaking hands. "There was a loud noise and she just ran."

"You've got her now," says Kian. "Can you find your way to the gangplank from here?"

The woman nods, more tears spilling from her eyes.

"Good." Kian points the way behind her. "You need to move quickly. Tell anyone else you see along the way."

Clutching her child to her, the woman turns and runs. Nova grips Kian's arm. "We have to find that guy." Going up is the last thing anyone should be doing right now.

Three more people come running down the corridor, and Nova and Kian direct them to the gangplank. At least with the smoke being thinner down here it'll be easier for them to navigate.

They reach the bottom of the stairs and Nova's heart stops. Smoke is trickling down like mist, the toxic smell of burning paint making her cough. There's a shout and then the man comes tumbling down, his body folding and toppling over itself.

He stops at their feet, crumpled and groaning. Nova kneels down. "Don't move. Tell me where it hurts."

But the man pushes her hands away. "Get him away from me! The fool, the fire is going to kill us all!"

Concerned he's knocked his head, Nova tries to scan his scalp and face. The man struggles to stand and Kian reaches down, helping him up. "Once we know you're okay, you need to get to the gangplank."

The man looks back up the stairs. "The fire, it's up there. How can it move so fast? And that crazy man is—" The thumping of boots above them has the man jerking away. "You need to get out of here!"

He's gone before they can ask what's going on. But then someone appears on the stairs and Nova realizes what had the man freaking just as much as the fire.

Cain's eyes light up when he sees Nova below him. He lifts the spear in his hand and points the sharpened tip at her. "Now, you're just the person I was looking for. I need a ticket off this death trap."

He launches himself down the steps, the same violence that Nova saw in the Outlands flashing across his face. Ice floods her veins as she braces herself. She can't run. There's nowhere to go.

And she didn't run for the bear. She's not running now.

"No!" Kian roars, catapulting past her.

But Cain must've been expecting it, because he lifts the spear mid-flight and strikes it across Kian's face. The stick cracks in half from the force and Kian's head snaps to the side, altering his trajectory and he crashes into the wall.

It's all Cain needs. He shoulders Kian out of the way and grabs Nova. She struggles, fear and fury powering her movements. Every offensive strike Phoenix taught them flashes through her mind. Cain grunts when a punch slams into his gut, and roars when the second collides with his jaw.

The pain only infuriates him more. He grabs Nova by the hair and spins her around. In a blink, she's pinned against him, her back to his front, the shattered half of the spear pulled hard against her throat.

"Nova!" Kian pushes from the wall but Cain jerks the choking length of wood higher and Nova gasps in pain.

"Not another step closer," warns Cain.

Kian freezes, his hands extended. A trickle of blood snakes its way down his face and along his jaw. "Cain—"

"Shut up! I'm the one doing the talking for a change."

Nova lifts her hands to pull at the spear across her throat but Cain jerks it again. Agony jolts through her and her head swims as her airway's compressed. She drops her hands, keeping her gaze on Kian. She wants him to know she loves him.

She wants him to know she's sorry.

Kian's hands drop an inch. "Fine, you do the talking. What do you want, Cain?"

"You're one of those High Bound." Cain shuffles along the corridor, creating more distance between himself and Kian. "You can open the doors."

Nova holds Kian's gaze, wondering what Cain is talking about. The doors are all open. He doesn't need Kian to do that.

Kian slides slowly forward. "Yes, I can. But anyone from Askala is able to."

"No, they can't!" screams Cain and Nova closes her eyes as her ears ring. Cain is sounding as crazy as Ronan. "I've tried. Unbound can't open the doors. You bastards are trying to kill us all!"

The young man. Nova didn't want to notice—the world of Bound and Unbound has ceased to exist in her mind—but it was almost instinctive. His left hand. It only had four fingers.

The corridor is progressively filling with smoke. It makes Nova want to cough, and her eyes water in the attempt to suppress it. She can barely breathe right now, plus Cain is going to take any sharp movement as a threat.

Kian raises his palms again, keeping his arms wide and relaxed. "Okay. I can open the doors. Just let Nova go."

"You don't live as long as I do in the Outlands by being stupid. She ain't going nowhere until I'm off this corpse maker." Cain jerks his head. "You walk ahead, we'll be right behind."

Kian shuffles by, his eyes flicking to the ground but then jolting straight back up. Nova realizes he probably just passed the other half of the spear. But she'd be dead by the time he reached down and grabbed it. As if to prove it, Cain tightens his grip as Kian passes them and Nova can't help the grimace. The hall spins for long moments and all she sees is Kian's agonized gaze.

But then he's ahead of them and Cain relaxes. Nova draws in precious air, sucking in ash and smoke. Each inhale draws in the harbingers of destruction.

They're running out of time.

"Attaboy," sneers Cain. "Now start walking. Navigate this godforsaken maze and get us out of here, and your girl will be fine."

Kian goes to glance over his shoulder, but Cain jerks the spear again and Nova gasps. Kian's body freezes and he keeps his gaze straight, his whole body vibrating with tension.

Cain thrusts his hips forward, chuckling as he starts them moving. Nova allows her eyes to shut. At least Luca got to safety. And hopefully as many others as possible.

And once they get to the gangplank, so will they. Cain will have his freedom. He'll see that no one was trying to kill anyone.

"You know," Cain whispers. "All I wanted was some food. I didn't ask for any of this."

Nova doesn't answer. Her throat is being stretched and crushed. For a moment, sympathy flashes through her. Cain was molded by the fight for survival. That's all he's trying to do now. Survive.

He chuckles, the sound crawling into her ear. "But I got something better. You won't be escaping me this time. You'll never leave this ship, girl." He promises quietly, his breath smelling of smoke and meat. "No one holds a spear to my throat and lives."

Nova's eyes shoot open. When she'd held that spear to Cain's throat in training she'd been protecting Shiloh.

This isn't survival. It's revenge.

She looks frantically around. One violent jerk and Cain will snap her neck. But she's trapped. And Kian's trusting Cain's words. He'll open the door...and never see it coming.

He'll blame himself.

The sound of frantic voices carries from up ahead and Nova frowns. What are people still doing on the Oasis? Especially when the gangplank is just ahead.

"Sounds like your boyfriend is going to be opening the door for more than just me," breathes Cain, the words hot and threatening.

And if Kian has a reason to open the doors, Cain doesn't need Nova.

Nova decides in that moment that if she's going to die, she's not going without a fight. Maybe if she injures Cain somehow, she can buy some time.

Except there are no sharp movements. No grunts or gasps. Cain draws the broken spear closer to his chest as he simultaneously lifts it. Nova's feet rise from the ground as her airway is crushed closed.

Frantically, she scratches at the wood across her throat. She can't draw in air to cry out, can't call for help. Her body is hanging in the air, leaving her legs dangling helplessly. The edges of her vision blacken. Her mouth opens and closes like a fish on land.

Kian...

In a last burst of energy, Nova kicks out her legs. One foot hits the wall while the other connects with Cain's thigh, eliciting a grunt.

Kian spins around, his eyes widening with horror as he realizes what's happening. Cain staggers back, knowing he just needs a little more time...

Nova reaches out to Kian, but her arm feels too heavy. And then she can't feel it. Her whole body has gone numb.

Kian leaps toward them and Nova tries to keep her eyes open, but they flutter closed, suddenly as heavy as everything else. It's too late.

He'll be too late.

Through the haze stealing over her mind Nova hears a *crack* and then a grunt. And without warning, she's crumpled on the floor, sweet air filling her lungs. She gulps, the action hurting her bruised throat, but she doesn't care. With each gasping breath, death withdraws its icy fingers.

"You bitch!" screams Cain, blood pouring like a fountain down his head.

Nova looks up to find Shiloh behind him, holding the other half of the spear like a sword before her. "Leave them alone!"

Cain runs at her, his own shaft of wood extended. "You're going to die just like she will."

"Run!" croaks Nova.

Shiloh's eyes widen and she backs up, but then her gaze flickers to Nova. To Kian.

And she slams herself back against the wall, just like Nova did with the tree when the bear was coming at her, just as furious. Just as hell-bent on killing.

Shiloh lifts her fractured piece of wood just as Cain throws himself at her.

There's a gurgling cry as he arches backward, his momentum skewering him until the tip protrudes from his back. A breathless second later, Cain slumps, pinned to the wall with his own weapon.

Except Shiloh is trapped between him and the wall. Kian

launches into action, Nova scrabbling behind him. They yank Cain back and his body collapses to the ground.

Ignoring the slick blood at her feet, Nova looks up. And gasps. "Shiloh…"

She's gripping Cain's half of the spear in her crimson hands. Her gaze lifts from where it's impaled in her abdomen.

She killed Cain, but at a price.

Shiloh looks to Kian, her pale lips trying to smile. "All I want is for you to be happy."

She whispers the words, the smile never gaining life. With a last, hoarse breath, her head sags to the side. A lonely trickle of blood leaks from the corner of her mouth.

"No." Nova mouths the word, her bruised throat clogged with grief.

Kian's hands flutter up only to fall helplessly by his side. "She…"

Nova grips his arm. "She was brave and selfless and kind."

And she loved Kian enough to die for what mattered to him. Nova.

"Kian, we can't leave her—"

Several high-pitched screams carry down the corridor, and Nova spins around. One of those voices sounded familiar. But it can't be…

Above them, the ceiling starts to crackle, and Nova looks up to find the paint bubbling and flaking. Pale fragments fall around them like snow. The fire is just above them!

Suddenly, there's a trembling beneath their feet and Nova grips Kian. The floor is shuddering with whatever's coming.

Her eyes widen when she sees what it is. People. So many people.

And her mother is at the forefront, carrying Luca.

"Thea, what are you still doing here?" shouts Kian over the stampede. "You all need to get out of here."

But she's already shaking her head. "We can't. The doors."

Fear fractures in Nova's chest. Cain said something similar, and his eyes held the same frantic terror her mother's do.

Kian steps forward. "What do you mean, we can't?"

Amity pushes around Thea, chest heaving. "Kian. The doors. They're all locked shut!"

Sweet Terra! They're trapped.

KIAN

"What? That's not possible!" Kian scans the sea of frightened faces. It feels like half of Askala extends down the hall. "Callix ensured they were all open."

His mother shakes her head, his little brother, Jasper, wrapped tightly around her legs. "We tried. The door to the gangplank is shut and no one can get it open."

Kian's heart pummels his ribs as he tries to comprehend this. Every door they've passed so far has been open.

But the rows of wide, frightened eyes are undeniable. Thea holding Luca, his head pressed into her neck. His mother, Kian's three younger siblings trembling beside her. Men, women, children. His people wouldn't be here if they'd found a way to escape.

A crash sounds from above and more flakes of paint rain down. People gasp as they duck, one or two crying out. They can't stay here.

They have to find a way out.

Kian turns to his mother and Thea. If the fire's above them, they have to go down. "Take everyone to the ballroom. Once we find a way out, we'll come for you."

His mother nods but Thea hesitates. "But what if…"

Nova pulls her into a fierce hug, Luca pressed between them. "We'll be as quick as we can. You need to stay strong."

Thea's lip trembles but she nods.

Kian pushes up on tiptoes, calling out. "Go to the ballroom. We're going to find a way out."

His mother starts ushering people past. Many of them huddle in pairs, some carry a child, others follow blindly, their faces blank with shock.

Thea straightens, her face becoming resolute. She presses a lingering kiss to Nova's head, probably terrified she has to say goodbye again. Luca raises his head, his eyes large and luminous in the haze. He lifts his hand even though his arm is too short to reach Kian. He's asking him not to leave him.

Kian brushes his face, noting it's tear free unlike so many of those around him. "I'll be back. I promise."

With that, he grabs Nova's hand and they push past the tide of people. The door to the gangplank is their best chance of getting out of here quickly.

A bead of sweat trickles down Kian's temple, and he realizes how warm it's become. Heat is filtering through the walls, an ominous warning of what will come next.

Flames.

Fire.

Nothing left behind but destruction. And death.

Kian glances back at Nova. Neck bruised, face streaked with ash, she's reaching out to the people they pass, murmuring words of assurance.

There's still time.

There will be another door.

We'll find a way out.

And Kian finds himself nodding and agreeing. This is what they can give their people.

Hope.

And determination that it's not unfounded.

Once they're free of people, Kian and Nova break into a run. His eyes water as the smoke stings them and he brushes it away. The door isn't far.

They turn a corner and see it at the end of the corridor. And just like his mother said...it's closed.

Sprinting, they stop before it, Nova wheezing through her damaged throat. Kian lifts his hand and scans it over the sensor.

The door doesn't move.

He tries again, this time pressing his hand closer.

Still nothing.

He lets out his breath, knowing he was stupid for holding it. Others have tried, there's no reason it would've been different for him.

Nova moves closer to the door, fingers running around the edge. "Maybe we can override it."

Except these doors were designed to withstand storms. And a potential Remnant attack. But Kian knows they still have to try.

They wedge their fingers into the crevice where the door meets the wall and pull. Pain streaks up Kian's arm as he feels his nails lifting, but he doesn't let up the pressure. Suddenly, Nova tumbles to the side, her fingers slipping out.

Kian catches her and they hold each other, breath panting.

"There has to be a way," says Kian through gritted teeth. Callix had the doors open.

He moves back to the sensor, and gasps. He peers closer. Fine lines spear out on its surface like a spider's web.

"What is it?" asks Nova, moving in and grabbing his hand.

Kian shakes his head, not wanting to believe what he's seeing. "It's been damaged."

Nova's grip tightens. "Kian..."

It means they're wasting the one thing they don't have—time.

Somewhere, the scream of metal collapsing jolts through them, followed by a wall-trembling crash. Nova presses herself closer as she looks around.

What little protection the walls offered feels like it's about to combust any minute.

Nova's words echo in Kian's ears. *There's still time.* Although that prediction hasn't held, her next words have Kian grabbing her hand and running down the corridor.

There will be another door.

Nova's instantly by his side. "The door we sometimes use to access the gardens."

Kian nods. "Not all the sensors would be damaged."

The next entrance is only a short dash away. They're both coughing as they round the corner, but Kian tells himself once this door is open, their lungs can feast on fresh air.

And so will everyone else who's depending on them.

But the damage to this sensor is apparent at a distance. The fractured surface looks like someone punched it, shards of glass splintering from the center.

Kian slams the wall above it with his fist, welcoming the pain that shoots up his arm. Two sensors, both damaged.

"Why?" whispers Nova. "Why would someone do this?"

Kian scans his mental map of the Oasis. They grew up on this ship. Slipping out together through any available exit used to be a game they played. Each one that comes to mind is quickly struck off. They're all on the upper decks.

The upper decks that are being scorched and devoured by flames.

Which leaves only one door, one he doubts anyone would even remember exists. Except it's on the next level up. Kian glances down at Nova, hesitating. She's pregnant. How can he agree for her to join him? To take her closer to the inferno?

But Nova's already grabbed his hand. "We both know there's one more door we can try. We're doing this together, Kian." She tugs him to the nearest stairs, already shaking her head at the irony of what that door is.

A fire exit.

Boarded up because it led to nowhere useful, he and Nova used to loosen the bottom plank and sneak out. They didn't do it often, knowing their little secret would be discovered, but enough for Kian to remember it.

And for Nova.

The moment they take the first few steps up, the smoke thickens. Nova coughs harder, the sound rough and fractured in her damaged throat. Protectiveness wells in Kian and once they're at the top of the stairs, he pulls her in close.

If this door opens, she'll be the first person who'll be using it. He can go back for the others without her.

They reach the next level and sickly smoke envelops them, obscuring more than a few feet in front. Kian's shoulder bumps into the wall and he hisses at the heat that brands him. Above, the ceiling crackles, a subtle, ominous sound.

The fire is close.

Half-running, they head for the end of the corridor. Kian keeps his arm extended—with the thick smoke, they could run straight into the door. "Pull your shirt over your mouth!"

Nova jerks the material over her mouth but it doesn't stop the coughing. Kian picks up the pace, squinting in the haze. They need to find this door, fast.

His fingers feel it before he sees it and he halts them before they crash. Just like he remembered it, the door's boarded up, but now ash shivers in the spider webs that decorate the edges.

Kian steps in close, feeling for the sensor. Finding it, he draws back as pain slices through his finger. "No..."

He waves his hand, trying to clear the smoke. Eddies flutter, almost beautiful in their dance through the air, and a streak of air clears long enough for Kian to see what his bleeding finger already felt.

The surface is smashed.

"No!" Kian roars, just as the fire above them does the same.

Nova grabs his arm. "We can't open it. We need to get out of here."

But Kian shakes her off. This door was their last hope. They can't give up yet.

He reaches out, grabbing the ends of one of the planks nailed to the doorjamb. "Maybe we can smash our way through."

"Kian—"

"Stay back!" He has to try.

He jerks the board, and it comes away with a screech as rusted nails are yanked out. Another heave and it comes loose. Kian throws it to the floor, grabbing the next one, violently coughing.

"It's too late," Nova shouts over the roar that seems to be coming from all directions.

It can't be. Without this door, there are no options.

No way out.

Yanking off the next plank, Kian lifts it high. "Give me room."

Nova's gasp is cut off as he slams it against the door. The clang reverberates over Kian's eardrums, quickly muffled by what's coming at them from the other side of the walls. A dent appears in the metal door and he lifts the wood again. This has to work.

Kian hits the door over and over, his panting breaths choking on the cloying smoke. Behind him, Nova tugs on his shirt. "Please, Kian," she begs. "We have to get out of here."

But that would mean giving up. A death sentence for Nova and everyone else on the Oasis. His people.

His responsibility.

"The walls, Kian!"

But Kian doesn't look. The door is battered with dents. He raises his arms to hit it again. If he can only—

"No!" screams Nova. She pushes herself between Kian and the door, places her hands on his chest, and shoves.

The force has Kian tumbling back, and instinctively, he drops the wood and clasps her. He tries to keep them upright, and for a few stumbling steps, he manages it. But gravity wins out and he slams onto his back, Nova landing on top of him.

"What did you—"

His words are cut off by a *boom*. Kian's eyes widen as he watches the ceiling cave in over the door, crimson flames suddenly crawling over every exposed edge. As the fire finds fresh air, it billows and blooms, exploding outward.

Kian grabs Nova and they both clamber to their feet.

"Run," he screams.

They sprint down the corridor, the sound of destruction a heartbeat behind them. Heat scorches Kian's back and he grabs Nova's hand. "Faster!"

Acrid smoke scorches Kian's lungs as they scream for oxygen. But it's being devoured by the monster behind them. The fiery demon that wants to burn them next.

It feels like it takes a lifetime to reach the stairs. Kian pushes Nova ahead so she can go down first. He glances over his shoulder and freezes.

The ceiling is gone, exposing a cavernous hole of nothing but blackened remains. And the corridor...it's alive. Feverish and ravenous, scarlet flames dance and devour over the half-eaten walls. Flames which are the color of blood and war.

Turning and running, Kian follows Nova down the stairs, knowing they've outrun it this time.

But with no way out of the Oasis, they'll eventually be cornered.

And there'll be no escaping the flames then.

At the bottom of the stairs, the smoke is thinner. It pours down like ashen fluid around their feet, a promise that the fire is coming.

Kian stops, chest heaving. What now?

Nova presses her hand to his chest. "We need to go to the ballroom."

His heart contracts painfully beneath her palm. And tell the others they've failed. That Ronan won.

Kian nods, his agony echoed in the eyes of the girl who just saved his life. "Together."

He presses a kiss to her forehead as her hand clenches over his chest, every shred of his being wishing this had ended differently.

And then they're running.

The smoke thins the further away from the fire and with each flight of stairs further into the bowels of the Oasis. Kian knows it's a false sense of security, but it gives his lungs a reprieve. And his mind a break from the pulse-rocketing panic.

They're about to turn a corner when Kian stops. "My father! He's in the brig!"

And last time Kian saw him, he was weak with hunger.

Nova glances at the direction they were just heading in, then the corridor they'd have to take. She nods. "We can bring him to the ballroom."

At least he'll be with his people.

They change direction, sprinting to the brig. The empty corridors echo with the sounds of their frantic footsteps. A ship that was once alive with people and movement is now a hull being progressively charred from one end to the other.

They reach the brig and Kian bursts into the cell that was his father's only to find it empty.

Nova joins him a second later, discovering they're the only two in there. "Maybe he got out in time."

"Maybe."

Kian hopes so. It would give their decimated population some hope if their former leader survived.

He tugs Nova's hand, pulling her to him. They don't have

222

much time, but before they have to say this hopeless situation aloud, there are other words that need to be said. Stroking his fingers over her ash-streaked cheek, he brings his forehead down to hers. "Thank you, Nova. You've saved me more than once."

Long before that moment when she pushed him out of the way of the collapsing ceiling, Nova rescued him from a much slower death. A life without her. A life without heart.

Her hand lifts, pressing her fingertips against his lips. "Life doesn't exist without you, Kian."

This kiss is brief. Achingly sweet. Everything they feel for each other is captured in the press of their lips.

And just like this moment, it's too short.

It's a touch that will never be enough to encompass the yearning in their souls. The wish that this wasn't the end.

Kian pulls back, weaving his fingers through Nova's. "Let's get back to the ballroom."

Nova takes a moment to open her eyes. When she does, they shimmer with tears. And yet they're unwavering in the depth of the love they hold. She nods. "We need to go."

They run through the haze that's now everywhere. Inescapable. Like their fate.

The noises from the ballroom reach them as they round the corner. Frantic conversations. Children asking when they're leaving. Sobbing. Kian doesn't pause as they enter, keeping his shoulders straight despite the weight of the words he's carrying.

His mother rushes toward him, clasping him tightly. "Thank goodness."

And then Thea is hugging Nova. She pulls back just in time for Luca to leap into Nova's arms. "You came back," he cries.

"Of course, we did." Nova chokes out. "We're family."

Luca buries her head into the curve of her neck. "I didn't think you were coming back."

His mother looks at Kian. "You got back just in time. It's been hard to keep everyone calm. Which door are we going to?"

A crash somewhere behind them has Kian wincing. His mother is looking at him with such faith. She believes he's going to get them out of here.

Nova presses into his side. "We tried them all, Amity."

His mother looks from Kian to Nova and back again. "What are you saying? How are we going to get off the Oasis?"

Kian tries to speak, but his throat's too tight. The news that they're standing in their coffin winds through his chest, suffocating him. His knees almost buckle and he grips Nova's hand like a lifeline.

His mother needs to know. Every face that's slowly turning toward him, each so familiar, so trusting, deserves to know.

"You can't," comes a voice from the doorway. "There's no way out."

Kian spins around, disbelief detonating as he recognizes the voice.

His father strides through the doorway, stopping a few feet away. He looks pale and thin, but his eyes burn as if he's just come straight from the bowels of the fire.

"Magnus!"

Kian's mother flies into his arms and he holds her tight. "I'm so sorry, Amity."

His mother buries her head in his chest. "Magnus. I'm so glad you're here."

He pulls away, raising his gaze to Kian. "We're trapped. The fire isn't far away."

He says the words loud enough for them to ring through the ballroom. Several people gasp. Some cry out. One or two wail a denial.

Kian's body goes completely still. How does his father know this? He almost shakes his head, hating the suspicion that climbs up his spine. His father's words snake through him.

Human extinction is the best thing that can happen to planet Earth.

"What have you done?" he asks, aghast.

His father's lips thin. "I made sure we'll be staying here when I damaged the sensors."

Nova gasps, clutching Luca closer to her. "Magnus, what are you talking about?"

But his father doesn't even glance at Nova, keeping his dark gaze on Kian. "I tried, I really did, son. For a long time, I believed this was going to work. That Askala would make a difference." His left eye twitches. "But long before Ronan arrived I realized I was wrong."

Dread punches Kian in the gut. "When I chose a different direction."

"When you chose Nova!" his father screams. "When you forgot what we were doing this for!"

"I was doing this for the people we said we would care for!" Kian shouts back. Surely his father can't think what he's saying is right? It's so...wrong.

But his father shakes his head. "Askala was going to heal Earth. It was going to end human selfishness. But it failed." His shoulders slump. "I failed."

"This isn't selfishness, Dad. This is the part of humanity that counts—our heart! It's our heart that will heal. Our capacity to love makes us strong."

As if to add weight to his words, Nova moves in closer, weaving her fingers through his, Luca still in her arms. This is what Kian's proud of. Connections forged. Love won. A foundation for a future he was willing to fight for.

The show of solidarity isn't missed by his father. His face crumples as his body sags. "It was a war I never could've won. I see that now."

"What are you saying, Magnus?" Kian's mother whispers. When he doesn't look at her, she steps in front of him. "Our people." Her hand lifts, trembling. "Our children."

Willow and Holly and Jasper. And Kian. The terrified faces surrounding them. He's going to let them all burn to death.

His father clasps his mother to him. "I'm so sorry, Amity. Don't you see? This is the only way. It's the ultimate sacrifice for Mother Earth."

Not even the people of Askala were worth saving.

With a wrenching howl, his father breaks into sobs. He says the same words over and over again. "I'm so sorry. I'm so sorry." He clings to her as they heave through him, shaking the gaunt body that he was already sacrificing.

But his mother steps back, watching the man she loves crumple to the ground. He curls into himself, wrapping his arms around his head. Kian's mother trembles, her hand coming up to her mouth. "No, Magnus. This time, you're wrong."

The next crash as the Oasis combusts is visible from the doorway. A billow of ash and smoke is blasted into the room. People scream as they run for the other end of the room.

Kian's hands spear into his hair. How can he watch this happen? How can he live knowing his father chose this?

"Kian," Nova whispers urgently. "There's another door."

Kian turns to her. "What? Where?"

But then he remembers.

The door at the other end of the ballroom! Kian turns and runs, realizing as he reaches it why the frantic sprint was a waste.

It's the ultimate irony. A door to the outside. To safety.

But this one was installed for the Provings. For people to enter the bosom of Askala and everything it stands for. Symbolically, there's only one sensor.

On the outside.

You can enter. But you can't leave.

"No," Nova moans, beating her fist on the door they can't open.

Luca releases her, turning so he can beat on it, too. "Let us out! Please, save my family!"

Kian and Nova glance at each other, eyes wide with realization. This door leads directly to the outside. To the path to the remains of the lab.

"Everyone, come to the wall!" shouts Kian. "Start banging! Maybe someone will hear us!"

At first, the scared faces of his people do nothing but blink at him. But then one person jolts into action, throwing themselves at the wall as they start pounding it. Then another joins them, begging for someone to hear them. In the space of a breath, every body trapped in the ballroom is pummeling the wall of the ballroom, screaming for help.

The cacophony drowns out the approaching roar of the fire. It matches the thundering of Kian's heart.

This is their only chance. Please, let someone hear them.

And if not, they'll die fighting for their survival.

Just as his father would expect them to.

DEX

*D*ex's heart is pumping so hard it feels like it's going to jump out of his chest. Either that or it's going to stop in protest of what Dex is demanding of it.

His father is ahead of him. And he's running fast. Dex isn't even sure if he realizes he's being followed. He hasn't looked back once. It's like he's trying to pound his guilt into the soil with each frustrated step he takes.

With no lab to take sanctuary in, he's headed in the direction of the beach. Which suits Dex just fine. The angry sea will be the perfect witness for what Dex has to say.

They hit the sand and Dex slows his pace, waiting to see which direction his father will turn.

But he doesn't turn. He runs straight ahead, plunging into the shallows of the water, pushing himself forward until the water is up to his knees, his waist and then his chest.

What in sweet Terra is he doing? Has he lost his mind?

Dex barrels forward when he realizes what's happening. His father has lived with his guilt for sixteen years. Now that it's been exposed, it's too much. He can't carry the burden of what he did for another moment.

"You don't get to do this!" Dex reaches the water, wincing as the acid stings his feet. But he presses on. "You need to face what you did!"

He's lived his whole life with so many questions. What Dean told him in the ballroom answered most of them. The trouble is that it also brought up a whole lot more. And now's the time to have them answered.

"Dad!" he screams. "Stop!"

His father still doesn't turn, although he has to be aware of him now. He's choosing to ignore him. Not all that different to how he behaved for most of Dex's life.

"Why, Dad?" Dex is waist deep in the water now. His father is up to his shoulders. "Why did you do it?"

His father takes another step and plunges under the acidic depths of the ocean. He'd rather die than face Dex's questions, which somehow seems even more of a betrayal than what he'd done in the first place.

Dex surges forward and grabs hold of him. He hauls him back up to the surface and drags him to shallower waters, surprised his father doesn't fight him. It's like his touch has snapped him out of whatever trance he'd been in.

They're face to face now, the water lapping at their legs, his father unwilling to meet his gaze.

"Why?" Dex asks again. "Why did you do it?"

His father shakes his head. "I didn't mean for it to happen like that. I never meant…"

"Dean said you asked him to do it." Dex rubs at his thighs as the acid starts to sting. But he's afraid of losing this moment. "Why would Dean make that up?"

Very slowly, his father lifts his gaze, giving Dex a window to his broken soul.

He swallows and Dex can't tell if those are tears pouring down his face or droplets trailing from his hair. "I asked him to take off your finger. That's all."

"That's *all*? Are you serious? That's...*all*?" Dex takes a step back. Maybe some questions are better left unanswered.

His father blinks but doesn't shift his gaze.

"It wasn't meant to happen. Dean—"

"*You* did this," Dex spits out. "*You* caused it. *You* killed Mom just as much as Dean."

"You're right. It's my fault." His father rubs at his bloodshot eyes. "I was trying to protect you. I was worried."

"About what?" Venom slides into Dex's words, but he's powerless to stop it. "That I'd be Unbound? Because let me tell you that if I had a choice, I'd take having Mom here over being a precious Bound any day."

"I know." His father chokes on his words. "And I've had to live with that every day of your life. Why do you think I spent so much time in the lab? It was so hard for me to even look at you knowing what I'd done."

Dex remembers the way his father had avoided looking at his hand while he'd been growing up. And how Amity had raised him like the mother he'd never had the chance to know.

"I can never forgive myself," his father says. "I want you to know how sorry I am. There's not a day that goes by where I don't regret what I did."

"Did you really have such little faith in me?" Dex takes another step back, knowing he needs to get out of this water soon. "How could you be so certain I'd be Unbound? You said yourself that my results in the Proving were correct. That I'm a true Bound. Or was that a lie, too?"

"No! That is true." His father wades through the water to get closer to him and Dex continues to head for shore. "You *are* a Bound. You're the smartest and kindest and most amazing person I've ever known."

"Then why, Dad?" he asks again, still feeling like he doesn't have an answer.

"Because I didn't know that when you were a baby. You weren't...you weren't you yet."

Dex remembers the video message his mother left him. She'd believed in him. She'd seen in him all the things his father hadn't. She'd known what kind of person he was going to become.

"Maybe that's because you were never there. Maybe that's because you never gave me a chance." Dex presses forward until he reaches shallower water. Each step he takes is a relief to the part of his body being released from the water.

"I'm sorry!" his father calls from right behind him.

This time it's Dex who doesn't turn around. He has his answers and now it seems he has a whole lot more in common with Wren than he'd realized.

Both had their mothers stolen from them by their fathers. Both grew up thinking their fathers loved them, only to find out that they didn't.

It's just lucky they have each other now.

Thoughts of Wren have Dex increasing his pace, his need to see her adding to the necessity to get out of this crimson sea before it eats him alive. His legs feel like a thousand needles are being stabbed into him at once. But the pain is a reminder that he's alive. Dean may have robbed his mother of life, but he's still here. And he's determined to make her proud.

Which means he has to get back to Wren.

"Dex!" His father grabs him by the shoulder.

Dex shakes him off as they get to dry land. "Get away from me! You've done more than enough. Never talk to me again."

"I love you, Dex." His father's voice is filled with anguish. "I've always loved you, it was just shadowed by my guilt. I never meant for any of this to happen. You have to believe me."

But Dex is only half listening and it's not just because he doesn't believe a word his father is saying.

He can see smoke. Big black plumes of it are trailing into the sky from the direction of the Oasis. He blinks, certain he must be imagining it. He'd only just come from there. Surely, Ronan isn't foolish enough to have set the ship on fire?

He runs hard for the tree line, knowing he has to get to Wren. And Kian and Nova. Everyone he loves is on the Oasis.

But as soon as he breaks through the trees he slams straight into the last person he wants to see. Or perhaps it's exactly the person he needs to see most.

Dean.

"You!" Dex screams, hardly even able to get that one word out. "You!"

"Get out of my way." Dean pushes past him only to slam directly into Dex's father who seizes him by the collar.

"My son is talking to you," he sneers. "Pay him the respect of listening."

"Who died and made you the King of Respect?" Dean shoves Dex's father away. "What happened was your fault. You told me to make the cut."

"His finger, not his hand!" Dex's father pulls back his shoulders.

"How the hell could anyone cut off a hand instead of a finger?" Dex asks, finding his voice again and asking yet another question he hadn't been aware he had.

"Have you seen how small a baby's hand is?" Dean is screeching now as if the volume of his voice will make his words more convincing. "I had the knife all lined up when your mother jumped on my back and made me slip. I did you a favor taking it all off instead of leaving it hanging off the bone like a hunk of rubber flesh."

Dex hadn't expected such a vivid description and his stomach heaves. But now isn't the time to be weak. This man destroyed his life.

Dex grabs Dean by the throat. "Why did you have to kill my mother?"

"She saw my face." Dean is grappling at his throat but Dex has a tight grip on him. Using only one hand all his life has meant his fingers are stronger than most people's. A strength that Dean is responsible for. And he's going to use it to get his revenge. "She wouldn't have rested until I was dead. I had to kill her."

Dean's face turns purple and he tries harder to pry Dex's fingers away.

A force hits Dex from the side and he's sent flying, his hand breaking contact with Dean's throat. He watches helplessly from the ground as Dean scuttles off toward the beach.

"What did you do that for?" Dex glares up at his father, realizing he shoved him away from Dean.

"You were going to kill him." His father stands and offers Dex a hand to help him up.

Dex gets up on his own, not needing another thing from the man who calls himself his father. "And you have a problem with that?"

"You don't need that on your conscience. Trust me." His hand falls to his side. "I've thought about killing Dean a million times over the years. If I thought it would solve anything, I'd have done it already."

"Well, I wish you had." Dex runs toward the beach. Going to the Oasis is going to have to wait a few more minutes. He has business to attend to first. He's not a coward like his father. His mother deserves more than to have her death brushed aside like that.

He scans the beach, seeing Dean on the rocks several yards away. He has a raft, the same one he'd arrived on with his turncoat army.

Dex races over to him, but Dean's too fast. He has the raft on the water and is using an oar to paddle away.

"Get back here!" Dex scrambles over the rocks until he reaches the one at the very end. Without giving it much thought, he dives into the ocean, his skin screaming as the acid gets to work on finishing the job it started.

He knows it's foolish to go back in here. It could well be the last decision he ever makes. But he'd rather die than let Dean get away.

He powers through the water, the raft seeming to get further away until a wave picks it up and pushes it back toward the rocks.

Knowing this might be the only chance he gets, Dex kicks at the water, his determination fueling his tired muscles as he closes the gap.

Dean is working hard, but that raft was designed to transport a hoard of men. Paddling it out to sea solo is a slow, laborious task. He hasn't even had time to notice he's being followed yet.

Another wave pushes the raft back and Dex surges forward, making contact as he slaps his palm down hard on the edge.

Hoisting himself onto the raft, Dex crawls forward. One good shove and Dean will be in the ocean. If he can grab his oar before he topples, he'll be able to knock him out and let the angry sea do what his father should've taken care of years ago.

But just before Dex can throw himself at Dean, he rises and turns like he'd been given an invitation to his own ambush.

He lets go of his oar and grips Dex hard on both arms, forcing him close to the edge of the raft. Dex makes another grab for Dean's throat but he's ready for that, too, and evades him.

"You bastard!" Dex roars, anger consuming every one of his cells. "You're not getting away with this."

A wave hits the raft, tossing it toward the rocks and Dean is forced to let go of Dex to keep his balance. Seeing this an opportunity instead of an obstacle, Dex launches himself at Dean while the raft is still in the grip of the wave.

But in the tumble of the violent ocean, Dex's aim is off and it's Dean who ends up with his hands around Dex's neck. His fingers find the pendant that Wren had given him and he pulls hard. It unbalances Dex and he winces at the tight feeling across this throat. Wren has always been the one to save him. He hates that this symbol of their love is being used against him like this.

Feeling his air supply being cut off as Dean grips the leather strap harder, Dex shoves him as hard as he can, sending them both sailing off the edge of the raft and plunging back into the ocean.

Dean's hands slip from Dex's neck and he drags in some oxygen as he fights to keep his head above the water.

"Are you crazy?" Dean screams over the crashing of the waves on the nearby rocks. "Now we're both good as dead."

But Dex doesn't intend for some water to get in the way of the revenge he's craving. He kicks ahead, his eyes stinging and the back of his throat burning. He reaches Dean and wraps his legs around his torso from behind, trying to push him underneath the water.

Dean turns himself around, their bodies slippery in the water, and now they're face to face, pure hatred passing between them. They both know there's no room for more than one survivor here. They're either both going down or one will take out the other. Far too much has passed between them for both of them to live.

A huge wave washes over them, sending them hurtling toward shore. Dex holds on tight as they're slammed into the rocks, the impact jerking their bodies apart. They scramble up the rough surface and out of the water, and Dex wastes no time in landing a punch directly in the fleshy part of Dean's nose. Blood spurts out, soaking his shirt and dripping onto the rocks below.

Dean roars as he maneuvers himself on top of Dex and pummels him hard in the ribs. Dex may have the advantage in terms of anger to fuel him, but as an Unbound, Dean has the experience when it comes to fighting. He lands punch after punch in Dex's middle, cracking open the ribs that have only just had a chance to heal after the torture that Ronan put him through.

The pain is so intense that Dex can't fight back. Every time he takes a breath, Dean has slammed the air right back out of his lungs, flashing black spots before his eyes. Just when he thinks he's able to predict the next blow and shield himself from it, he realizes he can't. Dean is too fast for him. And far too strong.

This isn't how he's going to win this fight. It doesn't matter how much blood is pouring from Dean's nose, he's going to hit Dex until there's nothing left to punch except the same rubber flesh he'd used to describe his hand earlier.

He screams in agony as the next blow lands on his chest, his thoughts turning to Wren. She's not here to save him this time. And if he can't find a way to fight back, she won't be able to save him ever again.

Dean raises his fist again, this time right above Dex's face. But just as it's powering through the air, he's thrown backward onto the rocks and Dex sees his father standing above him, radiating pure fury.

His father turns and picks Dean up as if he weighs nothing at all and tosses him into the ocean, jumping in straight after him. He lands directly on top of Dean, forcing his head under the surface. Blood pools around them, which Dex can only assume is continuing to pour from Dean's nose. A dark crimson circle forever expanding in the pale red water of the ocean. Mingling and merging as the two liquids become one.

Dex scrambles to the edge of the rocks, every part of his body aching. He wants to dive in after them and help his father finish the job he started, but he knows he can't. He'll only end up going under himself and then his dad will be forced to rescue him instead of dealing with Dean.

He watches as his father holds Dean under the water, unaware he had this kind of strength. But then again, he's being fueled by as much anger as Dex. And he knows how powerful that can be.

But more than that, Dex knows his father is being fueled by the need to make things right. He hadn't just saved Dex from certain death by picking up the fight with Dean. He's trying to grant Dex his wish for revenge.

Is it possible his father actually does love him?

Dean is thrashing under the water. Giant air bubbles rise to the surface as he fights to regain control. But Dex's father has too firm a grip on him.

Dex wants to call out to his father to stop. That it's not worth it. That they can find a way to move past this without another person having to die.

But he remains quiet.

Mute.

Unable to say the words that he knows would make him a good person. Perhaps he's not a true Bound after all? Because he can't deny that he wants Dean dead. What kind of person does that make him?

When his father releases his hands from Dean and looks up at the rocks, Dex knows the job has been done. Finally, after all these years, his mother's death has been avenged.

But it's a hollow feeling that sits in the pit of Dex's bruised gut. When he'd climbed aboard that raft, he'd thought Dean's death would feel like a victory. So why does it still feel like he's lost? Perhaps there are no winners here. Everyone involved has paid too high a price.

Dean's body bobs to the surface and Dex's father pushes it away as he waits for a wave to wash over them so he can make his way back to the rocks.

But it seems someone else is waiting for this wave.

Or rather, something else...

A huge gray fin slices through the water, heading directly for the pool of blood. And straight for the man whose only real crime was a misjudged act that he thought would protect his son.

"Dad!" Dex cries out, forcing himself to his feet and pointing. "Leatherskin!"

His father's eyes widen as he turns and starts swimming for shore. With any luck the leatherskin will make a start on Dean's remains, giving his dad a chance to get to safety.

Dex picks up a rock and hurls it at the giant shark, knowing it won't do anything but feeling like at least he's trying. It bounces off the beast's thick skin and Dex doubts it even felt the impact.

The leatherskin's massive body streaks through the water, heading for Dean. When it gets close, it opens its huge jaws, revealing a wall of teeth. Thank goodness Dean's already dead. That sight would be enough to stop your heart in an instant.

"Swim faster!" Dex squats down and leans over the edge of the rocks, ready to help scoop his father to safety the moment he gets close.

The leatherskin tosses Dean's body in the air and catches it, chomping it cleanly in half, then tossing one of the halves up again.

Dex looks away, bile rising in his throat. It was the end Dean deserved but he doesn't want to watch it. He'd already witnessed Jay die in the Proving when the leatherskin had rushed at him. He has no desire for a repeat performance.

He gasps when he turns his head to see something he hadn't expected. Another leatherskin is approaching from the other direction, no doubt attracted by the blood. Or perhaps it had been circling all this time.

"Faster!" Dex screams to his father, who's almost at the rocks now, his arms propelling through the air as they hit the water and push him further ahead. "There's another—"

His words fall short as the leatherskin comes at his father with impossible speed, its jaws opening and taking his father by the middle. It dives down under the water until they're both lost from sight.

"Dad!" Dex straightens up, trying to get a better view as he scans for any sign of his father. Or a fin. Anything to indicate where that creature has taken him. "Dad!"

Bubbles of air rise to the surface a few yards away and the water turns a deep red.

A fin slices through the oncoming wave and swims away from the rocks to deeper water, closely followed by the leatherskin who'd feasted on Dean.

"Dad!" Dex cries again, knowing it's all over.

He'd thought his father hadn't loved him, but he'd died protecting him, just like his mother had. He'd proven his love in the bravest possible way and now it's too late for Dex to ever forgive him. That's something he knows he's going to have to live with.

He turns away from the ocean, looking back at the heavy smoke rising from the direction of the Oasis.

It's too late to save his father. Too late to take back the fateful minutes that just passed. But it's not too late to make sure his friends are okay.

Clutching at his ribs, he stumbles over the rocks, heading toward the Oasis.

A thunderous explosion echoes through the forest. Dex halts his steps as he watches a mushroom cloud rise into the sky.

Another explosion sends Dex's gut churning as he faces the possibility that checking on his friends might be another thing to add to his list of things he's too late to do.

WREN

The second explosion is worse than the first. It launches Wren out of her mother's arms and sends her running toward the beach.

She's fairly certain Dex got out of the ship in time. And surely the others did, too. Every last door on that ship had been open. There should have been plenty of time for everyone to get themselves to safety. But she has to make sure.

Which is exactly why she needs to get to the beach. She can't think where else Dex would be, unless he's gone back to the camp. But she doubts he'd go there without her.

She takes the worn path that not all that long ago was so foreign to her. Now it's like a fold of skin in the palm of one of her hands. She knows this island almost as well as she knows the village she grew up in. This is her home now. She can't imagine ever going back to the Outlands.

Halfway down the path, she slows her steps, certain that Dex is approaching. She's not sure if it's because she hears his familiar footsteps or if she feels his presence. Maybe it's both.

She rounds the corner, ready to throw herself into his arms, until she sees him limping toward her. He's clutching his ribs and his skin is bright pink. He's also dripping wet.

"Dex!" She rushes up to him and he draws to a stop, looking at her with red-rimmed eyes. "What happened to you?"

"Thought I'd go for a swim." He lifts his arms and draws her into his damp chest, wincing as she gently folds herself into him. "Thank goodness you're okay."

"What happened?" she asks again. "I tried to follow you but Phee and Kian convinced me to leave you to sort it out alone. Where's Callix?"

Dex releases her to run a finger down her cheek, his eyes spilling over with raw grief. "He's dead, Wren. So is Dean."

"You killed them?" Wren's eyes widen as she tries to take this in.

"Technically Dad killed Dean. And a leatherskin killed Dad. But none of it would have happened without me. If I'd stayed in the ballroom, they'd both be alive." His voice is calm. Almost robotic. She understands immediately why. He hasn't processed whatever trauma he just lived through. A feeling she knows only too well.

"My dad's dead, too," she says, hoping this might ease some of his pain.

Dex's fingers pause on the line he'd been trailing down her cheek. "Who did it?"

"Technically my mother did…" Wren gives him a sad smile. "But just like you, it wouldn't have happened without me there."

"How did it happen?" His question is simple. Unfortunately, the answer isn't.

"He started a fire. It got…hectic. He jumped from the top deck."

"Kian and Nova got out okay, though?" He glances up to the smoke billowing above their heads. "Please tell me they did."

"I think so." She presses her hands to his chest, noticing how bruised his neck is. "Dex, what happened to you?"

"Later." He brushes her hands away. "I can't talk about it now. We should check on Kian and Nova."

"We should." There's no way they can take any chances. Assuming people are okay is usually the best way to ensure they're not.

Dex drapes an arm around her shoulders, leaning on her far more than he normally would.

"Are you okay to walk?" She supports him around the waist, and they head toward the Oasis, his steps slow but determined.

"I'll be okay," he insists. "Just as soon as this is all over."

A scream pierces the air and Dex and Wren pick up their pace.

"You go ahead," says Dex, his breath seeming to catch in his lungs as he lets go of her to wrap his arms across his chest. "Go find Kian and Nova."

"I'm not leaving you again." She loops her hand in the crook of his arm and drags him forward. "How many more times do we have to make that mistake before we learn?"

He nods, pulling back his shoulders and marching forward. She knows he'll pay for that later. But if they don't move now there might not be a later.

The air thickens with smoke the closer they get to the ship. Far worse than when Wren had left only minutes before.

A group of people pass them on the path.

"Don't go that way!" the people shout. "Get down to the beach. It's safe there!"

More people are behind them. But not as many as there should be. Where is everyone else?

"What's happening?" Dex asks a woman Wren recognizes from the encampment. "Have you seen Kian?"

The woman shakes her head. "People are trapped on the ship. We can hear them screaming. But we can't get close enough to open the doors. It's far too hot."

"Go, Wren," Dex begs as he limps forward. "Please! We have to open the doors. I'm too slow right now."

"My chip doesn't work." Wren's shoulders slump. "You have to come with me. It's the only way."

"Urgh!" Dex slaps himself on the forehead, knowing he was the one who deactivated her chip. A decision that could end up costing Kian and Nova their lives. But he couldn't have known it would come to this.

They stumble forward, bursting out of the trees and the Oasis comes into sight. It's a glowing shadow in the heavy smoke, lighting up the early morning sky. The noise of it is almost as intense as the heat, and the smell winds its way up Wren's nostrils as she practically drags Dex along the path. It's the scent of the evidence of hundreds of lives going up in smoke. Not the people themselves, but everything they owned that made them who they were.

Wren goes to clasp Dex's hand, then realizes she's standing on his left. She switches to his other side and slips her hand into his, only to find it's far too painful with her missing finger. Fighting the feeling the universe is working against them, she loops her hand in Dex's elbow and they push forward.

"Which door?" she asks, scanning the ship from left to right.

"The ballroom." Dex urges her to the left. "If Kian's still on board he'll gather everyone there. I'm certain of it."

Wren nods. If anyone knows what Kian would do, it's the guy who grew up beside him.

As they make their way past the gangplank, Wren strains her eyes in the smoke and sees Phoenix and Felicia running down it toward them.

"What's going on?" she calls out.

"It's no use!" Phee shouts. "We opened the door but there's too much smoke. We couldn't get inside."

"We're going to the ballroom!" Wren raises her voice over

the crackling of the fire, but her words are swallowed by the booming sound of more of the ship collapsing.

"It's starting to cave in!" Wren grips Dex's hand, no longer caring how much pain it causes her. They have to get to Kian and Nova. And she needs Dex's touch more than she needs to be free of pain.

They wind around the ship, staying as close to it as they dare. Sweat is pouring off Wren's forehead now and she wipes it away to see her hand come away black. There's so much soot in the air, it's plastering itself to their skin. Dex is fast going from bright pink to ash gray. It's no wonder those people they passed hadn't been able to get close enough to open any doors.

If there really are more people stuck inside this inferno, Wren doesn't like their chances. But she's not prepared to give up, either. Kian and Nova hadn't given up on them when they were stuck in the burning lab. She owes it to them to do the same.

"Up there!" Dex points in the haze and at first Wren thinks he's confused. But she blinks and sees that through the smoke there's a door.

A banging noise drags them up the ramp. It's the sound of desperation. The sound of people fighting for their lives to be saved.

"They're in there!" Wren shouts, as Phoenix and Felicia catch up to them. "I can hear them."

Dex slams his stump to the sensor and the door jolts a couple of inches then stops. "It's stuck!" he cries out. "The heat is melting the doorframe."

Several sets of fingers claw out of the small gap and Phoenix shoulders his way past them into the space, gripping the door and heaving it back with a force neither Wren nor Dex are physically capable of exerting.

It shifts back a few more inches and Phoenix heaves again, creating a gap that might just be enough.

A child is pushed through and Felicia scoops her up and runs down the ramp to safety. More people follow, squeezing their way out of the gap as Phoenix tugs at the door again, managing to get it wide open this time.

And now people are pouring down the ramp. More people than Wren can believe managed to find themselves trapped. What happened to stop them getting out?

Wren and Dex stand back as they wait, knowing that if Nova and Kian are there, they'll be the last to exit. There's no way Kian would leave before anybody else. And Nova won't leave him, no matter how much they all know he'll be begging her to.

Thea emerges next, carrying Luca in a firm grasp.

"Thank you," she breathes as she passes them. "Thank you."

As the people start to thin out, Amity exits with Kian's siblings. She seems torn, like she's left a part of herself onboard the ship, but knows she has to save the three young lives that are clinging to her legs.

The heartbreaking sight of the look on her face makes Wren unsure if she ever wants to become a mother. It was hard enough growing up with just herself to worry about. Life's been even more difficult since she opened up her heart to let more people in. To have a child to have to worry about is unthinkable. Wren doubts she'd ever sleep again with the anxiety it would cause her.

"Is Kian in there?" Dex asks Amity.

Amity nods. "Please, you have to convince him to come out. Please!"

Dex and Wren tilt their heads. Why wouldn't Kian want to come out? Nothing about this situation is making any sense.

"I'll go after him," Dex says, touching Amity on the shoulder. "I promise."

The last of the people come through the door and sure enough there's no Kian. Or Nova.

Dex is through the door first, holding his elbow to his

mouth, trying to breathe through his shirt. Wren is right behind him.

But nothing can prepare her for the intensity of the heat. It's like they've stepped directly into the core of the sun. The walls are warping and the chandeliers are glowing white above them.

Wren lets her elbow fall. Breathing through her shirt isn't going to help in here. Any oxygen she gets in the next few minutes will be a bonus.

"Kian! Nova!" Dex shouts.

"Over here!" Nova comes running to them. She's barely recognizable with the coating of ash stuck to her hair and face. "You have to help me. Kian won't leave Magnus."

They follow her into thicker smoke and see Kian standing with his back to them.

"Dad!" Kian is pleading. "Come with us. We still have time. Please!"

But Magnus shakes his head. "You let them all out! This was how we could prove what we're willing to sacrifice!"

He steps closer to the inner door of the ballroom, which must be just about to explode inwards. Wren can hear the fire on the other side. And when that blast happens, nobody in this room has any hope.

But she can't turn away and leave Kian here. And nor can Dex. They just have to hope they can do what they need to do and get the hell out of here in time.

Kian turns to them and Wren sees a large gash down one side of his face, blood seeping steadily out. But otherwise, he seems intact. Certainly in better shape than Dex.

Wren grips Dex's hand and slips her other hand into Nova's.

Nova reaches for Kian with her free hand and they stand facing Magnus.

A line of friendship forged in ways they could never have imagined, the bond between these four is unbreakable. They've saved each other, fought beside each other, laughed with each other and helped each other grow. Wren never expected to be part of anything as special as this.

Protective Kian with his fierce loyalty to Askala. Sweet Nova with a kind heart twice the size of anyone Wren's ever met. Beautiful, funny Dex with his unwavering ability to make anybody smile.

And Wren.

She knows what the others think of her. She's the wild girl who came from the Outlands, doing her best to push every one of them away, only to bring them right in close. She was the final piece of this puzzle and now that she's in place, they fit together in ways that would never be possible otherwise.

Which means nobody is going to die here. She's not going to let them.

"Magnus!" Dex screams over the roar of the fire. "Come with us!"

But Magnus shakes his head as he takes another step away from them.

"We need to grab him!" shouts Wren, already fed up with this. "We can carry him out!"

"He has a knife," says Kian, pointing.

Wren looks to see the knife clutched in Magnus's hand and realizes how Kian got the cut on his face. Magnus means business. Nobody will be dragging him out of here against his will.

Nova lets out a hacking cough and Wren's hand is tugged down as Nova collapses onto the floor.

"Get her out of here!" Kian shouts. "Please, get her outside where she can breathe. For the baby! I'm right behind you."

Wren hauls Nova back up to her feet and with Dex's help they stumble toward the door.

"Kian!" Nova is struggling against them, but she's weak. "Kian!"

"He'll follow us." Dex has a pained expression on his face

now. Wren isn't sure how he's managing to hold himself up, let alone Nova. "We need to get you and the baby to safety."

Wren tries to take more of Nova's weight, but it's difficult given Dex is taller. They drag Nova to the door, one arduous step at a time.

"Kian!" Nova screams as they pull her through the exit and out onto the ramp.

Thea is right there waiting, her face crumpling when she sees Nova looking so unwell. Wren motions for her to take her place and Thea slips right in beside Nova to support her.

They continue down the ramp for a few more paces and Wren falls behind, waiting for the gap to widen. Dex is distracted by the task at hand as well as his own crippling injuries, which is exactly what she needs right now.

She turns and runs back onto the burning ship.

Kian isn't behind them. He had no intention of following them. Not without his father. And Magnus had a crazed look Wren's seen before. He's a man more interested in what comes after death than before. He's given up. There's nothing Kian will be able to do to convince him otherwise. She's not sure what happened to Magnus. Maybe he went insane when Cy threw him in the brig, but it's clear to Wren that the Magnus they know is already dead.

And she'll be damned if he's going to take Kian down with him!

Fighting her way through the smoke, she reaches Kian and grips him by the back of his shirt.

"Wren!" He turns to her with fear radiating from his eyes. "Where's Nova?"

"She's safe but she needs you. We all do. Come with me!"

Kian looks at her for a long moment and she wonders if he's thinking what she is. They're two of the most unlikely allies. They'd hated each other at first sight, thinking it was because they were different, not realizing it was because they were so much alike. Both fighting for what they believed was right. Both desperate for their father's approval. Both determined to make the world a fairer place.

"You have to leave him." Wren pulls on Kian's shirt. "Don't let your baby grow up without a father."

"I can't leave him." The anguish in Kian's voice pulls at Wren's heart. "I can't."

"You can, Kian. This is his choice. Not yours. Come with me."

There's a crash outside the internal door and Wren tugs harder on his shirt. "I know it's hard. I had to turn my back on my own dad. It was hard but I did it. You can, too."

Kian shifts his gaze back to his father and the flames break through the wall behind Magnus, getting to work on devouring the ancient timber floor.

Getting closer. And closer still.

"Dad!" Kian cries, knowing they're out of time. "Please."

Magnus holds up his hand, letting his knife fall to the floor and Wren lights with hope. It seems Kian had been right in persisting. They can all walk out of here alive.

Or perhaps run...

But as Kian takes a step toward his father, Magnus holds up his other hand. "This is what we should all do."

"What?" asks Kian, not understanding.

With a shake of his head, Magnus turns and races toward the flames, leaping into them like he's jumping off a cliff.

And just like that, he's gone.

"Dad!" Kian shouts after him. "Dad!"

Wren stands on the tips of her toes and shakes Kian, trying to bring him back to the reality of their situation. "You're the dad now! And you need to get your ass moving!"

She reaches for his hand, pleased to find he grips her back.

They run from the flames, hand in hand. No longer enemies. So much more than friends. He's another brother to her now.

Someone who she'd walk into a fire for every day of her life if it meant keeping him safe.

They emerge through the exit just as a large blast behind them sends out a rush of intense heat. It knocks them from their feet, sending them skittling down the ramp.

"Magnus!" There's a scream. Wren doesn't need to look up to know it's coming from Amity. Wren's heart bleeds at the sound of her mourning. Once Magnus and Amity had been young and in love. They'd had their whole lives stretching out before them just like Wren has with Dex. They didn't know this was how it would end.

Amity had chosen to save her children. Magnus had chosen to die for his cause. Kian had been trapped in the middle, not prepared to accept either option.

Kian gets to his feet and pulls Wren up beside him, just as Nova and Dex come running toward them.

Wren opens her arms and waits for Dex. Kian does the same, his eyes focused only on the girl he loves.

They fall into each other and stand two by two, holding each other tight.

And Wren knows that when she came here to Askala, she didn't just find salvation.

She also found love.

FIVE YEARS LATER

NOVA

"*M*ommy! What does this say?"

Nova sighs, pushing the hair out of her face as she adjusts the sling on her back. She turns to her daughter to find she's holding the battered book Nova hoped she'd leave back in the hut.

Sam trots up to her, lifting it higher. Nova scans the text on the worn, water-damaged page. The sooner Sam learns to read fluently, the better. "It's talking about World War Five."

Sam frowns, her young face scrunching. "Over the oil reserves?"

There's a muffled mewling from behind her and Nova jiggles on the spot. Baby Sebastian needs to stay asleep for a little bit longer. Today's a big day and there are preparations to complete.

"Yes, honey. The oil reserves." Nova sighs. "Quick, we don't want to be late."

But Sam stays where she is, staring at the page her young mind desperately wants to decipher. "But that oil was the carbon they put into the atmosphere."

Five-year olds aren't supposed to talk about this stuff. And yet these books are Sam's bedtime stories. She and Kian snuggle up in her bed, and he reads her the history of Earth until her little eyes can't stay open any longer. Then, the next day, come the questions.

Why didn't they stop?

How long will it take to fix it?

Will sea levels go back down again?

Before Sam can ask anything else, Nova realizes they're alone. "Luca?" Nova calls out, spinning around. She took her eyes off him for five seconds, which means he could be anywhere.

"Up ahead!" comes his young voice. He barrels back down the path they're taking to the ballroom. "You guys are too slow!"

Nova shakes her head ruefully. "Maybe you could piggyback Sam? Then we'll be quicker."

Sam frowns as she regards her brother. "But what about my book?"

Luca strides over to her, pulling himself up to his full height as if he's twenty and not nine years old. "I'll carry it."

Sam hesitates, her small hands tightening around the twisted hardcover. "It's precious, you know."

Luca rolls his eyes. "You showed me how to carry them." He holds his hands out. "You've forgotten already, haven't you?"

Nova bites her lip as she watches the two siblings. Luca, the patient big brother...when he stands still long enough to be one. Sam...the serious little sister who gives him a reason to stop.

Sam's eyes widen as she realizes Luca's right. "Quick, we don't have time for this!" She passes him her precious book and Luca turns around. With a leap, Sam climbs on, the book tucked firmly under Luca's arm.

"Ready?" Luca grins over his shoulder.

"We can't run with the book, okay?"

Luca rolls his eyes again but does as he's asked. Nova's pretty sure the only time Luca walks or isn't up a tree is when Sam is clinging to his back.

She breathes a sigh of relief. They might get to the Oasis in time, after all. "Come on, Uncle Dex has been working on this for a very long time."

All year, in fact.

They strike out down the path, Sam and Luca igniting the well-worn discussion whether pods or cockroaches taste better. Nova allows herself a smile as the sounds of Sebastian sucking his thumb drift up from the sling behind her. She's pretty sure Luca's energy is the only thing that can keep up with Sam's insatiable mind.

Nova pulls in a deep breath, enjoying the scent of pine and earth. Her life is exhausting, but she wouldn't trade it for all the pods in the world. She and Kian lie in bed each night, holding each other, marveling at the family they've been graced with. Forged with love. Held together with patience and joy and laughter. It's everything they fought so hard for.

And as they listen to the sounds of people in the huts around them, they absorb the knowledge that it's not just their tight-knit family that's flourishing.

Askala is thriving.

There's a commotion ahead on the path and Luca launches forward before Nova has a chance to tell him to slow down. He comes to a halt when he sees Mercy skipping toward them.

Her face lights up when she sees Luca and Sam. "Daddy said you wouldn't be far away." She looks around, spotting Nova coming up behind them. "Hey, Auntie Nova. Daddy wanted you to know that another boat arrived today."

Nova's brows shoot up. "Another one?"

Mercy nods, her dark hair wild in that endearing way of hers. "Mommy said it's fine if you need to go to the infirmary."

Nova smiles, relieved she doesn't have to choose. She glances at Luca and Sam, knowing it's better if they don't come with her. "Why don't you three play and I'll meet you at the Oasis in a little bit?"

Mercy jumps up and down, clapping her hands. "Yes! We could play a game!"

Luca frowns. "Can't I just—"

"No, Luca." Nova keeps her voice firm. "I need you to stay with the girls."

Sam grabs her book from beneath Luca's arm, telling Nova that she'll be keeping herself occupied. Mercy slides closer to Luca, smiling up at him. "Maybe we can climb a tree?"

Luca snorts. "Except last time you wouldn't go past the first branch."

But Mercy isn't about to be deterred, which is exactly what Nova was counting on. The little girl with the face of an angel and her mother's determination won't be taking no for an answer. Sam won't get a chance to open her book, while Luca will find himself making mangrove pine tea and serving it to anyone unlucky enough to walk past before he realizes what's going on.

With a quick kiss on each of their heads, Nova heads to the infirmary. A boat arrived from the Outlands only a few days ago after not seeing one for months. They'd assumed there probably weren't many more of them left.

The infirmary isn't far, just like most of the essential buildings in Askala's village. Built from a combination of mangrove pine and the introduced and highly invasive varnish tree, it's bigger than most of the other huts, but just as sturdy. Recruiting a team, Phoenix had been busy over the past five years as he'd shelved his weapons and picked up tools. His skills are apparent in every building's strong, smooth lines.

Nova enters the infirmary, glad Sebastian is doing what he does best—sleeping. It's like this next child knew he needed to be easy-going to fit into the whirlwind family he was born into. Her eyes adjust to the gloom and she quickly finds her mother bending over a cot in the back corner. Nova's about to walk over to see if she needs a hand when she notices a man slouched in the corner.

Nova pauses, noting the way his head is slumped forward. Even if he's asleep, it's an odd place to be doing it.

She moves closer. "Hello? Is there some way I can help?" The man doesn't respond so she gently touches his shoulder. "Hi, my name's Nova. Are you okay?"

The man jolts awake, looking around frantically as he shrinks deeper in the chair. "I don't have anything to steal!"

Nova moves back, giving him some room as she smiles gently. "It's okay. You're in Askala now."

The man's gaze settles on her, slowly focusing. He gulps. "Oh yes. We made it…"

Nova's mother approaches them, absentmindedly stroking Sebastian snuggled on Nova's back as she stops beside her. "Five of them. Exhausted, with no food or water."

Nova scans the infirmary. "But only three here?"

Her mother shrugs. "Two of them felt they were well enough to go straight to the village."

Avis enters through the door carrying a jug of water. She pours a cup and sits it beside the man. "The two on the cots were the worst off."

Which means they prioritized fluids and food for those poor souls. Nova's been running the infirmary with her mother and Avis since it was built. Her mother has insisted Nova is far more in charge, but Nova won't hear of it. Avis's knowledge of plants and her mother's medical knowledge were accumulated over far more years, meaning Nova still has so much to learn.

Nova nods. "You two keep doing what you were doing. I'll help this gentleman."

The man bows his head. "Anything you have to spare will be appreciated."

Her mother and Avis go back to the cots as Nova smiles.

Most of the Outlanders are like this when they arrive. Thin. Desperate. Grateful. She picks up the cup that's beside him and holds it out. "What's ours is yours."

The man's brows shoot up and Nova realizes he isn't as old as she initially thought. She's not surprised, though. The harshness of the Outlands often ages the people unlucky enough to be born there.

She holds out the cup and waits. Cautiously, the man takes it. The moment it leaves her hands the cup dips and Nova quickly catches it. Her heart aches as she realizes even that's too heavy for him to lift.

Sliding onto the seat beside him, Nova brings the cup to his lips. The man gulps greedily, and Nova makes sure she doesn't tilt it too quickly. His brain might want this fluid, but his stomach is about to get a shock.

When it's finished, Nova stands. "I'll get you some more. And maybe something light to eat. We'll need to start slow." Maybe a pod and some tea. Easy to digest, packed with nutrients.

The man pants as if he's just run the perimeter of Askala. "More?"

"Of course." Nova turns back to face him. "Isn't that why you came here before the bridge is complete?"

Even with the knowledge of building the rafts from mangrove pine now being extended to hollowing basic boats, the trip from the Outlands to Askala can be treacherous. Rebuilding the bridge is the solution to that, but it's going to take time. It hasn't stopped the desperate from arriving the moment they learned Askala will welcome anyone who sets foot on its land.

The man blinks. "Well, yeah. I just figured the stories were more fairytale than real."

Nova smiles. "We want to help those who need it. The more

people who are well, the more people can heal the very land we depend on."

Slowly but undeniably, the man smiles back, revealing several missing teeth. "You feed me and I'm yours, love."

An arm slips around Nova's waist and for a brief second she jolts. But her heart recognizes the body as if it's an extension of her own and she relaxes into the man standing beside her.

Kian grins. "Unfortunately, she already has her hands full with me, but feeding you is a given."

Nova smiles right down to her soul as she fits herself to Kian. "This is Kian. One of our leaders."

Kian is actually the driving force behind the Askala they live in now, but he won't let anyone call him the sole leader. His determination to rid them of the division that was created by the Bound and Unbound has meant he wants Askala ruled by the minds of many.

The man extends a hand, his body still trembling for lack of food, and Kian shakes it, clasping it warmly. "You've arrived on an auspicious day. If you feel up to it, you might want to come and see the ceremony." He winks. "Next year, you might even want to take part."

The man blinks again, confused.

"I'll get you something to eat," Nova says to him before she pushes Kian away, shaking her head. "Give the man a second to breathe. Right now he needs rest and food."

He lets her push him backwards, his eyes twinkling. Once they're back near the door, he pulls her close, wrapping his arms around her. Glancing over her shoulder at little Sebastian, he whispers. "Has he even been awake today?"

"For a feed, then he promptly went back to sleep," Nova says fondly. "Amity says you were the same when you were a baby."

"He's probably exhausted just watching his older siblings," Kian chuckles. His eyes trace her face. "Are you doing okay?"

Nova pushes up to press her lips against his. "I have everything I need and more."

And it's true. There's still so much work to be done to heal the wounds history has wrought, but Nova's now part of the solution. Along with the man she loves.

Kian's grin pops up again. "How about I take the kids tomorrow morning for a walk to the lake?"

The thought of a couple of precious hours to herself has Nova filling with delight. "I knew I promised to love you forever for a reason."

With a chuckle, Kian plants a quick kiss on her nose. "It'll be fun, and just what we need once today is done."

Nova steps back, turning to the table beside her where some herbs are sitting in wooden bowls. "I was just on my way to help when I was called in here. Is everything sorted?"

"I think so. Dex only looked highly stressed when I saw him last. I'll stop off and check the breeders then head over." Kian glances over her shoulder at the three men in the infirmary. "You do what you need to do here."

Nova pauses the tea she was making. "There were five of them this time."

Kian's gaze turns thoughtful. "Maybe thinking there weren't many more wasn't realistic."

"Probably. We have so much, when they have so little."

Kian pushes away from the table. "Well, we'll welcome them like we have the rest." Pressing a sweet kiss to the fair-haired head tucked in the sling, he turns soulful eyes to Nova. "We learn, we move forward."

Nova cups his handsome face. "And as it turns out, you create something pretty special."

His face softens. "We're trying."

Nova knows what Kian's really saying is that he's trying. The loss of his father is a burden that he still carries and Nova wonders if it will always weigh on him, no matter how much she tells him it wasn't his fault.

She brushes her lips across his. "And you're succeeding." She pulls back, all business so he doesn't have time to reply. "Now, I'm going to work on fattening these guys up," she says loudly over her shoulder before turning back to Kian, "while you go check on your breeders. See if any new babies have been born."

Kian smiles. "You go do what you do best."

Nova's heart warms. "I was about to say the same to you."

As she turns with the cool brew in her hand, Nova allows her smile to grow. Starting deep within her, it feels like it could reach right to the Outlands.

She never would've dreamed this life was possible, but it's everything she's ever wanted.

KIAN

*K*ian pulls in a deep breath as he makes his way closer to the beach. Anticipation, cautious yet as bright as the sun, fills him at the prospect of what the day will bring. Today is the next Announcement, where those who have scored high enough in the Proving can be chosen as leaders. All thanks to Dex's tireless work to make the tests everything they should've been.

Fair.

Valid.

A reflection of the future, not the risk of losing it.

Kian picks up the pace toward the breeding area. To his right is the Oasis and he pauses to take in the riot of growth. After the decaying cruise ship they called home was burned to the ground, the ashen soil had become fertile in a way they hadn't seen before. Now, vines heavy with fruit climb up the steel skeleton left behind, while gardens they only dreamed of flourish around it.

Who would've thought so much good could come from such loss. Now, the ship named the Oasis has born an…Oasis. Kian still marvels at it, five years later.

But he keeps walking. A quick check of the breeders and he'll go see if Dex has lost all his hair yet. Between the Provings and the two females in his life, it's a wonder it's all there, let alone not gray. Although, he's never seen Dex happier. He never mentions his missing hand, he smiles even as he shakes his head in exasperation. He dotes on Mercy as much as he does Wren.

Kian reaches the breeding center, as he likes to call it. The timber fence that extends around the village isn't far behind. Phoenix's idea, it cordoned off a section of the island for the people of Askala. The rest is left to Mother Nature to heal and be healed.

Wooden barrels, built of timber and sealed with sap, are dotted around him. He's not surprised to find his mother there, dipping a vial into the water of one of the barrels. With her back to him, Kian's struck again at how she's thin in a way no one else is in Askala, that her stooped shoulders have her looking older than her years.

Because of Kian's father. The leader who molded Askala. Who had a vision that ended in flames.

Magnus.

It's hard to know whether he betrayed them, or they betrayed him. The look of disappointment, of overwhelming loss and failure, before his father leaped into the inferno is forever seared in Kian's mind.

His mother must hear him because she turns, her face lighting into a smile. "Kian. I didn't think you'd be here today, so I started the water testing without you."

But Nova knew he'd stop by. This is where Kian grounds himself. The life around him is evidence that he's on the right track.

Even though he tells himself this, Kian pauses. "What do you think he'd think of all this, Mom?"

Her hands drop, her eyes filling with understanding. She walks over to him, slipping her arm around his shoulder.

Slowly, she spins Kian around and he takes in the fertile gardens, the breeders, the skeleton of the bridge reaching to the Outlands.

"He'd be so proud of his son. Look at what you've achieved."

"We all have." The abundance they're surrounded by is the product of countless hands and even more hours of toil.

"He would love this Askala, Kian." His mother's eyes glow with certainty.

But somehow, Kian isn't convinced. And the more he thinks on it, the more he realizes Askala never thrived under his father's rule. The Unbound were dying, the Bound battling to survive.

It's like his father's subconscious was slowly killing them long before Ronan set the Oasis alight.

But his mother doesn't need to hear this. It's best to let her believe her beloved Magnus wanted this. The alternative—that he was willing to let her and their children die alongside the rest of humanity—still haunts Kian at night.

He smiles. "It would be one heck of a tour."

His mother's return smile is muted, but there nevertheless. "It certainly would."

Not wanting to wallow on questions that will never have an answer, Kian heads to the nearest barrel. A green island of phytoplankton floats on the top, protecting the precious pods below. Like all the others, a small pipe trickles water into it, allowing the water to aerate and recycle. "Everything okay down there?"

She nods. "It's much easier to keep an eye on numbers now that they're in smaller tanks."

The loss of the pool meant having to find a new way to contain the pteropods. Splitting them across multiple barrels had been logical. This way, one mistake doesn't have to mean the loss of the entire population.

Kian squats, inspecting the shelf beneath it. The successful breeding of the cockroaches had taken a lot of trial and error. Discovering the nymphs were far more particular with food than their parents had been the key.

But now, between the pods and the roaches, the protein needs of Askala are taken care of. They've even started experimenting with crickets, hoping this might provide an additional source of nutrition.

Kian raises his brows as he sees something new. "They're going well." There are far more eggs than there were just a few days ago.

His mother's eyes twinkle. "I raised the humidity a tad."

Kian straightens, impressed. "And here we thought we had the formula perfect."

Moving onto the next barrel, his mother shrugs. "I've found life has a way of surprising you…"

She trails off before she finishes the sentence and Kian suspects he knew what she was going to say—especially when you least expect it.

It's something they all discovered. What some people lost their life learning.

Kian opens his mouth to reply, but his mother looks up. "I've got this here, why don't you go help the others?"

He hesitates, but his mother's already turned away, dipping another vial into the water. This is how she copes. By doing what she can for others.

Kian turns and heads to the Oasis. He understands, because that's exactly what he's done. Work tirelessly to show that the world his father couldn't fathom can exist.

And as Kian reaches the edge of the gardens, he breathes in the scents that are all the proof he needs. Rich earth, pungent herbs and verdant vegetation. Corn towers to his left as he skirts the amaranth bed, wondering how the new bean variety is going. They've been selectively cultivating fast growing, quick flowering types. This year, there will be more than enough to feed the people of Askala along with any new Outlanders who arrive.

Kian's just about to turn left, making his way to the ballroom when he hears a rustle from the corn. Curious, he wonders who's in there considering the corn still has a week or so before it's ripe.

He takes a step forward and is about to push back a stalk when someone comes barreling out at him. The bearded man shoves Kian back, snarling. Shocked at the sudden violence, Kian stumbles back, raising his hands in the air.

A second man joins the first, and they stand side by side, faces twisted with aggression. And fear. "Get back, or it'll be the last thing you do."

Kian keeps his stance relaxed and his hands where the men can see them. These must be the two Outlanders who arrived with the others. Dirty and thin, their faces are smeared with corn juice.

He takes a slow step back. "I'll stay here, I promise. I'm here in peace."

One of the men snorts. "Yeah, me too." He pulls a knife out of the waistband of his pants. "You play nice, so will we."

Kian smiles. "Wonderful. Now, the corn isn't quite ready, but have you thought of trying the carrots? They're a little further in."

The men glance at each other. The first man deepens his scowl as he lifts the knife. "You got some friends there, waiting? So you can ambush us? I don't think so."

Kian keeps his open, unthreatening stance in place. These men are scared and hungry. They don't want to kill, they just want to ensure they get to live another day.

He shrugs nonchalantly. "There might be others there, actually. Many of the people from the Outlands like to work in the gardens."

Which is true. It's like they need to see the food growing and thriving to believe it.

The second man shakes his head, moving further behind the first. "I told you none of it was true. They take us as slaves."

"No one here works against their will—"

"What's with the fence, then?" The man waves the knife around in a crazy circle. "It looks like it goes all the way round."

"Yeah, like you're trying to keep us in," says the second man.

Kian inclines his head. "Or we're keeping the polar grizzlies out. Their numbers have been increasing."

As the forests have grown and flourished, so has the wildlife. With the fence, the children of Askala can run free without the threat of a bear coming too close thanks to the smorgasbord of people who now live here.

Kian opens his hands wide. "Askala is here to heal all—you, me, and everything on the other side of that wall."

The men hesitate, which Kian understands. The offer seems too good to be true. It would feel like a trap. Kian indicates with his chin toward the kitchen. "We have soup in the kitchen. And our flatbread is quite filling, too."

Slowly, the knife falls to the man's side. "If you're lying…"

"You're welcome to return to the corn," Kian grins. "Although our breeding center would probably be a better place to start. I'll show you where it is another time."

This time, when the men glance at each other, they're a little slack jawed. The first man tucks the knife back into his waistband. "Where do we go?"

Kian directs them further down the path, suggesting the knife may be more useful in the kitchens. The men don't answer, but Kian didn't expect them to. Sometimes it can take up to a week for the knife to leave their side.

But with time, with generosity and compassion, the knives are handed over. The people start to help. They want to be a part of this.

As the men head down the path, frequently checking over their shoulder whether Kian's moved, Kian turns to the sea. The acidic ocean, stained the color of rust, will take the longest to recover. But they've learned all they need is time.

Kindness can grow with time.

Change is inevitable with time.

And healing happens with time.

Shoving his hands in his pockets, Kian looks at the land that's a testament to that. Up ahead, the sound of children laughing dances through the gardens and Kian's heart smiles, recognizing the sound of his daughter among them.

Today is an Announcement. Another pool of people who will keep this legacy going.

Kian chuckles as he takes the path to the ballroom.

It's time to see Dex.

DEX

*D*ex paces as he checks everything is in place for the twentieth time. Had his father felt like this before the Announcement ceremonies? If only he were here to ask. He could really use his advice right now.

Thoughts of his father and all the regret that stirs up have him halting. He scans his eyes across the large clearing in the Oasis that they call the ballroom. Built on the same land where the ballroom once stood, he can feel the history in the soil through the soles of his feet.

The ballroom was once a large open space with timber boards that creaked, a stage that sagged, and broken chandeliers that swung above their heads, it couldn't be more different now.

Or more beautiful.

After the fire, families had claimed small patches of land and laid down the foundations for their new homes. The village quickly took shape, with houses being built not just from timber but a strong sense of hope for the future. It was healthier to live underneath the trees, waking to the sound of birdsong, than it had been when clustered together in their tiny stale cabins on the old cruise ship.

While most huts were constructed in groups dotted around Askala, Dex and Wren had built their home a little bit away from everyone else. Wren's need for solitude had outweighed Dex's need for connection. As long as he had her close by, he didn't mind.

But a concern had niggled at Dex the more huts that went up around the island. Where was their sense of community? In the Oasis they'd lived side-by-side, practically on top of each other. But in the new Askala, people retreated into their family groups, living like disconnected souls.

And this concern was where the idea for the ballroom had been born. So, as Zali had led a team of people to re-work the ash covered land into the lush Oasis it is now, Dex had marked out a rectangular section in the middle and claimed it as the ballroom. A space for people to gather. A memorial for all the lives that had been lost in Askala's bloody history.

As he walks around the space now, he's filled with a sense of enormous pride. Bordered by neatly laid stones, he looks at the names that have been lovingly engraved on each one of them.

Mercy. Callix. Magnus. Sam. Shiloh. Beatrice. Vern. Thom. Jay. Fern. Dorian...

One stone in remembrance of each sacrifice made. A small symbol to show that person had left a mark on someone's heart. There's even a stone that Flick laid for the baby she lost in the Outlands.

There are a few missing stones, of course. Nobody wants to remember Ronan, or Dean, or any members of their so-called army. Apart from Jagger, of course, although he's very much alive, working with Phoenix and his eager team of builders.

A huge arbor has been built over the new ballroom with grapevines winding their way over the beams. In the center hangs a giant twisted chandelier made from the charred remains of the original light fittings found in the ruins. All surrounded by the fertile gardens of the Oasis. It's even more spectacular in reality than it had been in Dex's imagination.

"Dex!" Phoenix calls out from the stage he's been building for today. "We're ready to go."

Dex wanders in his direction when the sound of giggling echoes across the ballroom.

Luca bursts through a row of corn stalks and runs into the open space, being chased by two little girls who are squealing with laughter.

Mercy and Sam.

Cousins, but in some ways more like sisters, these two are inseparable, despite how opposite their personalities are. That's the beauty of kids. The things that are the same are so much more important to them than what's different.

"Daddy!"

Dex squats down and opens his arms as his wild-haired bundle of adorableness flies at him.

Mercy plants a kiss on his cheek. "I missed you, Daddy!"

He laughs as he shakes his head. His daughter knows exactly what to say to ensure everyone remains firmly where she wants them. Cute for a four-year-old, but certain to be trouble when she grows into a teenager.

"Where have you been?" he asks.

"Playing with Sammy." She rolls her eyes as if that should have been obvious.

"You haven't been bothering Luca again, have you?"

She shakes her head in an over-exaggerated way that tells him she's been doing exactly that. "He kept trying to run away but we're too fast for him!"

"Maybe sometimes it's a good idea to let him get away, okay?" Dex lands a kiss on his daughter's forehead and she nods at him, full of false sincerity.

He needs to remember to thank Luca. He does a good job of

tolerating his younger sister and cousin when they all know he'd rather be climbing trees or following Phoenix around.

"Let's go see what Uncle Phoenix built for us." He swings Mercy into the air and holds her to his chest as she giggles.

Luca is already standing beside Phoenix, sizing up his massive biceps and mimicking the way he puffs out his chest. He could have worse role models, Dex decides. Phoenix has more than proven himself over the years.

Sam is sitting on the side of the new stage, her nose buried in a book, oblivious to all the things that fascinate her brother most.

"Hey there, Sammy," Dex calls, but she doesn't acknowledge him. He smiles knowing it's because she hasn't heard. He wishes that as a kid he'd been able to escape into a fantasy world like that.

He takes the stairs to the stage and marvels at what Phoenix has been able to achieve. Mercy wriggles from his arms and runs to Sam, who starts telling her a story about oil reserves. Mercy nods like she understands, even though Dex is certain she's plotting how to separate Sam from that book the next chance she gets.

"It's perfect," Dex says to Phoenix, looking from the elevated platform across the ballroom and imagining how it will look when it's filled with people.

Phoenix moves about the stage, pointing out various design features as Luca struts behind him, copying his every move. If Phoenix notices, he doesn't say anything. He's used to Luca by now and chooses to take it as a compliment.

Especially as his own son doesn't seem all that keen to follow in his footsteps.

"Got it done just in time," says Phoenix.

Dex suppresses a laugh. The stage had been perfect days ago. It was only Phoenix fussing over the small improvements that had apparently held it up. "You've done an awesome job."

Luca nods in agreement. "He used tongue and groove joins to make it extra strong."

They all startle as the sound of a horn being blown reverberates through the dense vegetation. Once used to alert Askala of Remnants approaching, it's now used to let people know when it's time to gather.

Kian comes through the trees first, smiling as Luca spots him and races over to him.

"I'd better go find Flick," says Phoenix, slapping him on the back. "Looks like you're up. Good luck."

Dex nods as Luca follows Phoenix off the stage, not realizing he's doing exactly what he complains Sam and Mercy do to him.

The horn sounds again. Wren will be finished with the Proving.

Which means it's time.

Even five years after embarking on their new life together, Wren still makes his stomach flip. The thought of seeing her again in a few moments has him bouncing from foot to foot as he keeps his eyes on the Oasis, wondering which bit of vegetation she'll emerge from.

Flick is the next to arrive. She must have already been on her way, as Dex has never seen anyone move so slowly. She has her son, Hawk, attached to one of her legs, her daughter, Robin, clinging to her hand, and little Dove strapped in a sling at her back. Her stomach is bulging with yet another child. Or twins if Wren's prediction is correct.

Phoenix rushes over to Flick, taking Dove from her sling and attaching her to his own back. He reaches for Robin who lets go of her mother to take his large hand, and Dex notices he doesn't try to lure away Hawk, who's still glued to Flick's legs.

Hawk is a quiet boy, even more so than little Sammy. Large for his age with masses of curly red hair, people often talk to him like he's far older than he is and wonder why he doesn't reply. Dex smiles at his nephew. He knows what it feels like when the world wants you to be someone you're not. If it weren't for the fact the Announcement is just about to start, he'd try to relieve Flick of Hawk for a while.

More people file into the ballroom, some stopping to pick a bunch of grapes to nibble on during the ceremony. It fills Dex with enormous pride to see people being able to eat whenever they're hungry. They find a place to sit on the soft ground and greet each other warmly as they look to the stage in anticipation.

Going to the center of the stage, Dex waits for Wren to bring in this year's participants. When he'd asked her to help him with the Provings all those years ago, he'd naively imagined she'd be his assistant. But it turns out Wren doesn't know the meaning of that word. So, they became partners.

Occasionally, Dex wonders if somehow he's become Wren's assistant...

He smiles as she emerges through the amaranth plants with six hopeful participants trailing behind her. Wren has tried to braid her hair into submission but it's still managing to fly in every direction as she marches forward, not returning Dex's smile. Her focus on the task ahead. That only makes Dex smile harder.

His feisty little bird has only gotten more stubborn and fierce as the years have passed. Thankfully, so has her love for him. Some nights she holds him so tightly, he can barely breathe, let alone sleep. But he wouldn't have it any other way. They make each other feel safe.

Kian and Nova step up to the stage, along with the other leaders who've been appointed at the previous Provings. There are nine of them in total and Dex already knows that two more will be joining them from this year's group.

There's no limit to the number of leaders, just like there's no limit to the number of times you're allowed to apply. It's not so much a different system to the one they went through themselves, more that it's been improved.

Vastly.

"Are we ready to start?" Kian asks, touching Dex gently on the back.

Dex nods. Sometimes their gatherings are run by Kian. Other times Nova or Zali. But this is the Proving and it's his time to shine. And for all Wren's courage and strength, it turns out that for her speaking in public is sort of like standing on the edge of a cliff. She's not especially keen...

"Welcome everyone." Dex holds up his hand and waits for the hush to spread across the crowd.

He nods at Wren who leads the participants to the front of the stage. Four males and two females, varying in ages from the minimum of sixteen right up to their oldest at age fifty-three.

"I'd like to thank this year's participants for their valiant efforts in the tests of the Proving," says Dex. "You all demonstrated your worth in so many ways and we're honored to have each and every one of you here in Askala."

A cheer erupts from the crowd and Dex watches as Wren shuffles her feet. She's about as good at standing still to listen as she is with public speaking.

"As you're aware, not everyone can be a leader." He smiles across the ballroom. "We've tested this year's participants for the kindness of their hearts and the sharpness of their minds, but that's not to say that those who don't succeed aren't worthy. This may just not be their year. As you're aware, you're welcome to enter the Proving as many times as you like."

There's some nervous laughter in the crowd as people jostle each other, daring each other to enter again. Most people only ever enter once. Some never enter at all. There are plenty of other important jobs to do in Askala.

As Dex waits for them to settle, he remembers the fear that had been present in the ballroom at his own Announcement. So much more had been at stake with those results. Fingers could be lost. Fertility could be stolen. Hearts could be broken.

Which is why as he calls the names of the two successful participants, his eyes are drawn to the four who were unsuccessful. They seem disappointed, as is expected, but not one of them is living through the gut-wrenching devastation that he'd witnessed Nova live through. And that's a relief.

There are no more Bound. No more Unbound. Finally, Askala has arrived at a place where *everyone* is worthy.

The eleven new leaders link hands and step to the front of the stage as the sound of drums starts up.

A cheer erupts as the people throw their hands in the air and dance to the beat. The joy is palpable. Perhaps that's what helps the Oasis to grow so prolifically.

This is what a ballroom is supposed to be like. This is what life is supposed to be like.

Wren squeezes his hand a little tighter than necessary and he looks across at her.

She beams up at him, giving him the smile he'd been waiting for, and his heart swells with love. Life is about as close to perfect as it can get.

Everything they've been through together has been worth it. He can't say he wouldn't change anything about it or that he'd willingly go through it all again, but there's no denying he's happy with the outcome.

The leaders step from the stage and join in the dancing. Dex encases Wren in his arms, laughing when he feels a furious banging on his legs.

Mercy is standing there, one hand on her hip and her foot tapping, demanding their attention.

"Remind you of anyone?" he asks Wren.

"I don't know what you're talking about." Wren laughs as she scoops up their daughter.

He wraps his arms around both of them and he realizes he was wrong. His life isn't close to perfect.

It is perfect.

WREN

ren wakes at dawn. In the dim light she can see Dex with his arms wrapped around Mercy. Her little body is turned into her father, her hand resting on his cheek.

Mercy often sneaks into their bed during the night. Always on Dex's side where she knows she won't be told to go back to her own bed. He'd have tucked her in beside him as if that's where she belongs and gone straight back to sleep. And Mercy would've drifted off, safe in the knowledge that she owns her father's heart.

Wren never once slept beside her own father. Instead, it was Phoenix she'd reached for until they got too old and she was forced to curl into herself. Sometimes she'd wrap her arms around her shoulders and pretend it was someone else.

It hadn't been an easy childhood and she's aware she still bears the scars.

Which is why she's padding across the small hut to the door. Sometimes, her need to be alone burns at her core. Just when she thinks she's adjusted to a life surrounded by people who love her, the feeling starts up. She'll dream that the cockroaches she ate for dinner have come to life inside her and are trying to claw their way out. And that's when she knows she has to escape.

Not forever. Just for a little while.

Just so she can breathe.

She slips out of the hut and closes the door quietly behind her, listening to the birds warming up their voices for their morning song. Some days they're so loud it's impossible to sleep. But nobody complains. It means the land is healing. That everything they've worked for is amounting to something bigger than what they can see.

Wren walks down the path toward a group of three huts in a small clearing. One for Kian, Nova, Luca and Sam. Another for Amity and her three children. And another shared by both Nova and Wren's moms who've become inseparable friends.

Breathing a sigh of relief that all is quiet, Wren walks on. She's not in the mood for much conversation today.

A little further down the path, she passes Phoenix and Flick's hut. Little Hawk is at the cut-out that serves as a window. He smiles and holds up his hand when he sees Wren, and she presses her finger to her lips. He nods solemnly, understanding her need to be alone in a way that's wise beyond his years.

She pauses her steps for a moment, then turns back and goes to her nephew.

"Do you want to come with me?" she asks.

His eyes open wide and he nods hard, making his curls bounce on top of his head. He doesn't even know where she's going, yet still he wants to come. That's a big compliment coming from a kid like Hawk.

"Phoenix!" she calls through the window. "I'm taking Hawk out."

"Thanks, Wren," comes Flick's tired reply. She doesn't sleep much lately. Those babies in her belly must be keeping her awake. Wren's certain it's twins this time. Flick doesn't believe her. Or maybe she just doesn't want to. Her hands are full enough already.

It's taken years, but Wren's finally come to an understanding with Flick. She's proven herself to be a loyal partner to Phoenix and a wonderful mother to Wren's nephew and nieces. It's hard to continue to dislike someone who takes such good care of the people you love. Phoenix could have done worse.

"Behave yourself, Hawk!" Flick calls as he climbs out the window, his sweet face beaming up at Wren.

They continue on down the path in silence, neither of them seeing the need to talk. Which is exactly why Wren decided to take him. Being with Hawk is like being with someone and being alone all at the same time. If Mercy were here, she'd have told Wren a dozen stories by now. If Dex were here he'd be telling her about an idea he had for next year's Proving. If Nova were here, she'd be asking how Wren's feeling. And if it were Kian, he'd be quizzing her about her old life in the Outlands.

Hawk doesn't need to do any of that. He just needs to *be*.

The path takes them into the trees and the smell of the ocean sharpens. It's a nice day to take a boat out. Running the Proving had been tiring. Day after day of tests and scores and conversations and decisions. But she's happy with the outcome. Their two new leaders will be a great addition to the team. They'll bring something new to keep their perspective fresh.

Hawk points to a branch lying across the path ahead and she nods at him. Without having to discuss what to do, they lift it from one end each and move it out of the way.

"You're strong for your age," she says, genuinely impressed.

"I get that from my dad." Hawk puffs out his chest as they continue walking.

"You've got a good dad."

Settling back into silence, they make their way onto the sand and over toward where the new bridge is being built. A bridge that will stretch all the way to the Outlands. Construction has started on the other side and one day they hope to meet in the middle. It will take years the way they're going but Kian says it will be worth it. Because then there won't be an Outlands. There will just be *lands*. One world, with people free to come or go as they please.

Wren isn't entirely sure about this idea. It seems too simplistic. Or perhaps optimistic. Their whole way of living right now is just too…perfect. And nothing is ever perfect. There's always someone who wants to bring it all down.

There are three small boats resting on the sand near the bridge. Built from the same mangrove pine that Wren used to construct the raft she'd arrived here on, the design has been adapted into something far safer. Sometimes, Kian and Amity use the boats to collect more pods to diversify their breeding pool. Other times, Wren and Phoenix fill a boat with food and seedlings and head over to the Outlands with their offerings so they can check on the bridge. A small village has taken root where the bridge-builders and their families live. Progress is being made, but these visits are more hostile than Wren would like. It seems that no matter how much you give someone, they always want more.

And on rare luxurious occasions like today, Wren takes out a boat with no plans to go anywhere at all. She just wants to go.

Hawk is looking from the boats, to Wren, and back to the boats again, his face alight as he dares to hope that his wish to go out on the water has finally come true. She's been promising to take him out for a long time now.

He reaches for her hand. "Are we…"

"We are." She smiles down at him. "We are, Hawk."

If it were Mercy having her greatest wish granted, she'd shriek and holler and do a little dance. But not Hawk. He just nods behind his smile, his too-big-body for his age quivering as the excitement tries to escape.

But as they get closer to the boats, Wren sees something inside two of them.

"Stay back." She puts a hand on Hawk's chest to steady him and marches forward to find two men asleep, taking one boat each as if they're a crib.

She recognizes them as two of the new arrivals from the Outlands. The ones Kian had pointed out at the Announcement ceremony as being the men whose anger he'd diffused with the promise of soup.

Maybe she can drag the third boat away without them waking. She's not in the mood for a fight. Nor does she have any soup to offer.

But as she takes hold of the gunwale of the boat, one of the men sits up.

"Hello, little lady." He winks at her, his eyes going directly to her chest as he reaches over and knocks on the hull of his friend's boat. "Wake up, Davey. Breakfast has arrived."

Ignoring him, she tugs on the vacant boat, sliding it across the sand toward the water.

"Get in!" she calls to Hawk, who's standing frozen, his excitement leaching into the sand as he tries to assess how scared he should be. Even at his young age he can tell these men mean no good. "Now!"

The men climb out of the other boats and make suggestive gestures in Wren's direction.

"Hawk! Get here now!" She points at the boat and Hawk launches into action, flying across the sand, diving in and sitting with his eyes focused on the men.

"It's okay," she says to him. "I just need to have a little chat with our visitors. Stay here."

She walks back to the men, wishing she'd thought to tuck her knife into her waistband. It's been so long since she's needed to use it.

"Hello there," one of them calls out, practically drooling as he scans her body. "Got rid of the kid so we can have a bit of fun?"

"See that bridge?" she asks. The men nod and she takes a few more steps. "Why don't you take a walk on it? And when you get to the end, jump off."

The men seem to find this hilarious instead of the threat it was meant to be.

"I like an angry woman, don't you?" the one called Davey says, elbowing his mate.

"Let me tell you something." Wren lowers her voice so Hawk can't hear. "Don't go thinking the people here are weak just because you've been treated with kindness. Your Commander came here with his strongest army and look what happened to them. They're all dead now. You'll be next if you're not careful."

That wipes the smiles from their faces.

"You reckon you're tougher than the Commander and his army?" she asks. "Because Kian may have gone easy on you yesterday, but I've seen him kill men twice his size with his bare hands. Snapped their necks like they were sparrows. He's not too keen on second chances."

The men shuffle their feet and she eyes them.

"So, you either learn to play nice, or you get back in those boats and return to where you came from." She takes another step toward them to show she's not scared. "Do you understand me?"

The men nod. "Sorry, miss. Didn't mean to bother you."

Wren gives them an icy cold glare then turns her back on them, another move to show she's not afraid. They're not to know how hard her heart is pumping.

She returns to the boat and pushes it from the shore into deeper water, shooting what she hopes is a reassuring smile in Hawk's direction. "I'll row us out, then I'll teach you how to do it."

He nods earnestly at her, his eyes returning to the men on the beach.

She picks up the oars and pulls hard, surging them toward the horizon. With each pump of her arms, she lets a little bit of her tension fly free. This was why she came here.

"Are they still there?" she asks Hawk, refusing to turn her head toward the beach.

He nods. "Aunt Wren, you were very brave."

She lets out a small laugh, realizing her young nephew had never seen this side of her before. To him, she's Mercy's mother. His father's sister. She's just Aunt Wren. The poor kid has no idea of what she's done in her past.

"Does Kian really snap necks like sparrows?" he asks.

Wren gasps. "I didn't think you could hear that."

He blinks at her, waiting for her answer.

She rows a little further before she responds, needing to think through what she's going to say. "No, Hawk. Kian's the kindest man you'll ever meet."

"Mommy says it's bad to lie."

"Your mommy's right. But sometimes grown-ups say things that aren't true to protect themselves."

"Will you teach me to tell lies like that?"

"Hawk!" She laughs, lifting her oar to knock him lightly on the arm. "No, I will not. But one day I'll teach you how to protect yourself. Is that a deal?"

He nods, a small smile on his lips.

She rows them past the end of the bridge, enjoying the look of astonishment on Hawk's face as he stares at it. His red hair is blowing in the breeze, sending his curls into his eyes. She loves his hair. His mother's curls and his father's color. He's managed to inherit the best from the both of them.

"Your dad helped design this bridge," she says, even though he must certainly know this. "There's nothing your dad can't build."

Hawk doesn't answer, but she knows his silence is no reflection of what's going on inside his busy mind.

"Maybe you'll be a builder one day." She bites her tongue as she says this, knowing Hawk's shown no interest in this. Perhaps it was better when they moved in silence.

"I'm going to be an explorer," he says, his eyes lighting with a spark she hasn't seen before. "I'm going to find new places, like the ones Sammy talks about before the water ate them up."

Wren rows on, surprised to have been given this window into her nephew's mind. Where does a child so young get ideas like that?

"Then how about we start now?" She changes direction to head east. "Let's go somewhere nobody's been before. Would you like that?"

Hawk nods enthusiastically then leans over the edge of the boat, knowing better than to reach out and run his fingers through the acidic water.

There's been a shadow on the horizon that Wren's noticed from the shore but never had a chance to check out. Now seems like the perfect time. A real adventure for Hawk.

"If you're going to be an explorer, you need to know how to row." She pats the seat beside her, and Hawk scrambles over.

He takes an oar from her like she's handed him the keys to heaven, and she shows him how to use it, aware that this will slow them down. But Hawk has surprising strength and sets to the task with gusto, his tongue poking out the side of his mouth as he concentrates on trying to keep up with her.

The further they travel, the more the shadow moves down from the horizon, growing larger until it becomes a dark spot on the water.

Wren points it out to Hawk. "What do you think that is, Mr. Explorer?"

He stares at it for several long seconds. "It's a secret island," he whispers back in awe.

She laughs, taking the oar from him so she can better steer them, surprised he'd stuck at the task for so long. He may not have his father's passion for building, but he sure has his stamina.

But the more she rows, the more she starts to wonder if Hawk could be right. Could that be an island? The stretch of sand on their beach has been growing wider over the years, causing Dex to speculate whether or not the ocean levels have started to retreat. She'd always shrugged him off, but now she wishes she'd paid more attention to his theories.

Perhaps she should've taken Sam out here instead of Hawk. She's probably read something about the oceans rising and falling in one of those books she carries around.

"It really is an island!" Hawk is hanging over the edge of the boat now, lying on his stomach with his feet jiggling behind him. She's not sure she's ever seen him so excited, making her certain she chose the right kid to accompany her today. "We've discovered a new land."

Wren doesn't reply. She's too busy trying to process this, certain the shadow on the horizon wasn't there when she first arrived in Askala. Which can only mean one thing.

Sea levels are receding.

New land is being exposed. Right here. And who knows where else.

The boat hits shallow water and beaches itself at the shore of the tiny island.

Wren climbs off and drags the boat further up onto the sand. Hawk jumps off, landing with a thud. They stand side by side, staring at their discovery.

The island is an irregular shape and covered in sandy soil held together by weeds and shrubs. It's only small, maybe fifty feet in one direction and a hundred in the other. But it's already the home to a number of squawking sea birds, who are clearly not impressed with the new arrivals.

"Can I run around it?" Hawk asks.

"An explorer has to explore."

She pats him on the back as he skips off, shaking her head in wonder. The ramifications of this discovery are beyond huge.

"Woo hoo!" Hawk runs past Wren, taking off on a second lap, but getting distracted by something and changing course.

He runs up to the middle of the island, raises his hands above his head and spins around.

"I'm a real explorer!" he shouts.

Wren wipes away the tear that just escaped down her cheek at the sight of this quiet boy finding the thing that makes his heart sing.

Perhaps Hawk is destined to discover new lands, just like he dreams of. Perhaps he'll go to places the world never thought they'd see again.

Perhaps this story has only just begun.

THE END

Ready for the next installment in The Thaw Chronicles?
Check out Book 5, EXTANT, now!
http://mybook.to/ExtantThaw

BOOK FIVE - EXTANT

BEYOND THE THAW

Here's what reviewers are saying about Extant:

★★★★★ Just wow. This is my favourite instalment of the series so far. Gruelling Proving tests that require every ounce of stamina and savoir-faire; gripping blossoming romances, superb action, and dynamic friendships, relationships... and life questions. The dream team that is Sloan and Catherine have pulled it off again!

★★★★★ Such a good book! I love these new characters. I also love seeing some of the old characters and seeing how their life has gone!

★★★★★ I read the previous series and thought that no other series could come close to how amazing it was. Reading Extant proved me wrong... This was just as great, if not better than the previous series! I had to recommend you read only one book series this year, this would be it.

Extant. Only the chosen shall seek.

Sea levels have receded, exposing fertile, untouched land. Virgin soil that everyone in a ravaged world is willing to fight for.

Askala knows it needs to stake a claim if they're going to continue healing the Earth. To do that, a team of Seekers will be sent to colonize it...and assimilate those who don't understand.

This year, the testing won't end at the Proving. Passing is no longer just about having a kind heart and a sharp mind. To spread Askala's word, Seekers also need to survive in this harsh new land. New tests will determine who's strong and tough enough to be the best of the best.

Sam is determined to prove her father's vision is what the world needs. Mercy is convinced she'll be able to win the Outlanders over with her smile. Hawk believes he was destined to be a Seeker, but will his gentle soul be his undoing? Luca knows he's never fitted in and isn't about to try.

Who will pass and have the honor of representing Askala? And how will a society founded on peace succeed in a world where violence is power? Four teens are about to find out.

Lovers of Divergent, The Hunger Games, and The Maze Runner series will be blown away by this breathtaking series from USA Today best-selling author Tamar Sloan and award-winning author Heidi Catherine.

Grab your copy now!
http://mybook.to/ExtantThaw

WANT TO STAY IN TOUCH?

If you'd like to be the first for to hear all the news from Tamar and Heidi, be sure to sign up to our newsletter. Subscribers receive bonus content, early cover reveals and sneaky snippets of upcoming books. We'd love you to join us!

SIGN UP HERE:

https://sendfox.com/tamarandheidi

ABOUT THE AUTHORS

Tamar Sloan hasn't decided whether she's a psychologist who loves writing, or a writer with a lifelong fascination with psychology. She must have been someone pretty awesome in a previous life (past life regression indicated a Care Bear), because she gets to do both. When not reading, writing or working with teens, Tamar can be found with her husband and two children enjoying country life in their small slice of the Australian bush.

Heidi Catherine loves the way her books give her the opportunity to escape into worlds vastly different to her own life in the burbs. While she quite enjoys killing her characters (especially the awful ones), she promises she's far better behaved in real life. Other than writing and reading, Heidi's current obsessions include watching far too much reality TV with the excuse that it's research for her books.